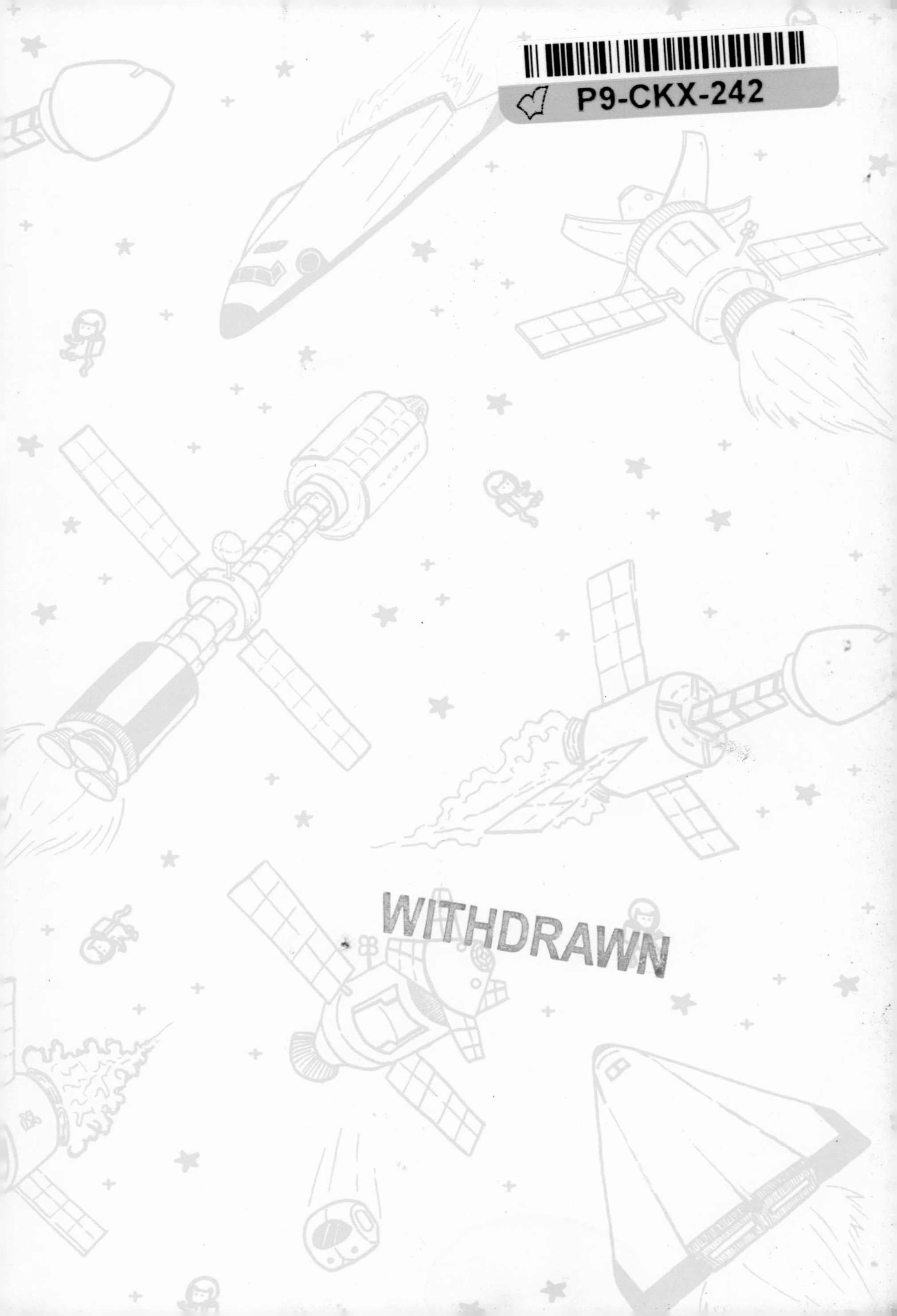

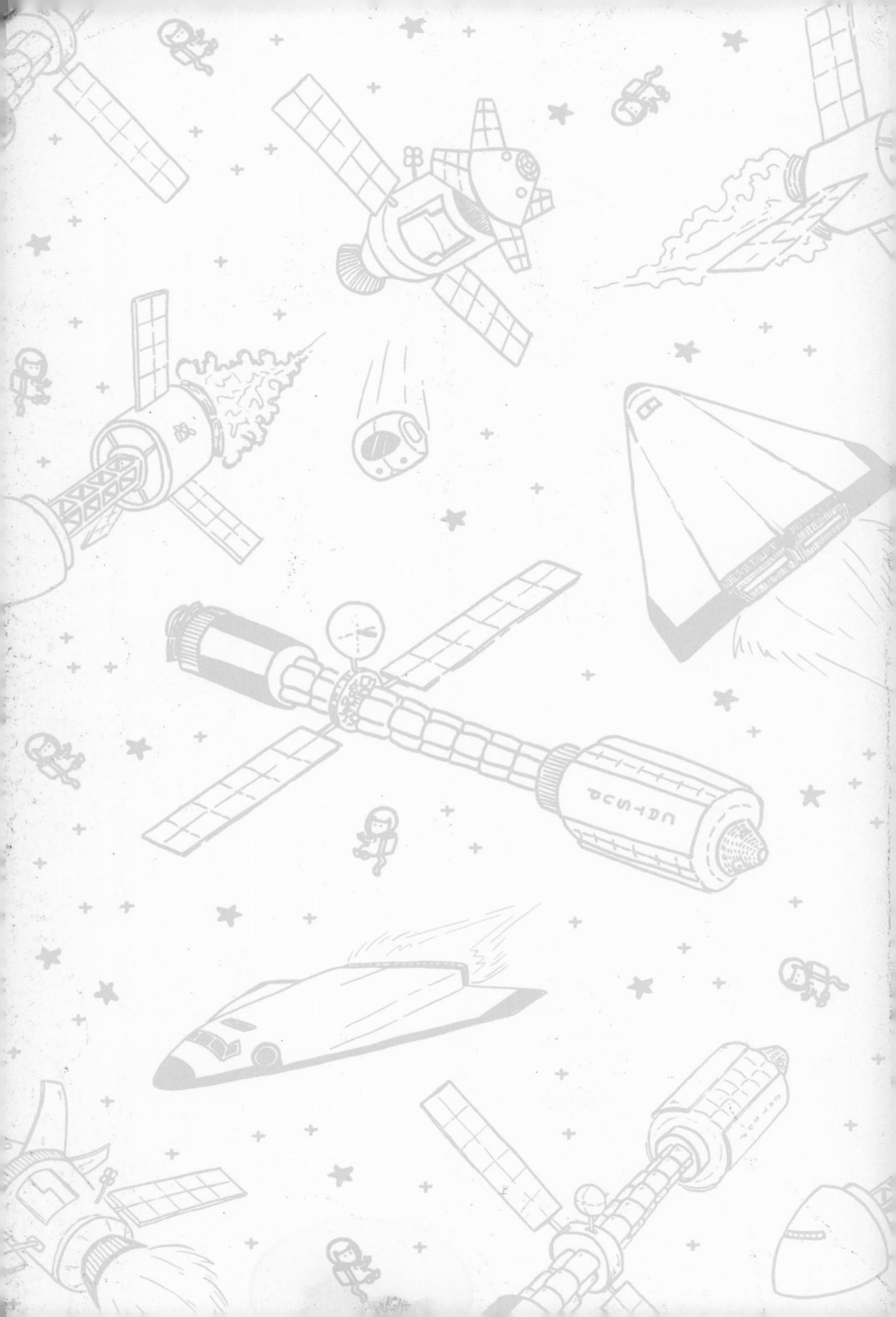

CatStronauts

RACE TO MARS

CatStronauts

RACE TO MARS

BY DREW BROCKINGTON

(L)(B)

Little, Brown and Company
New York Boston

Little, Brown and Company

Hachette Book Group
1290 Avenue of the Americas, New York, NY 10104
Visit us at lb-kids.com

Little, Brown and Company is a division of Hachette Book Group, Inc.
The Little, Brown name and logo are trademarks of Hachette Book Group, Inc.

The publisher is not responsible for websites (or their content) that are not owned by the publisher.

First Edition: April 2017

Library of Congress Cataloging-in-Publication Data
Names: Brockington, Drew, author, artist.
Title: CatStronauts : race to Mars / by Drew Brockington.
Description: First edition. | New York : Little, Brown and Company, 2017. |
Summary: "With national pride and valuable scientific research on the line, the CatStronauts race against the CosmoCats and others to be the first cats to Mars"— Provided by publisher.
Identifiers: LCCN 2016042317| ISBN 9780316307482 (hardcover) | ISBN 9780316307505 (trade pbk.) | ISBN 9780316307499 (ebook)
Subjects: LCSH: Graphic novels. | CYAC: Graphic novels. | Astronauts—Fiction. | Space flight to Mars—Fiction. | Cats—Fiction.
Classification: LCC PZ7.7.B76 Caw 2017 | DDC 741.5/973—dc23
LC record available at https://lccn.loc.gov/2016042317

10 9 8 7 6 5 4 3 2 1

1010

Printed in China

FOR
SIMON & MARCELINE

CatStronauts

RACE TO MARS

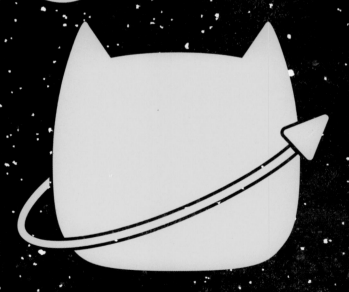

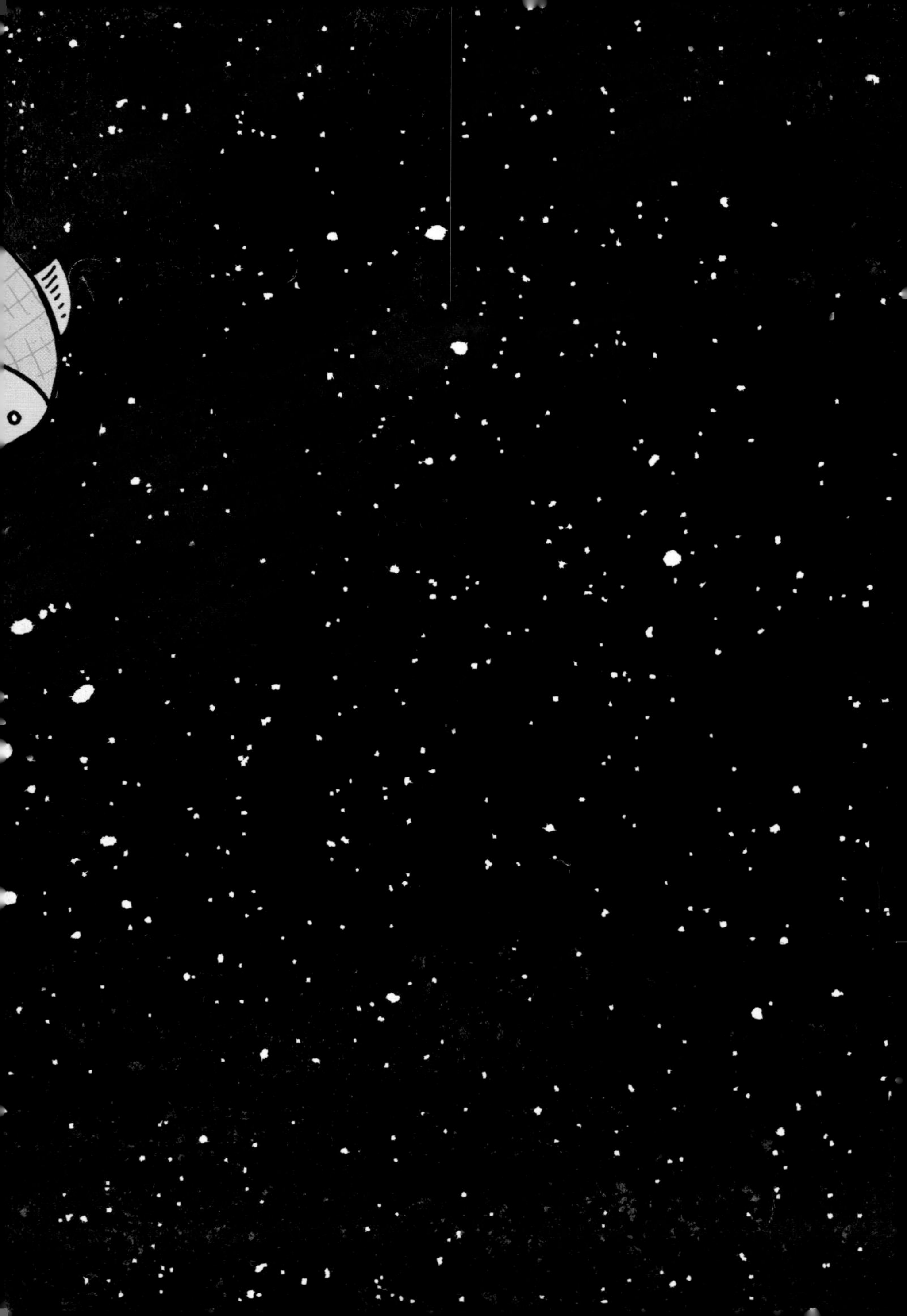

CHAPTER 1

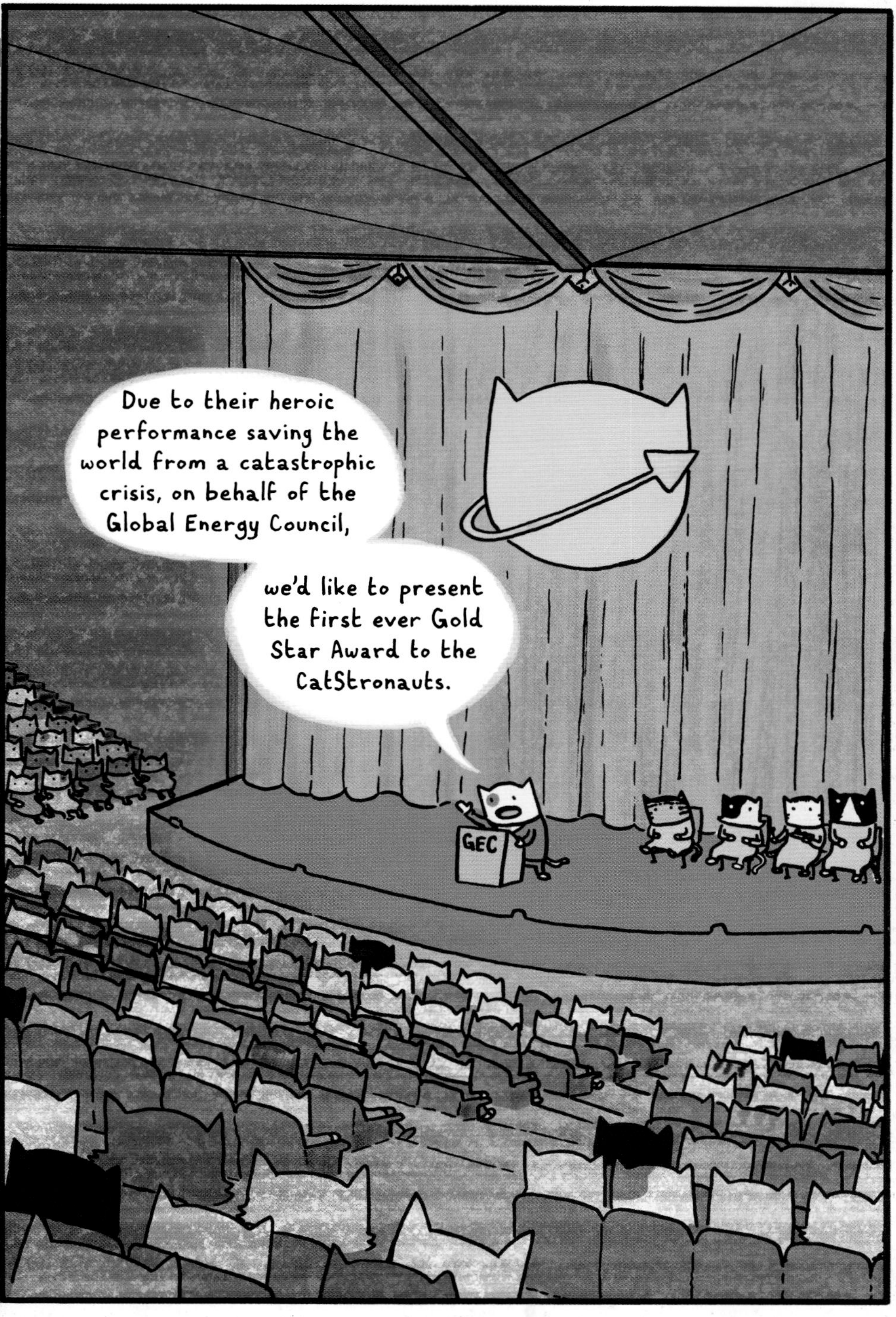
Due to their heroic performance saving the world from a catastrophic crisis, on behalf of the Global Energy Council,
we'd like to present the first ever Gold Star Award to the CatStronauts.
GEC

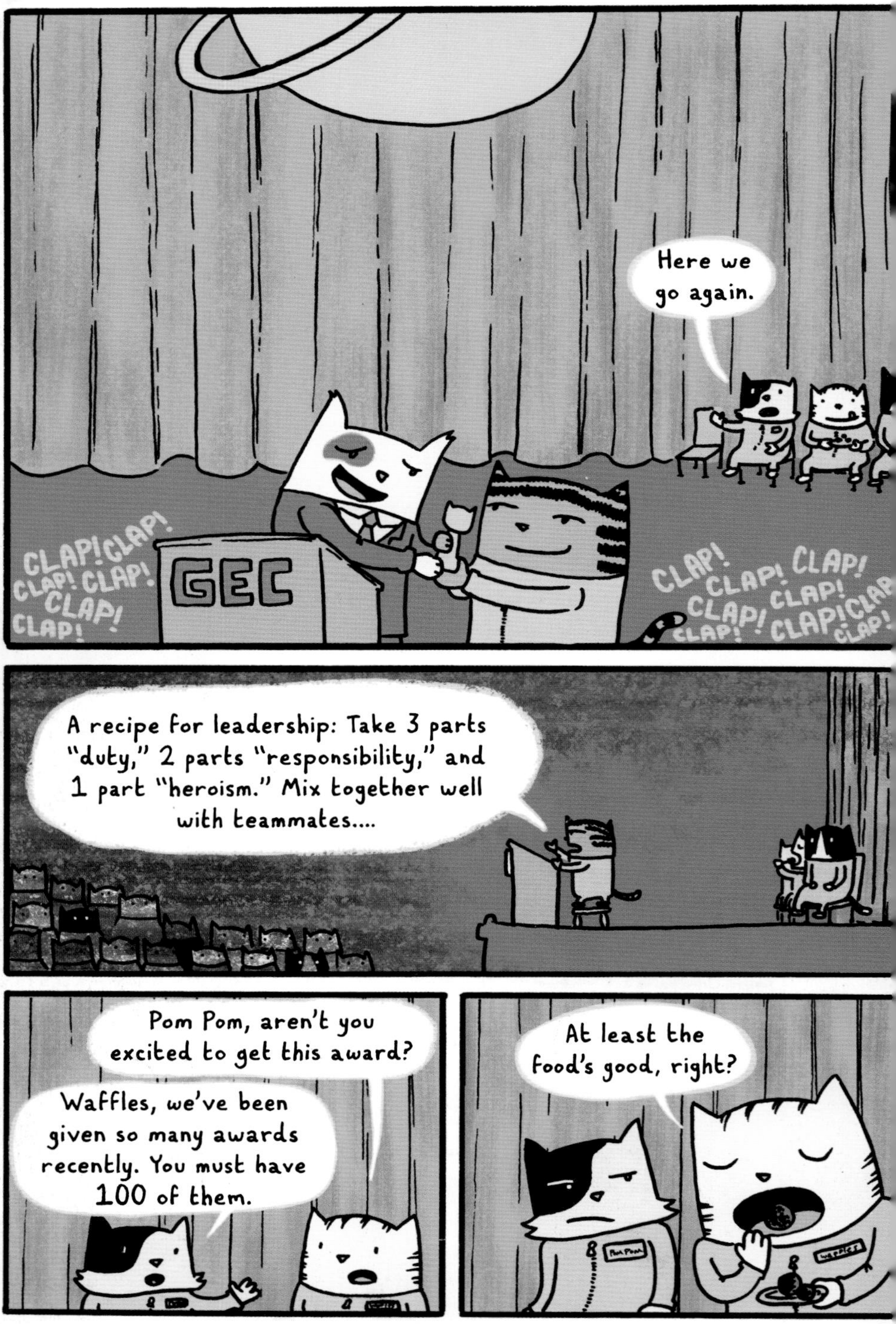
Here we go again.
CLAP! CLAP! CLAP! CLAP! CLAP! CLAP!
GEC
CLAP! CLAP! CLAP! CLAP! CLAP! CLAP! CLAP! CLAP!
A recipe for leadership: Take 3 parts "duty," 2 parts "responsibility," and 1 part "heroism." Mix together well with teammates....
Pom Pom, aren't you excited to get this award?
Waffles, we've been given so many awards recently. You must have 100 of them.
At least the food's good, right?

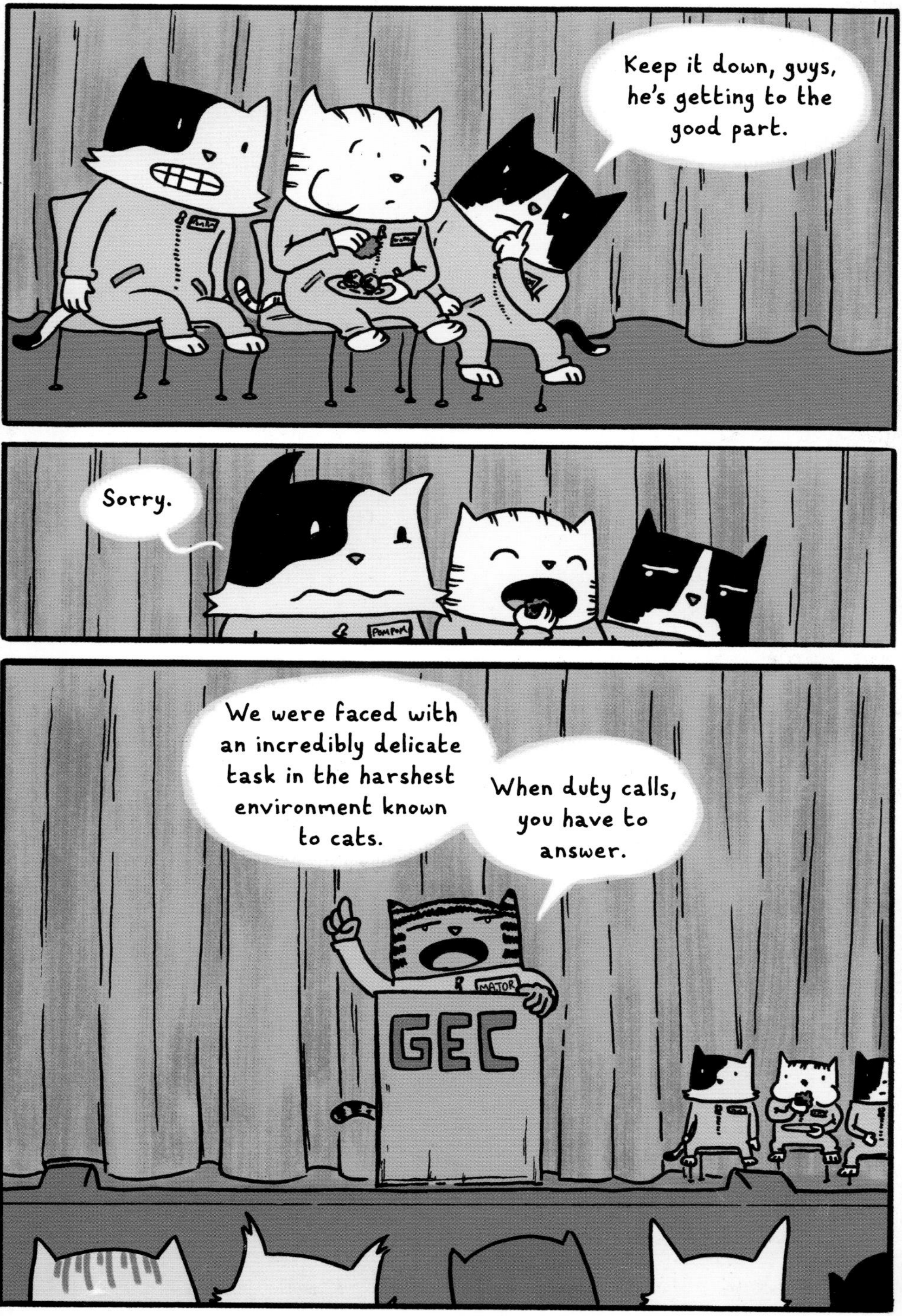
Keep it down, guys, he's getting to the good part.
Sorry.
We were faced with an incredibly delicate task in the harshest environment known to cats.
When duty calls, you have to answer.
POMPOM
MAJOR
GEC

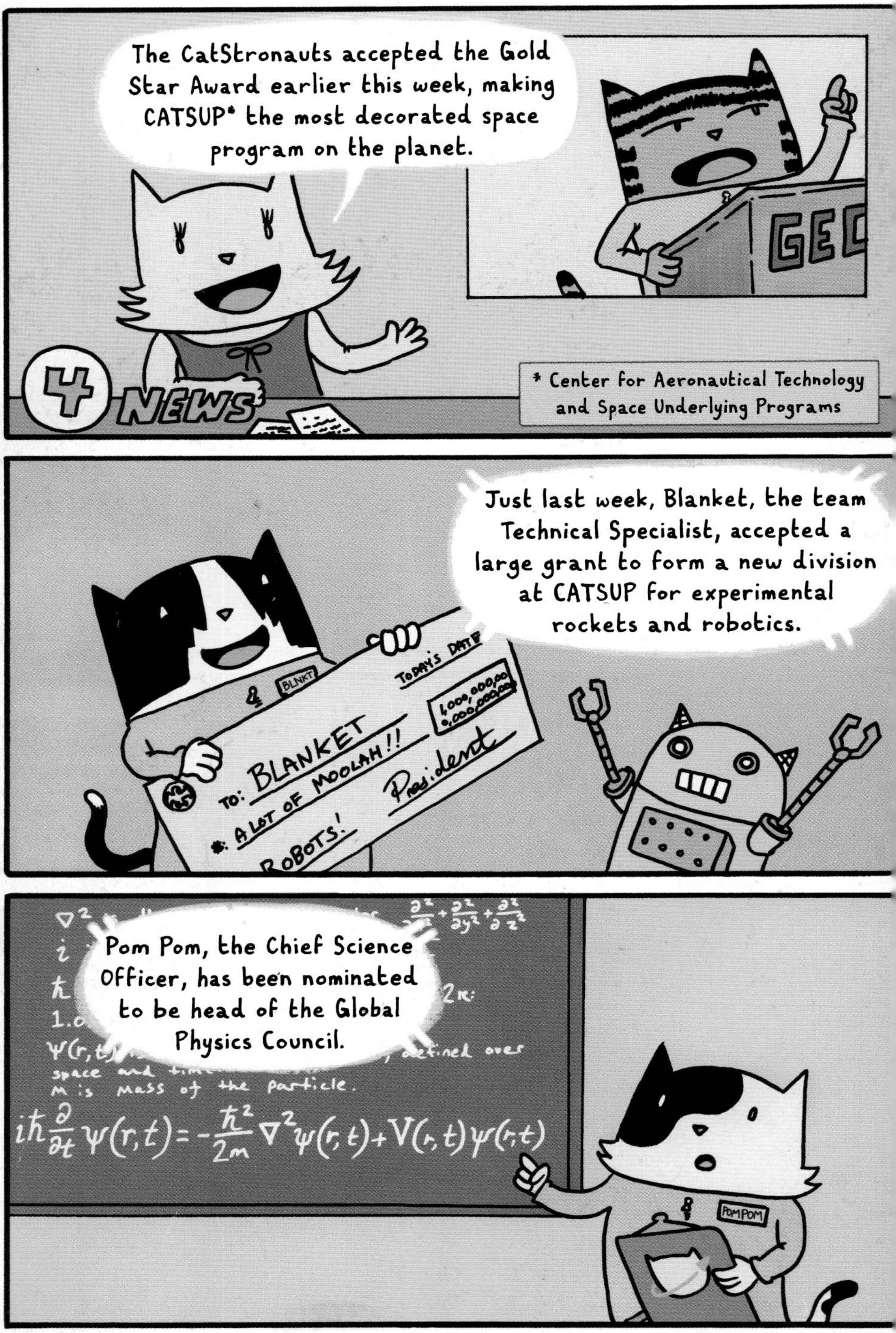
The CatStronauts accepted the Gold Star Award earlier this week, making CATSUP* the most decorated space program on the planet.
4 NEWS
GEC
* Center for Aeronautical Technology and Space Underlying Programs
Just last week, Blanket, the team Technical Specialist, accepted a large grant to form a new division at CATSUP for experimental rockets and robotics.
BLNKT
TODAY'S DATE
TO: BLANKET
A LOT OF MOOLAH!!
President
ROBOTS!
Pom Pom, the Chief Science Officer, has been nominated to be head of the Global Physics Council.
M is mass of the particle.
$i\hbar\frac{\partial}{\partial t}\psi(r,t) = -\frac{\hbar^2}{2m}\nabla^2\psi(r,t) + V(r,t)\psi(r,t)$
POMPOM

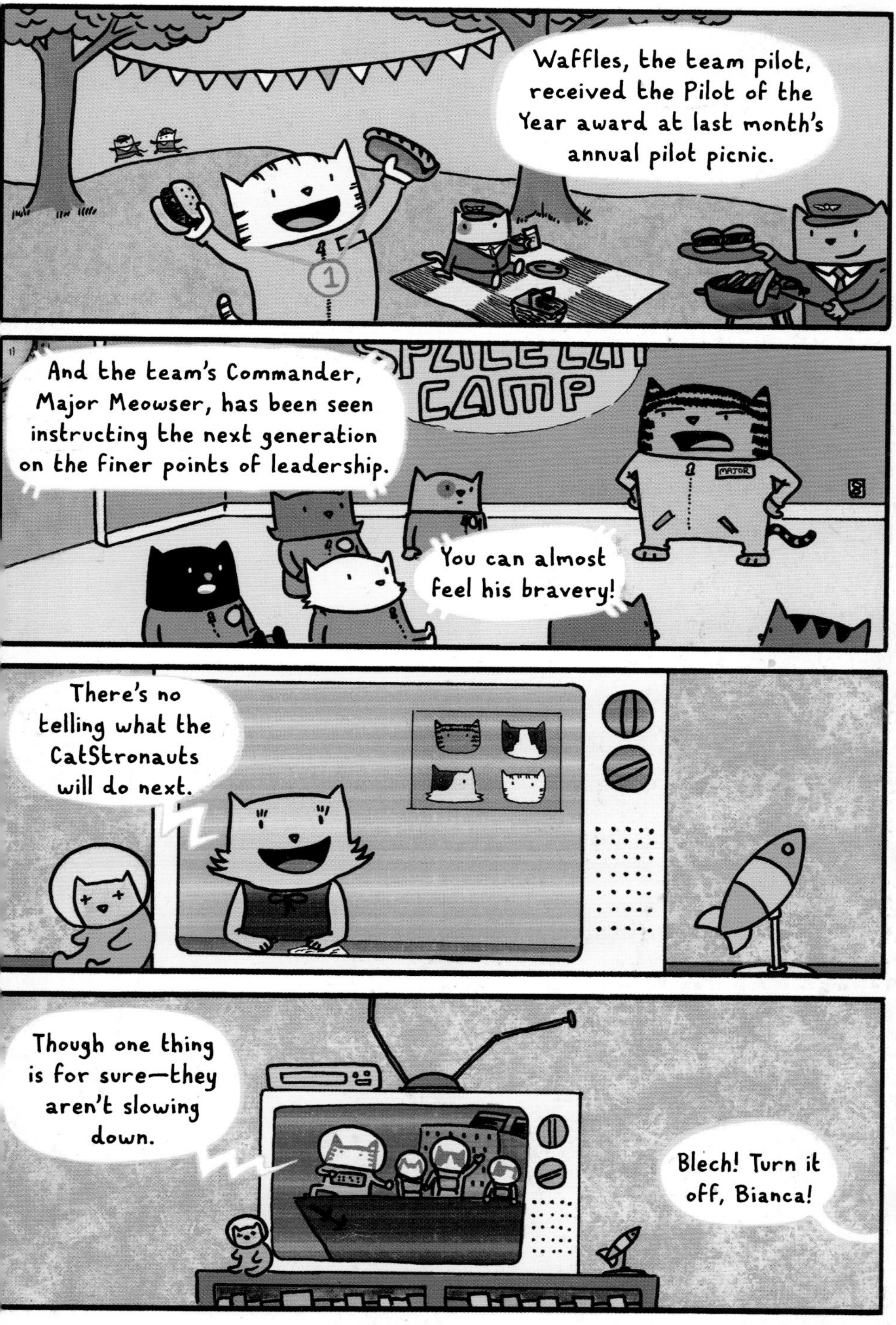

Waffles, the team pilot, received the Pilot of the Year award at last month's annual pilot picnic.
And the team's Commander, Major Meowser, has been seen instructing the next generation on the finer points of leadership.
CAMP
MAJOR
You can almost feel his bravery!
There's no telling what the CatStronauts will do next.
Though one thing is for sure—they aren't slowing down.
Blech! Turn it off, Bianca!

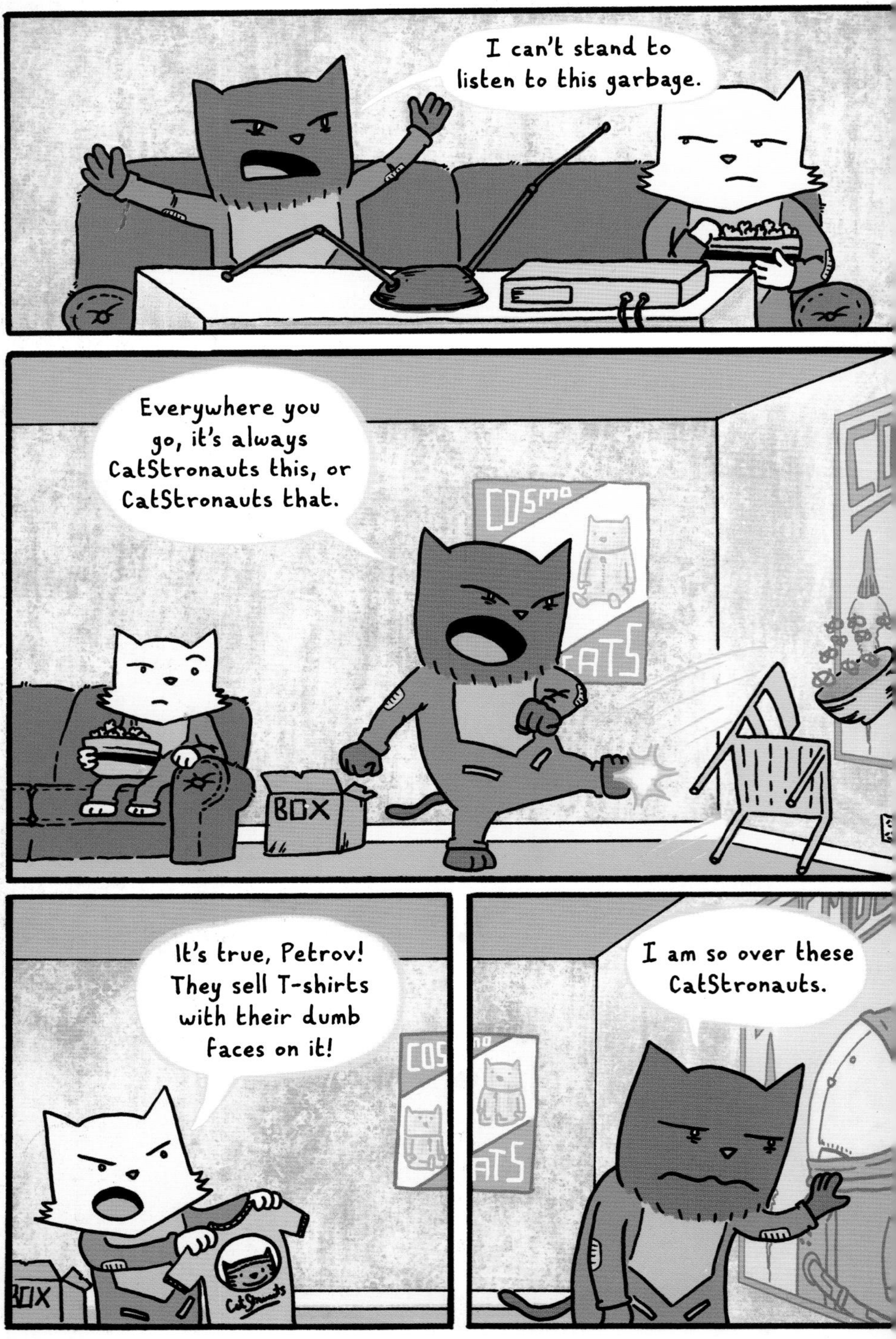

I can't stand to listen to this garbage.
Everywhere you go, it's always CatStronauts this, or CatStronauts that.
COSMO CATS
BOX
It's true, Petrov! They sell T-shirts with their dumb faces on it!
I am so over these CatStronauts.

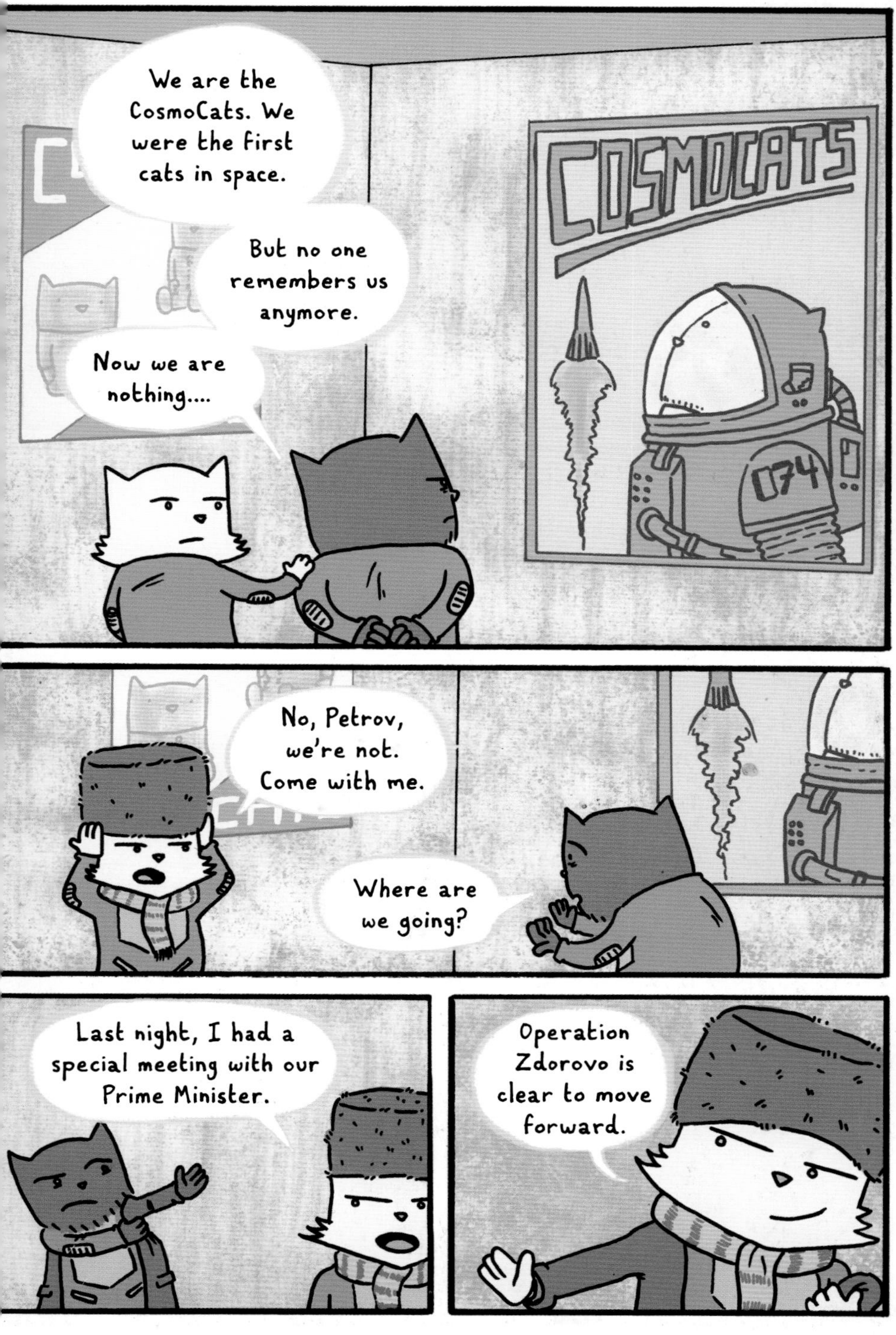
We are the CosmoCats. We were the first cats in space.
But no one remembers us anymore.
Now we are nothing....
COSMOCATS
074
No, Petrov, we're not. Come with me.
Where are we going?
Last night, I had a special meeting with our Prime Minister.
Operation Zdorovo is clear to move forward.

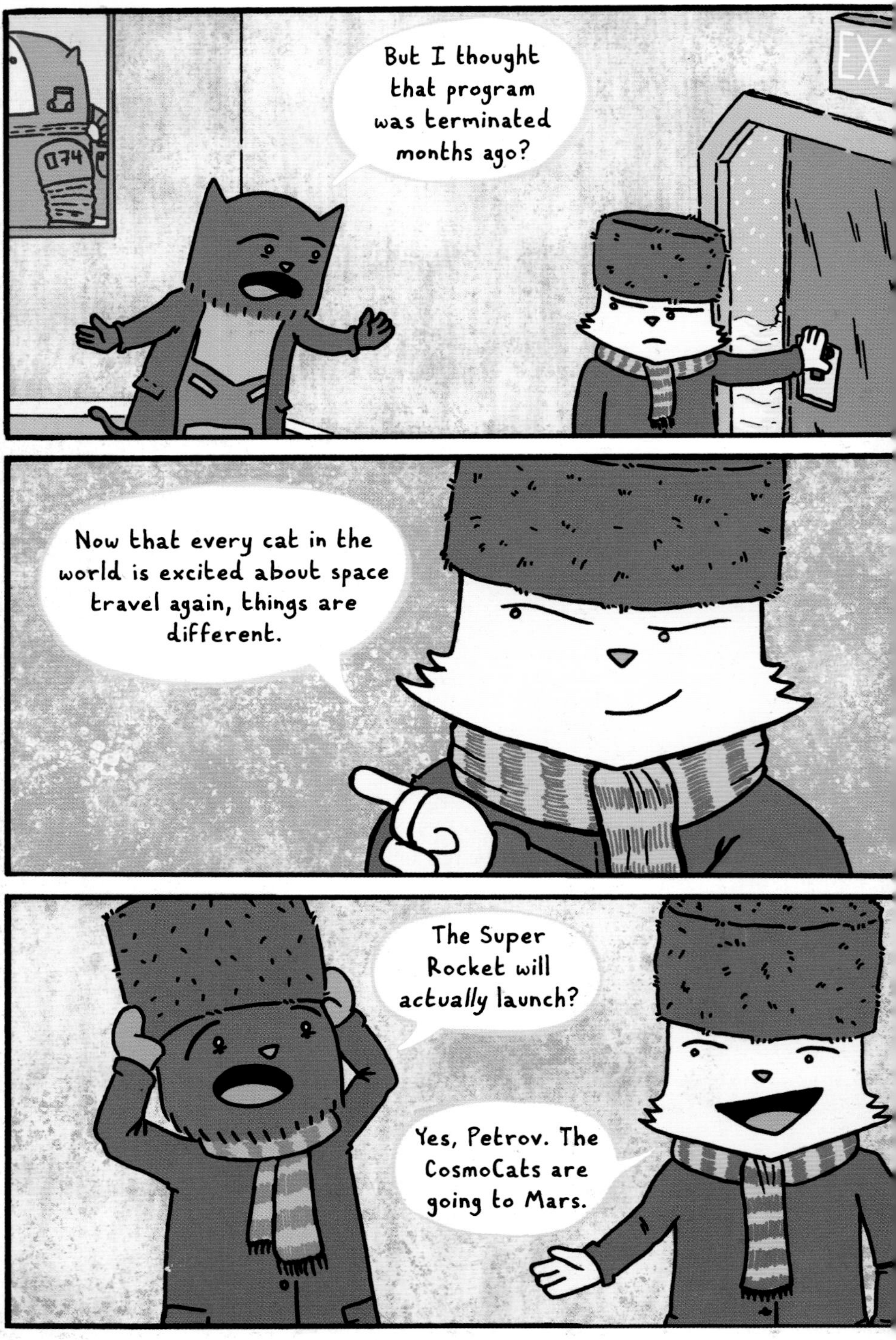
But I thought that program was terminated months ago?
Now that every cat in the world is excited about space travel again, things are different.
The Super Rocket will *actually* launch?
Yes, Petrov. The CosmoCats are going to Mars.

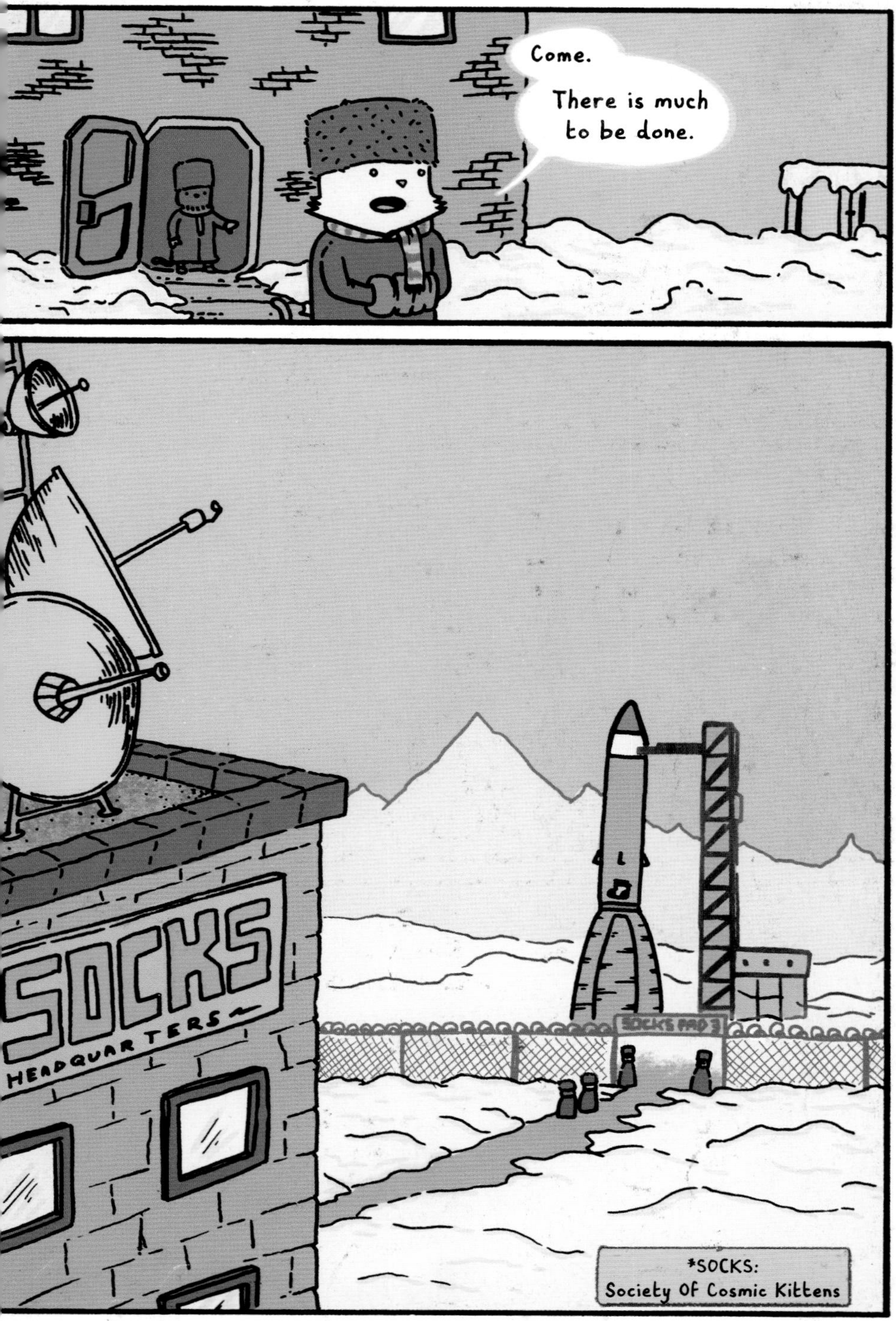
Come.
There is much to be done.
SOCKS
HEADQUARTERS
SOCKS PAD 3
*SOCKS:
Society Of Cosmic Kittens

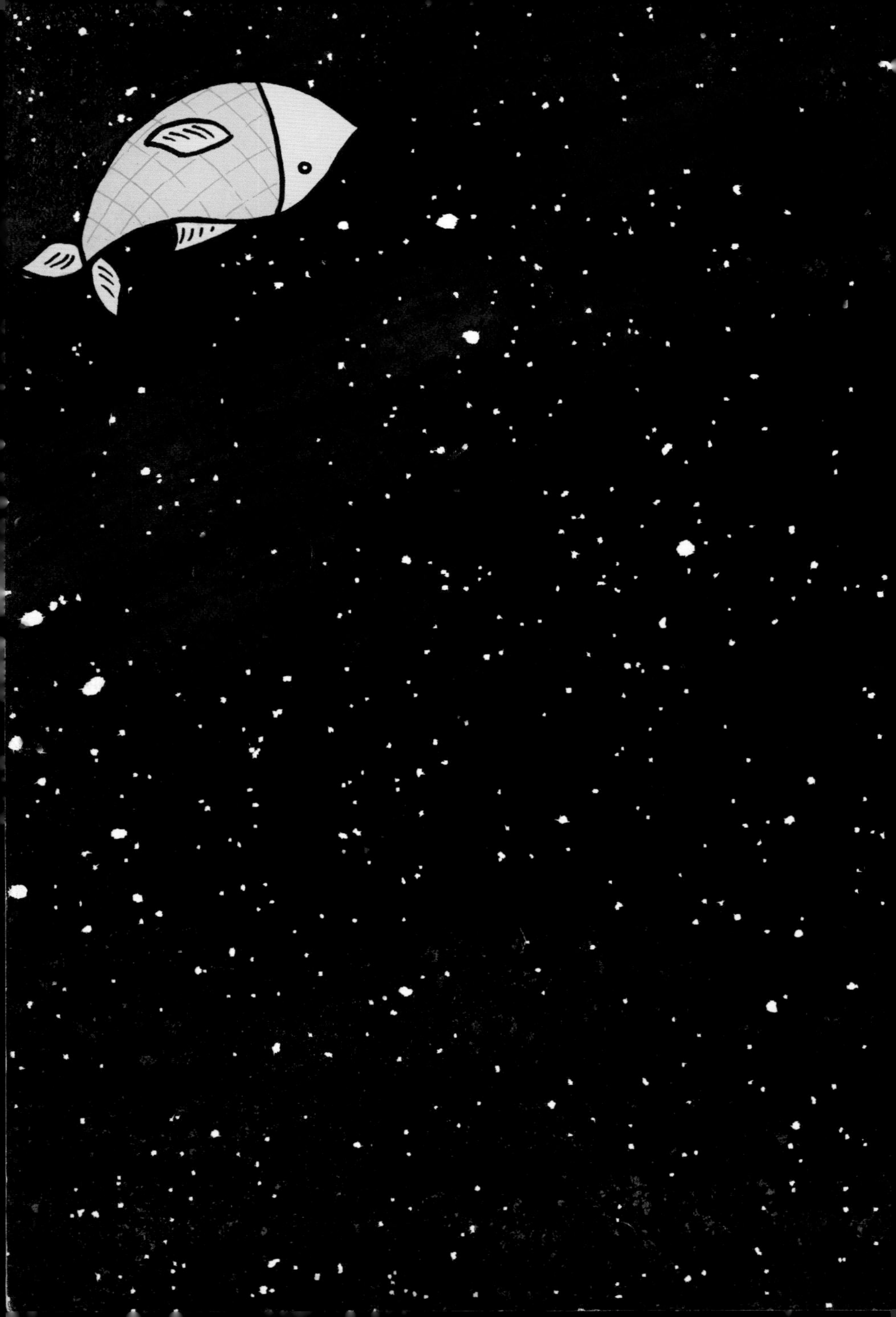

CHAPTER 2

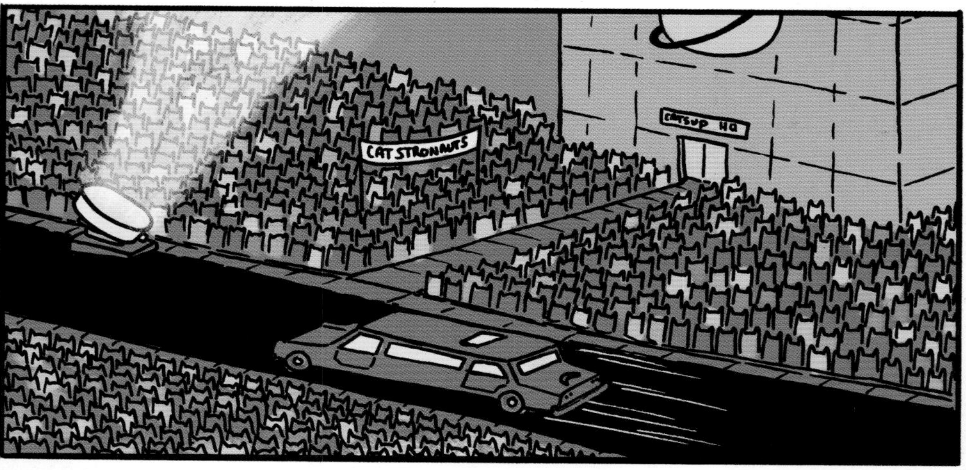
CATSTRONAUTS
CATSUP HQ

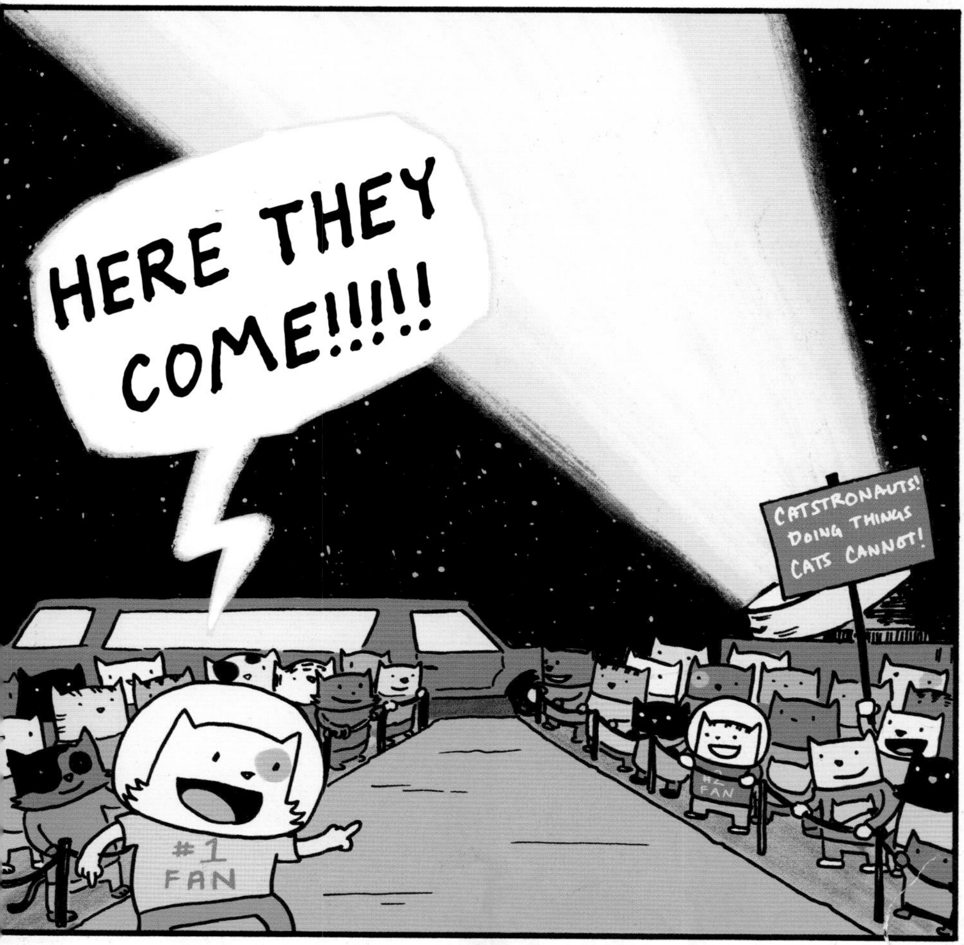
HERE THEY COME!!!!!
CATSTRONAUTS! DOING THINGS CATS CANNOT!
#1 FAN
#2 FAN

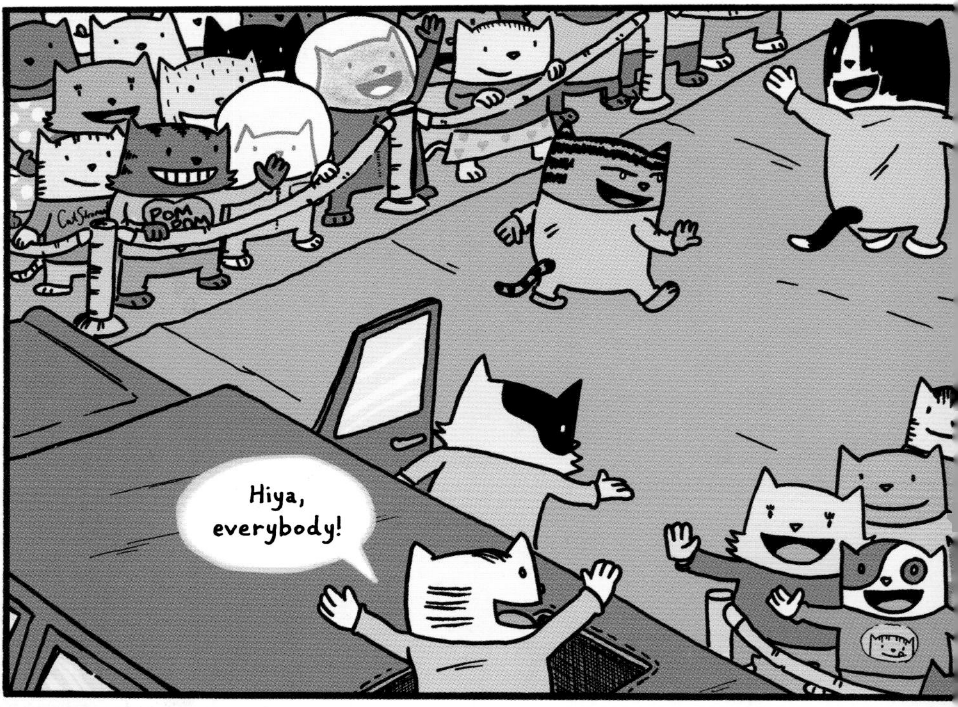
POM POM
Hiya, everybody!

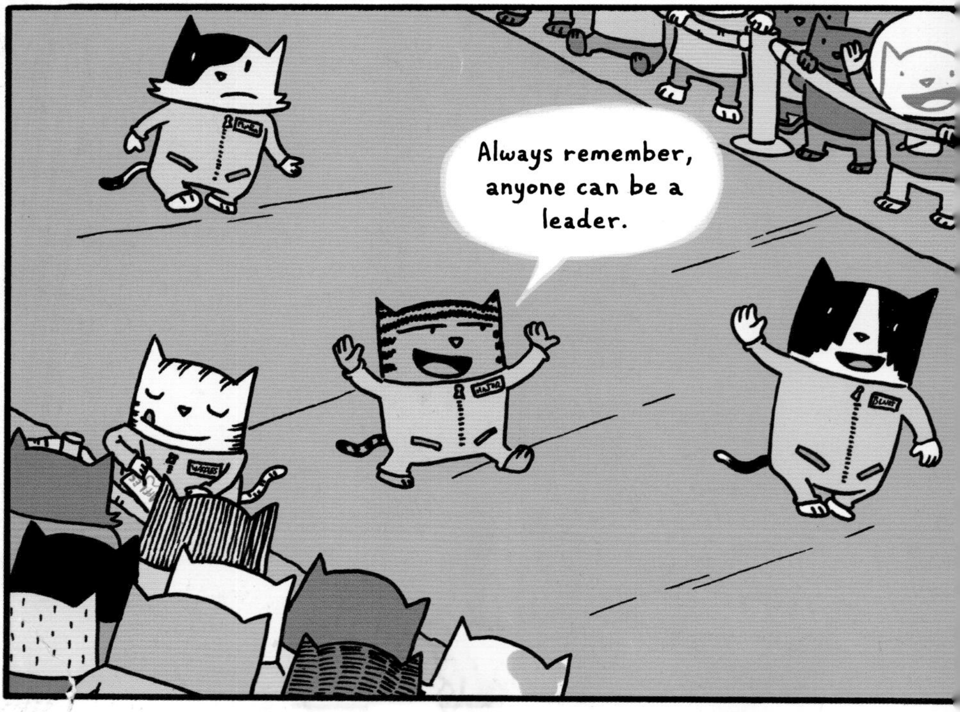
Always remember, anyone can be a leader.

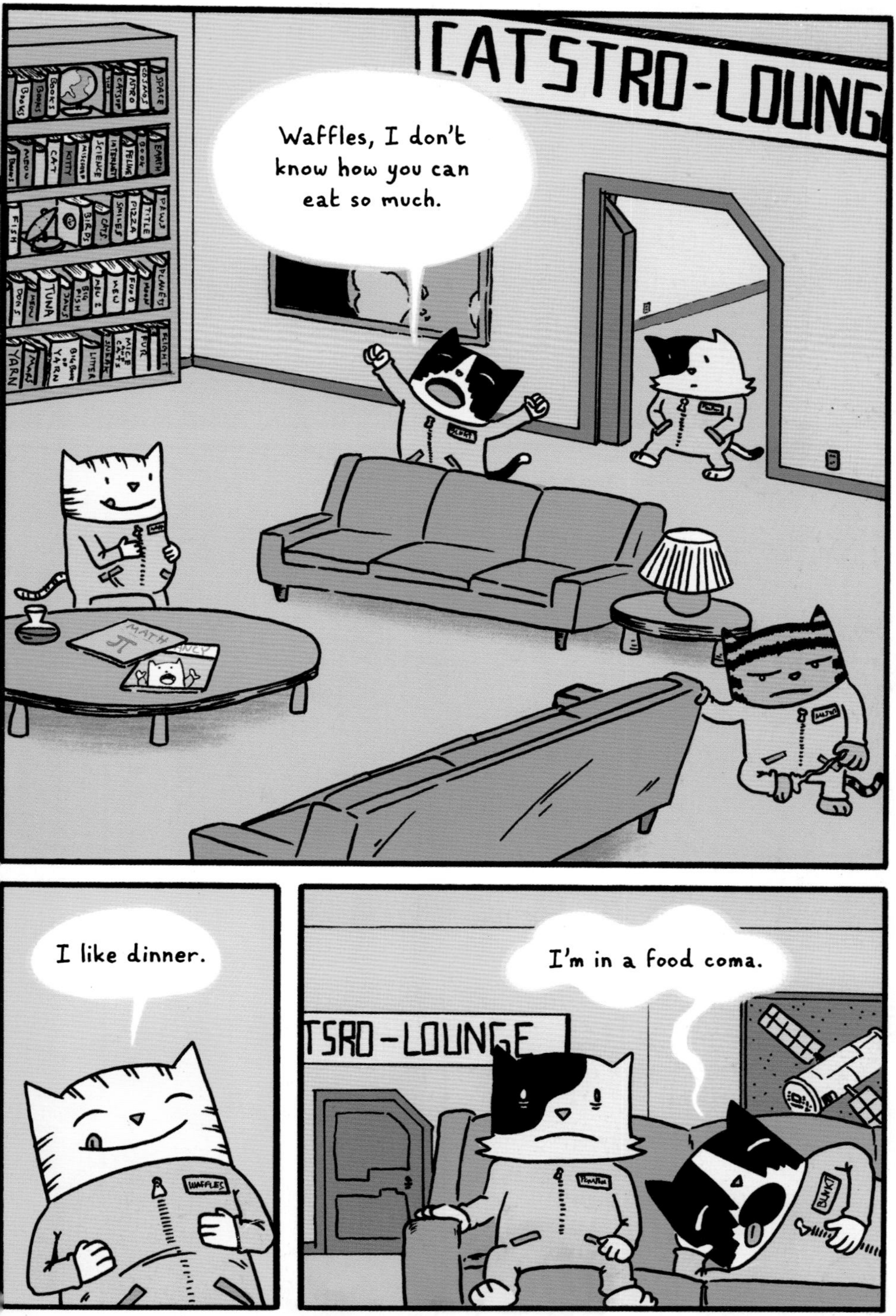
CATSTRO-LOUNG
Waffles, I don't know how you can eat so much.
I like dinner.
TSRO-LOUNGE
I'm in a food coma.

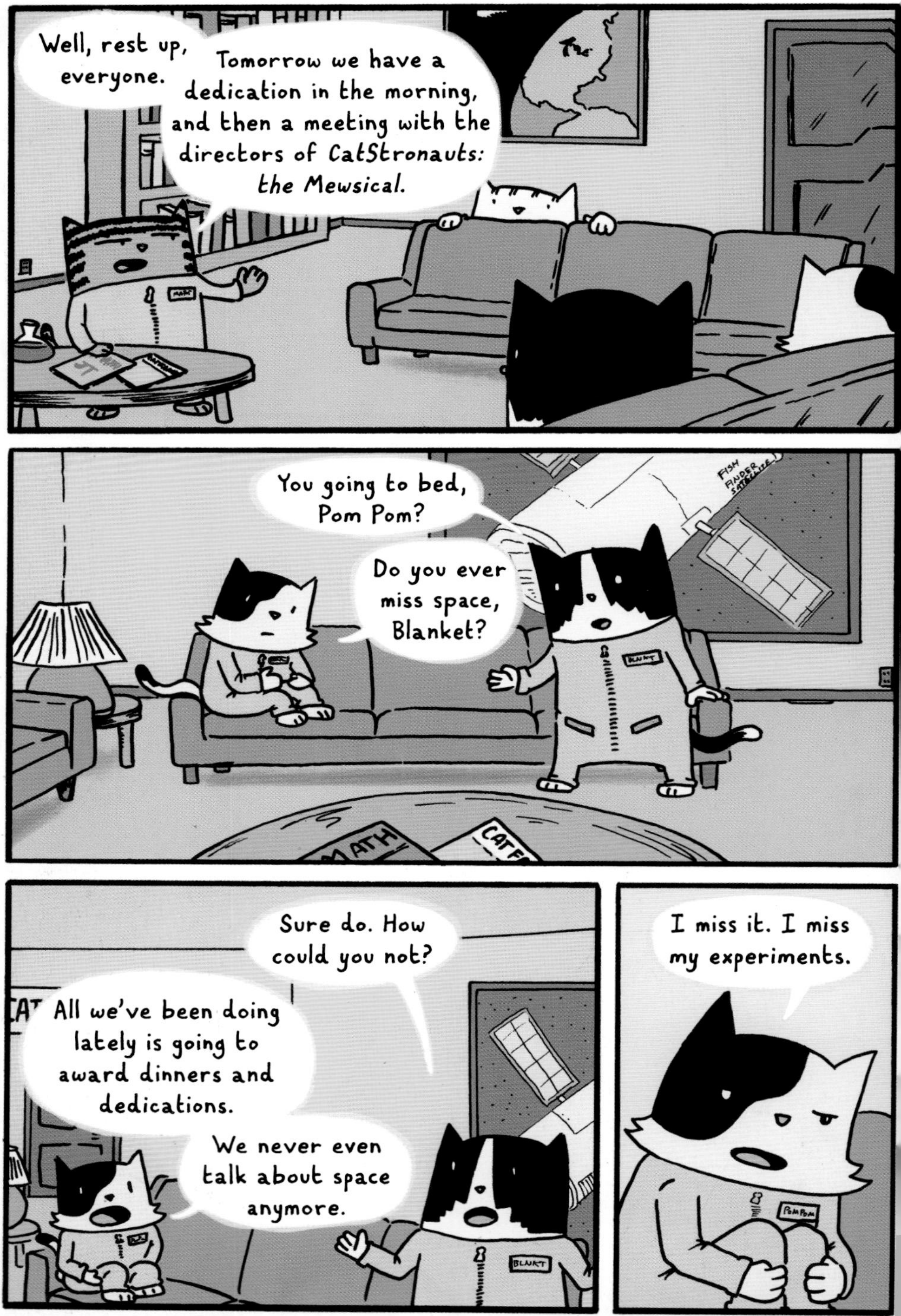

Well, rest up, everyone.
Tomorrow we have a dedication in the morning, and then a meeting with the directors of CatStronauts: the Mewsical.
You going to bed, Pom Pom?
Do you ever miss space, Blanket?
Sure do. How could you not?
All we've been doing lately is going to award dinners and dedications.
We never even talk about space anymore.
I miss it. I miss my experiments.

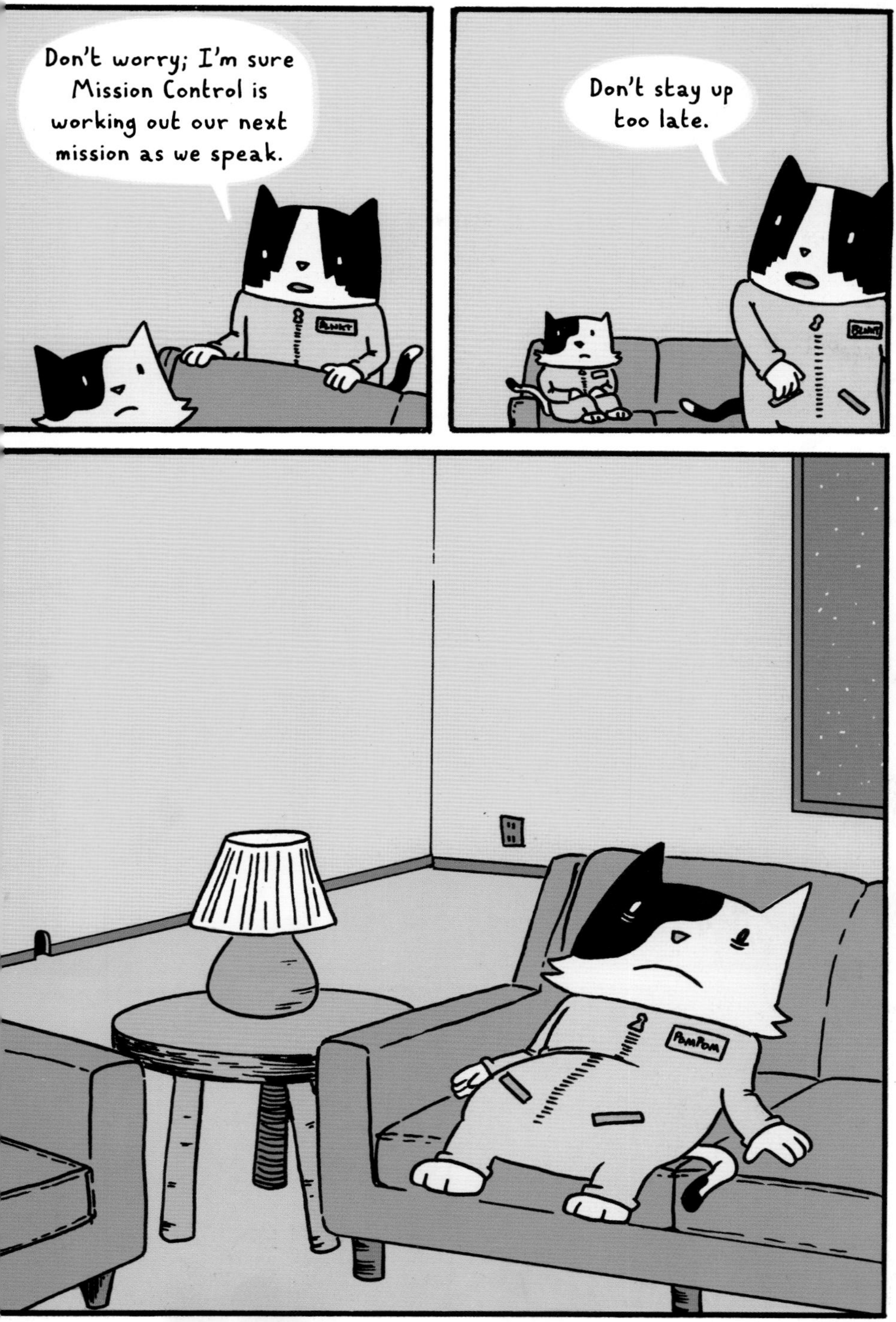

Don't worry; I'm sure Mission Control is working out our next mission as we speak.
Don't stay up too late.
POMPOM

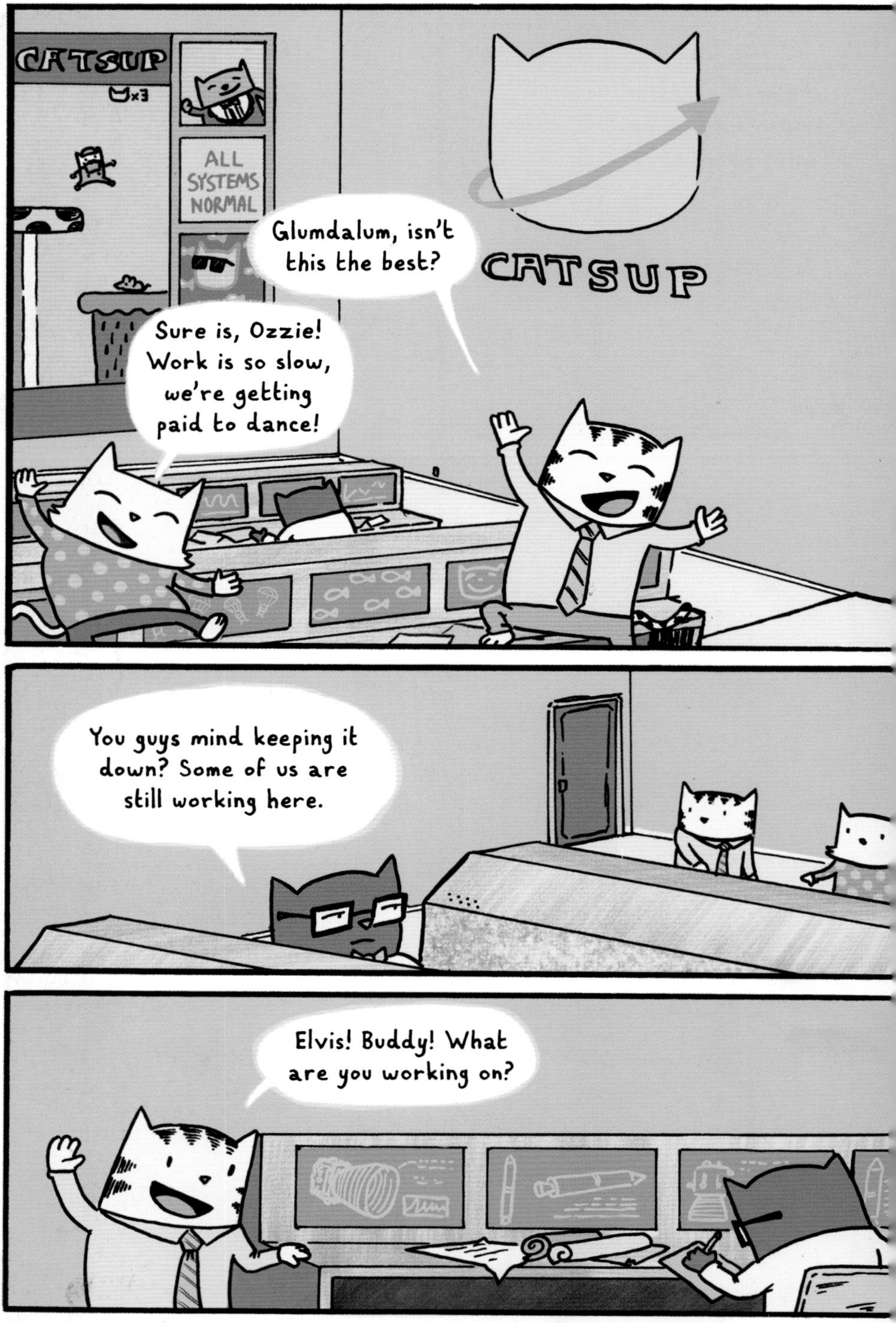
CATSUP
ALL SYSTEMS NORMAL
CATSUP
Glumdalum, isn't this the best?
Sure is, Ozzie! Work is so slow, we're getting paid to dance!
You guys mind keeping it down? Some of us are still working here.
Elvis! Buddy! What are you working on?

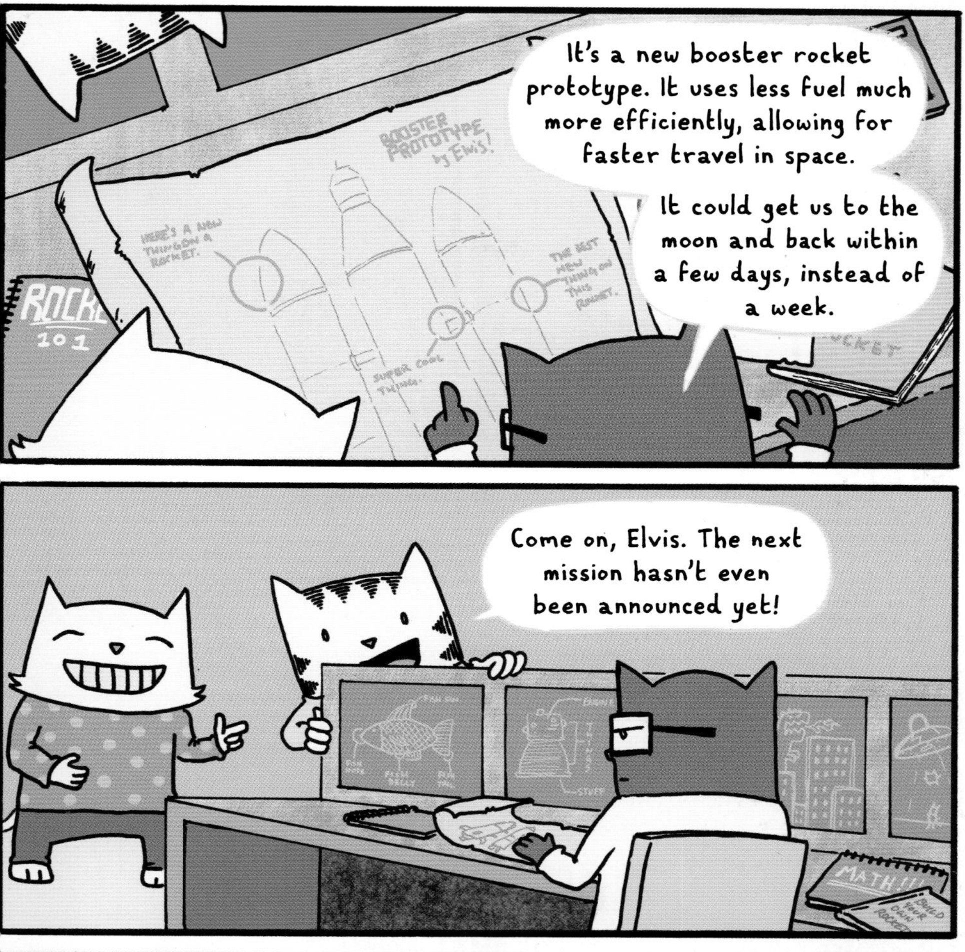
BOOSTER PROTOTYPE
It's a new booster rocket prototype. It uses less fuel much more efficiently, allowing for faster travel in space.
It could get us to the moon and back within a few days, instead of a week.
Come on, Elvis. The next mission hasn't even been announced yet!
MATH!!!
Yeah, quit working so hard! Take a break and have a little fun.

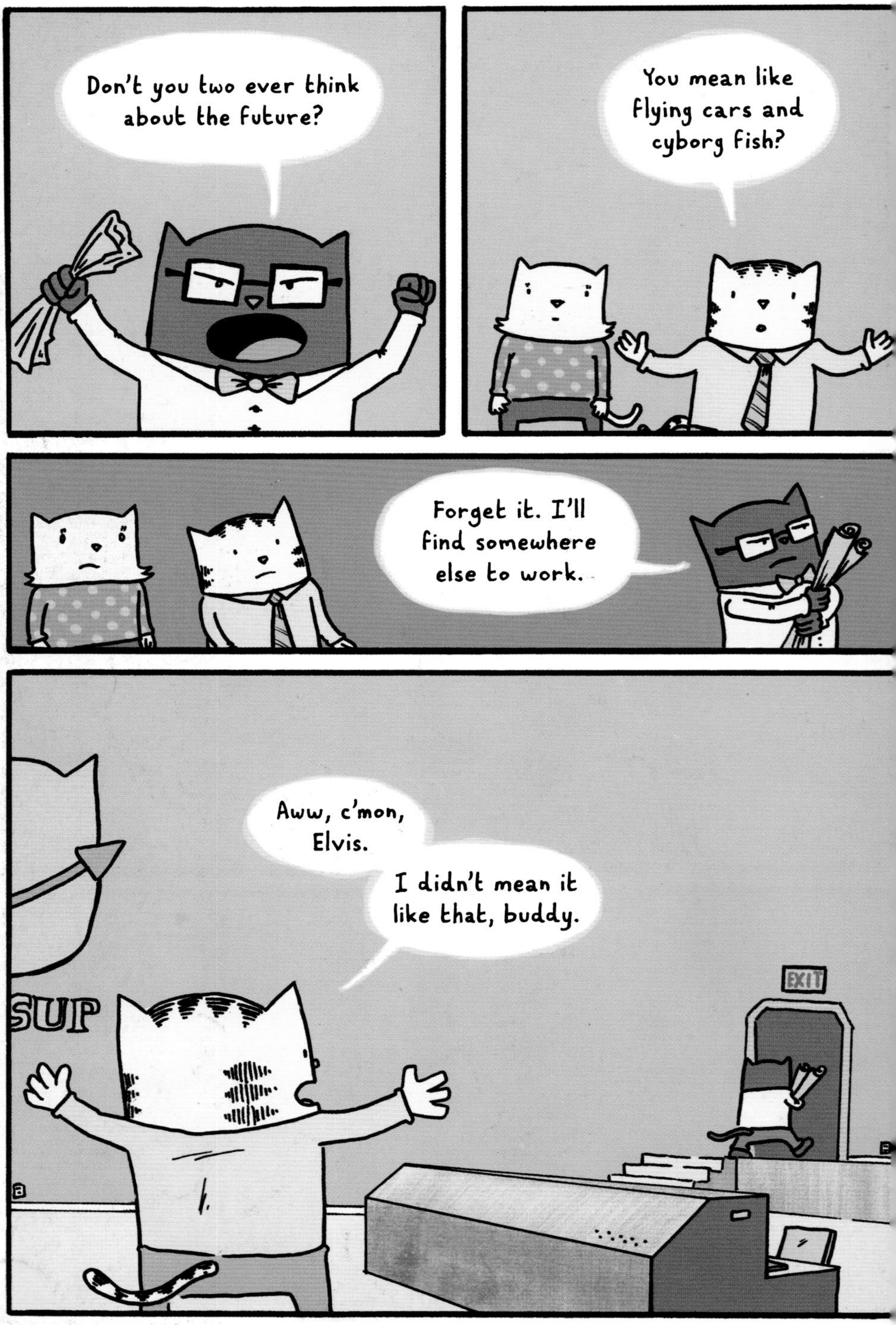
Don't you two ever think about the future?
You mean like flying cars and cyborg fish?
Forget it. I'll find somewhere else to work.
Aww, c'mon, Elvis.
I didn't mean it like that, buddy.
SUP
EXIT

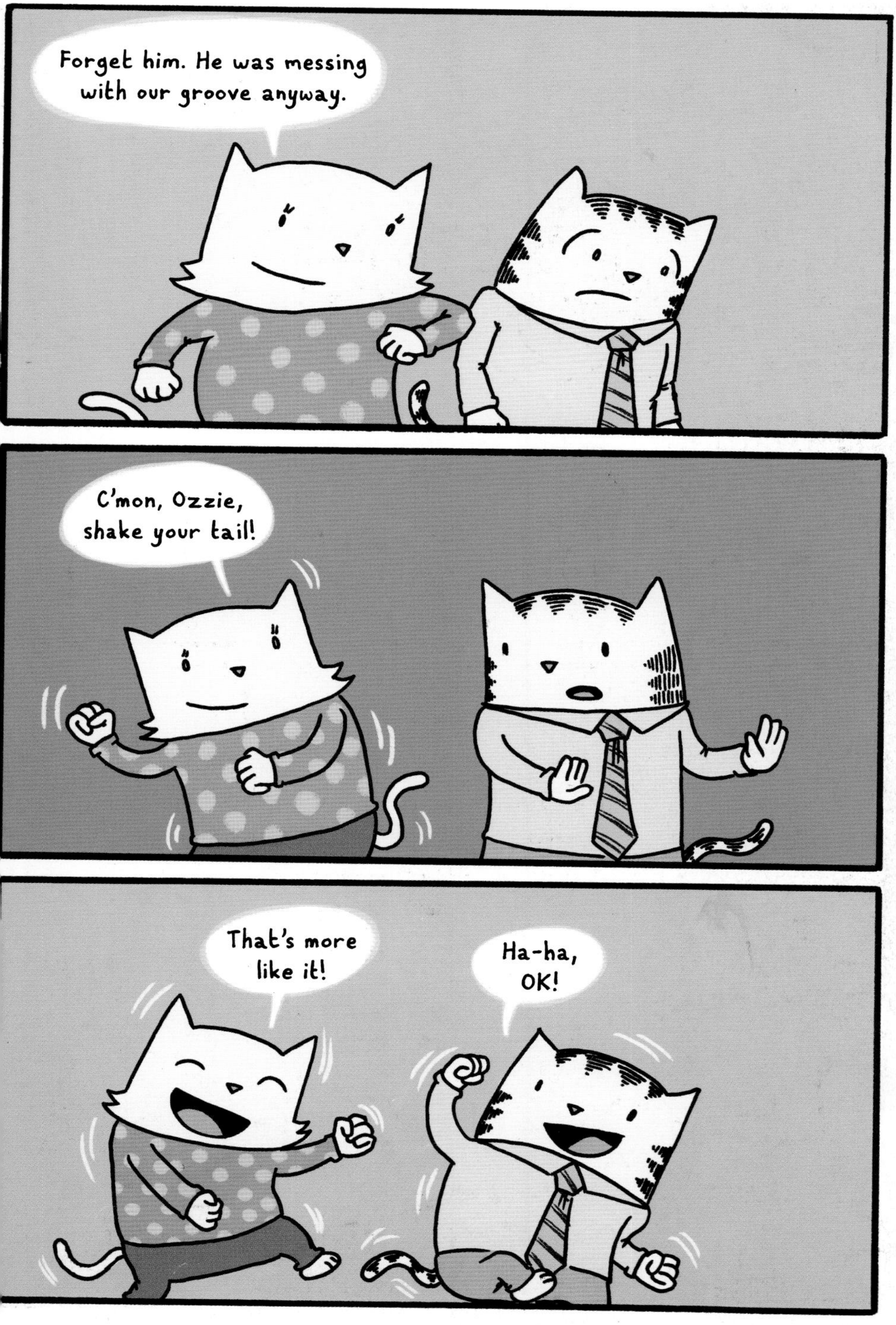
Forget him. He was messing with our groove anyway.
C'mon, Ozzie, shake your tail!
That's more like it!
Ha-ha, OK!

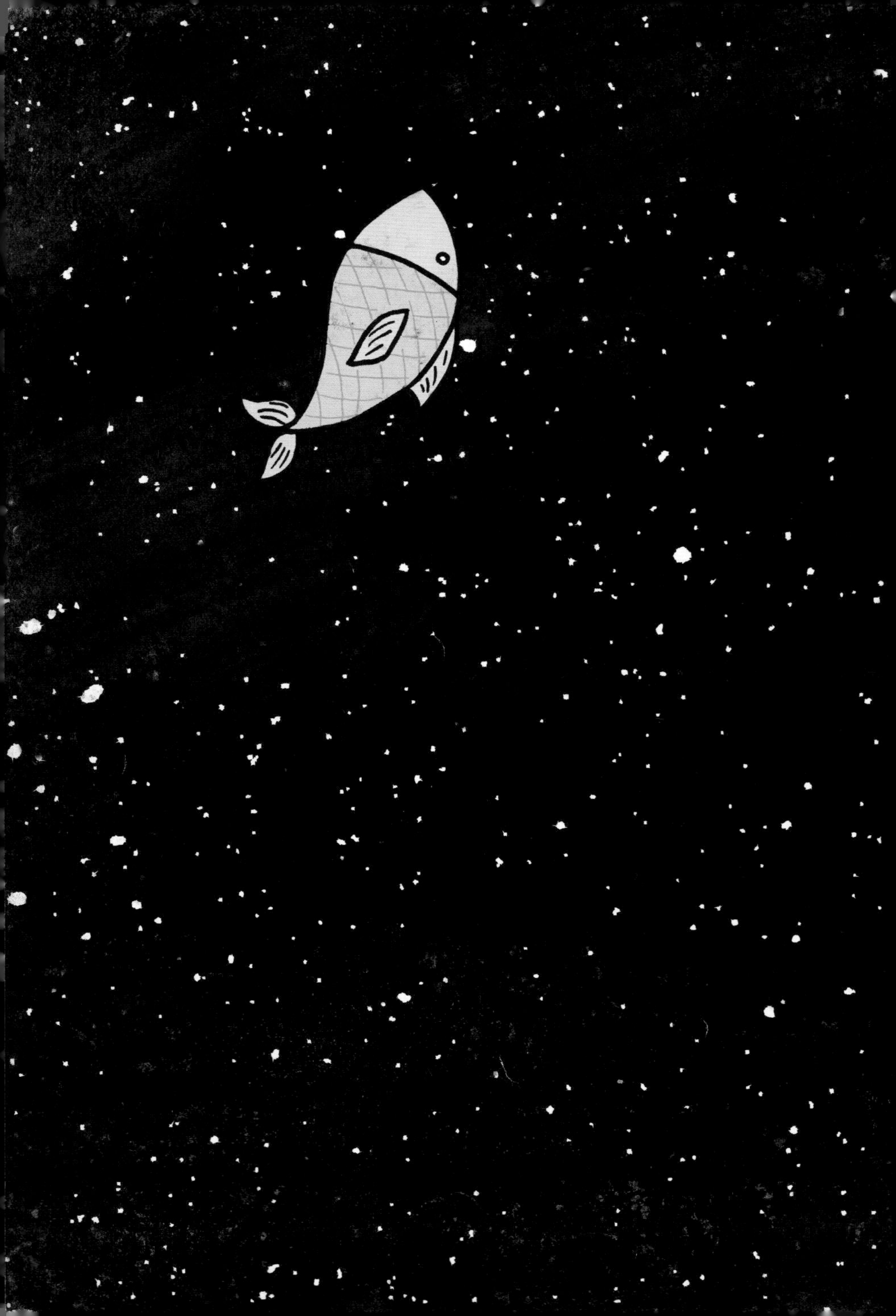

CHAPTER 3

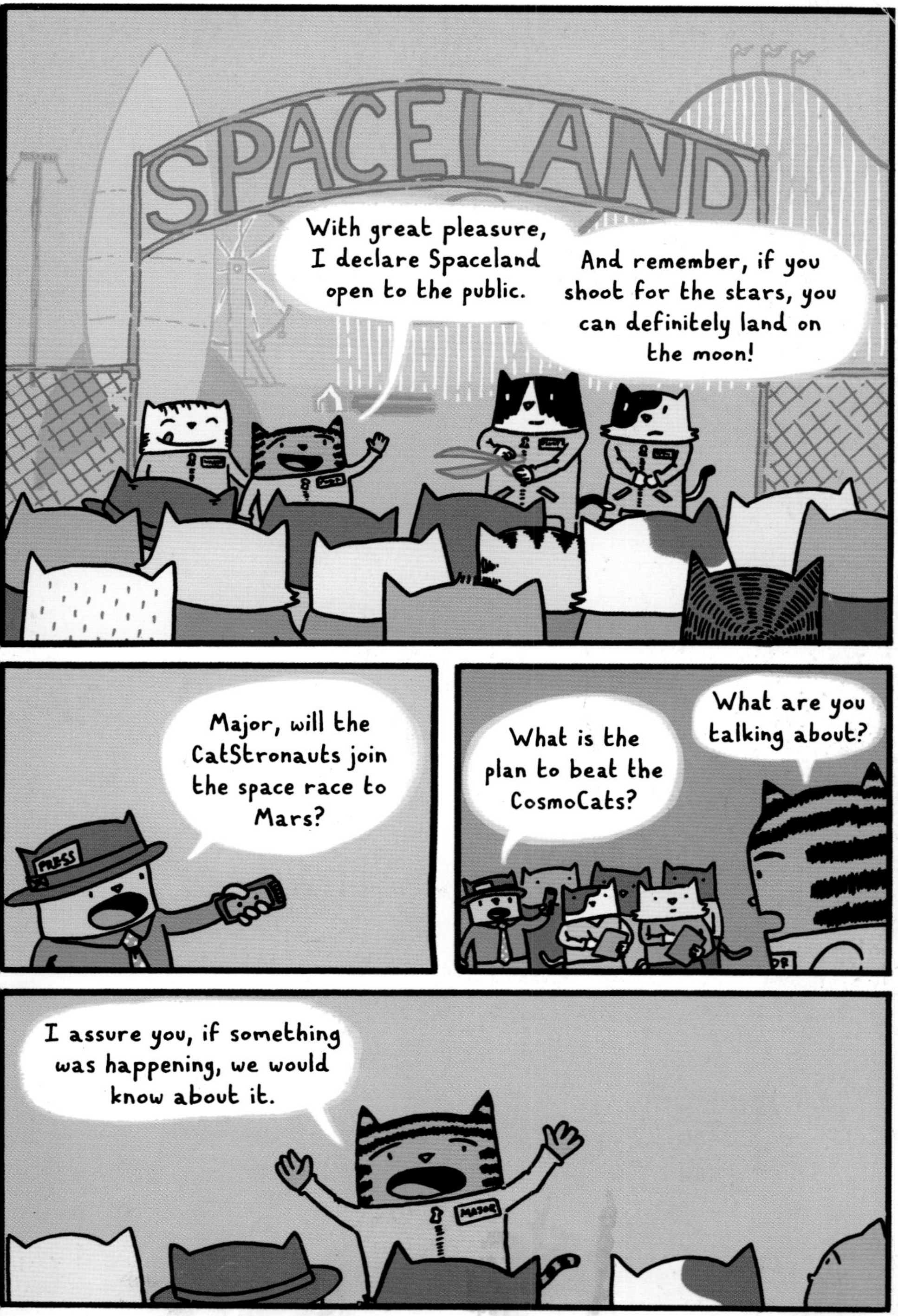
SPACELAND
With great pleasure, I declare Spaceland open to the public.
And remember, if you shoot for the stars, you can definitely land on the moon!
PRESS
Major, will the CatStronauts join the space race to Mars?
What is the plan to beat the CosmoCats?
What are you talking about?
I assure you, if something was happening, we would know about it.
MAJOR

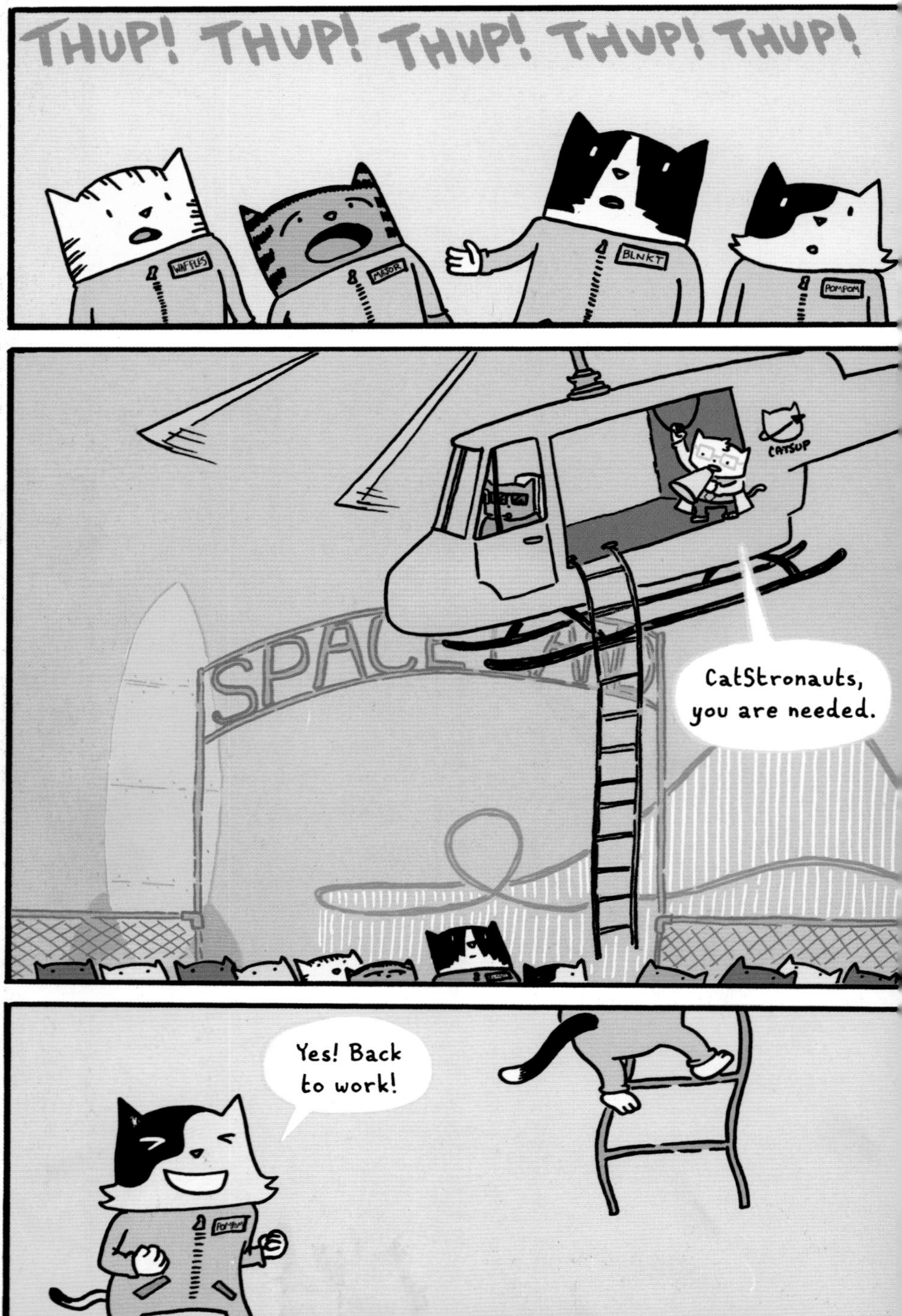
THUP! THUP! THUP! THUP! THUP!
WAFFLES
MAJOR
BLNKT
POMPOM
CATSUP
SPACE
CatStronauts, you are needed.
Yes! Back to work!

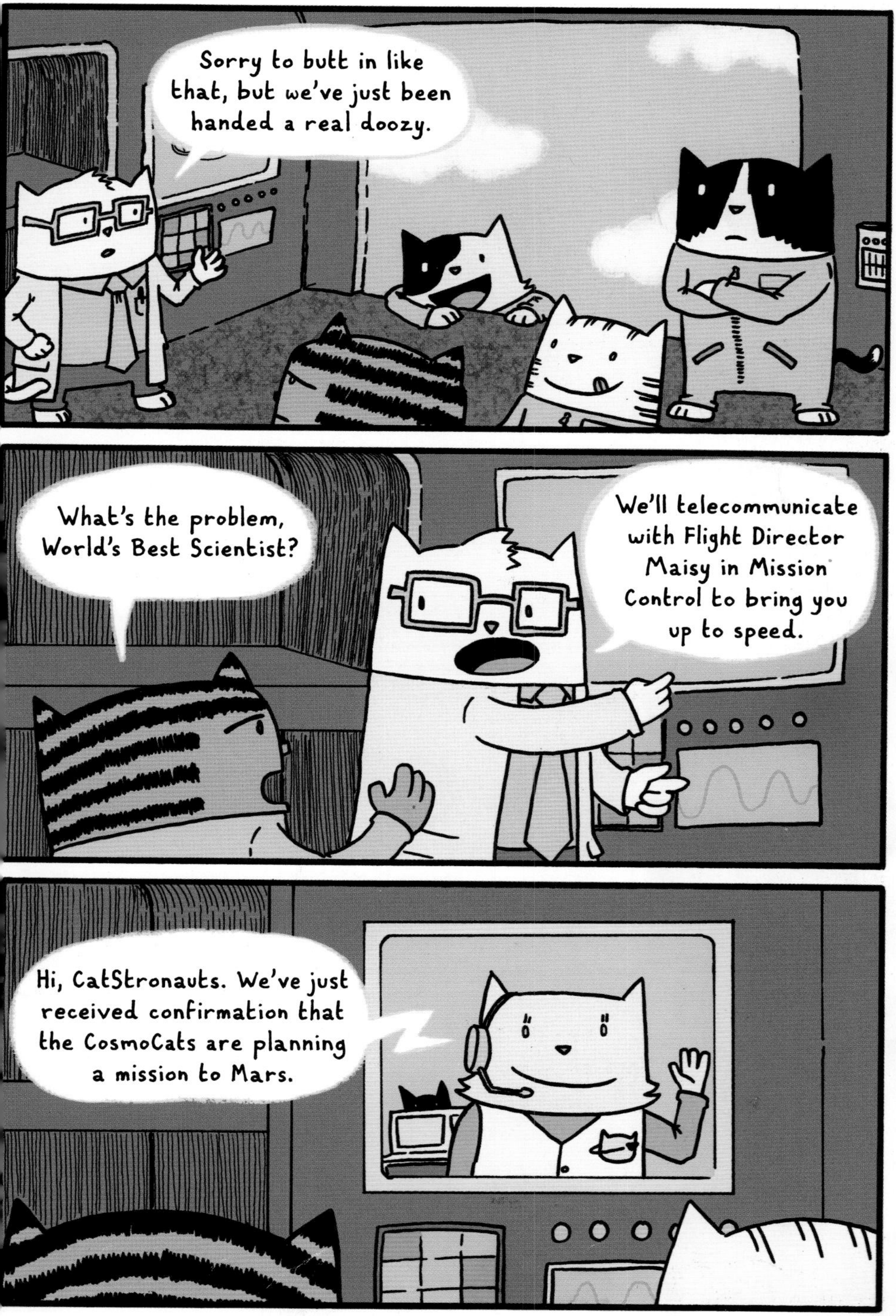
Sorry to butt in like that, but we've just been handed a real doozy.
What's the problem, World's Best Scientist?
We'll telecommunicate with Flight Director Maisy in Mission Control to bring you up to speed.
Hi, CatStronauts. We've just received confirmation that the CosmoCats are planning a mission to Mars.

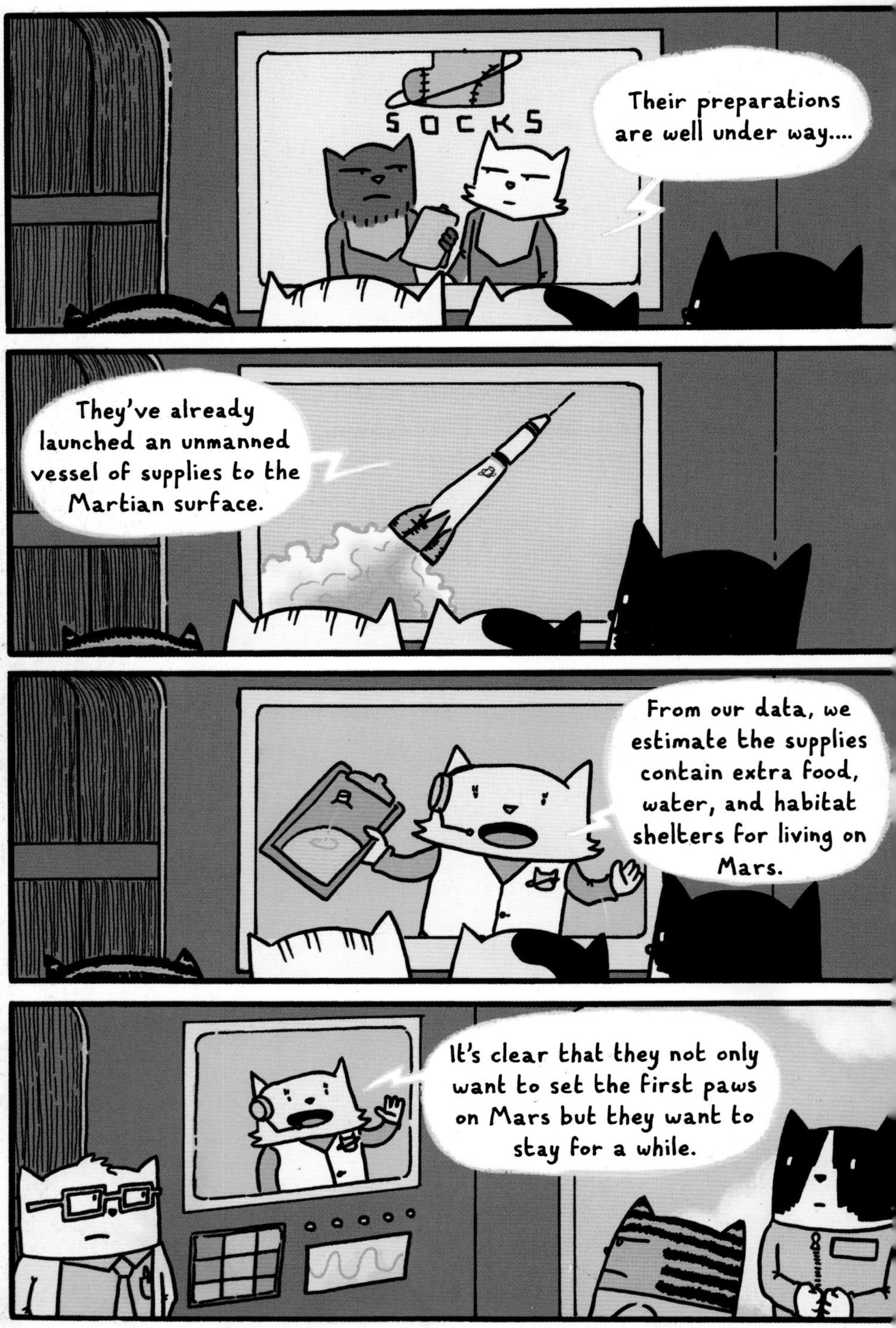
SOCKS
Their preparations are well under way....
They've already launched an unmanned vessel of supplies to the Martian surface.
From our data, we estimate the supplies contain extra food, water, and habitat shelters for living on Mars.
It's clear that they not only want to set the first paws on Mars but they want to stay for a while.

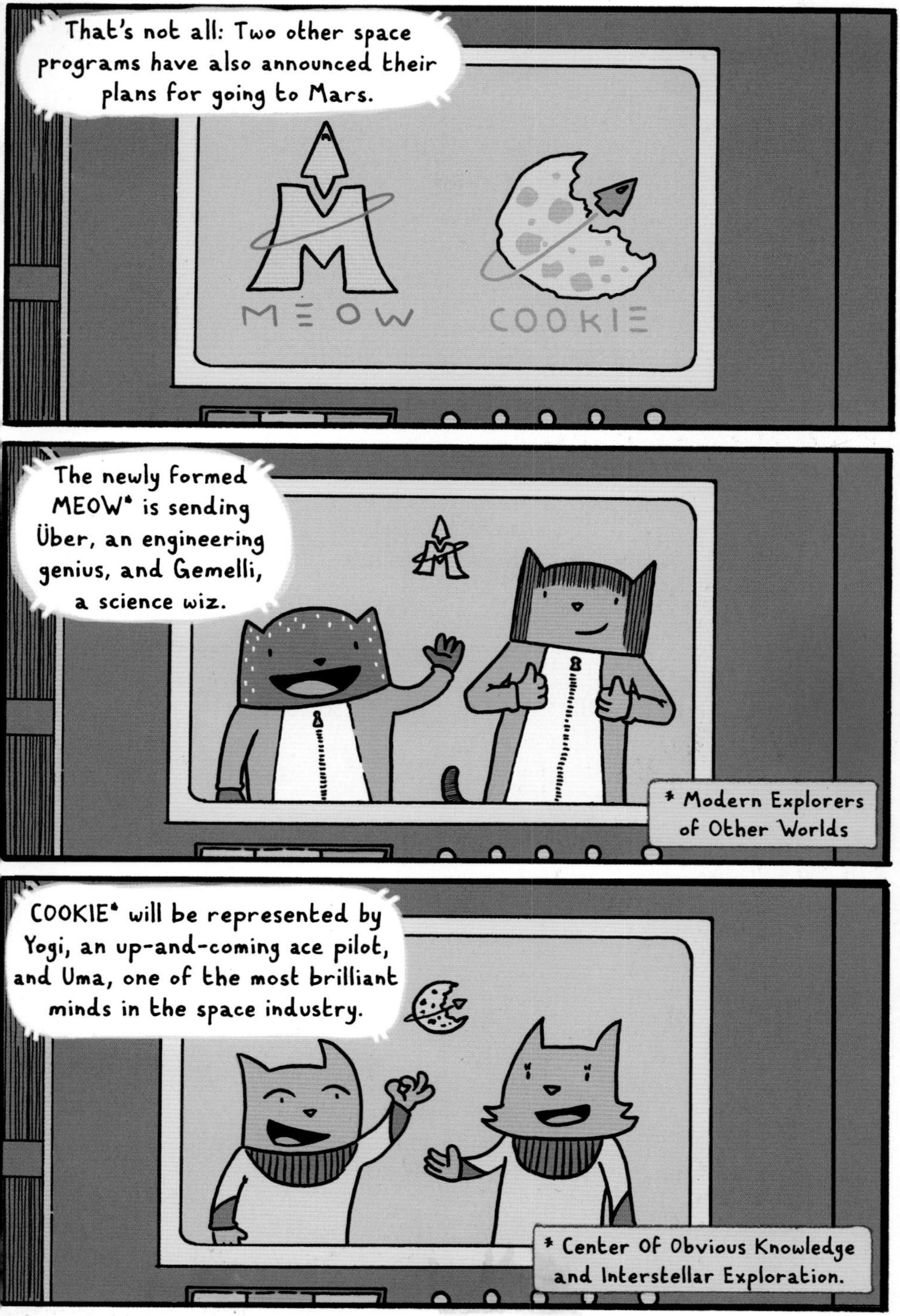
That's not all: Two other space programs have also announced their plans for going to Mars.
MEOW
COOKIE
The newly formed MEOW* is sending Über, an engineering genius, and Gemelli, a science wiz.
* Modern Explorers of Other Worlds
COOKIE* will be represented by Yogi, an up-and-coming ace pilot, and Uma, one of the most brilliant minds in the space industry.
* Center Of Obvious Knowledge and Interstellar Exploration.

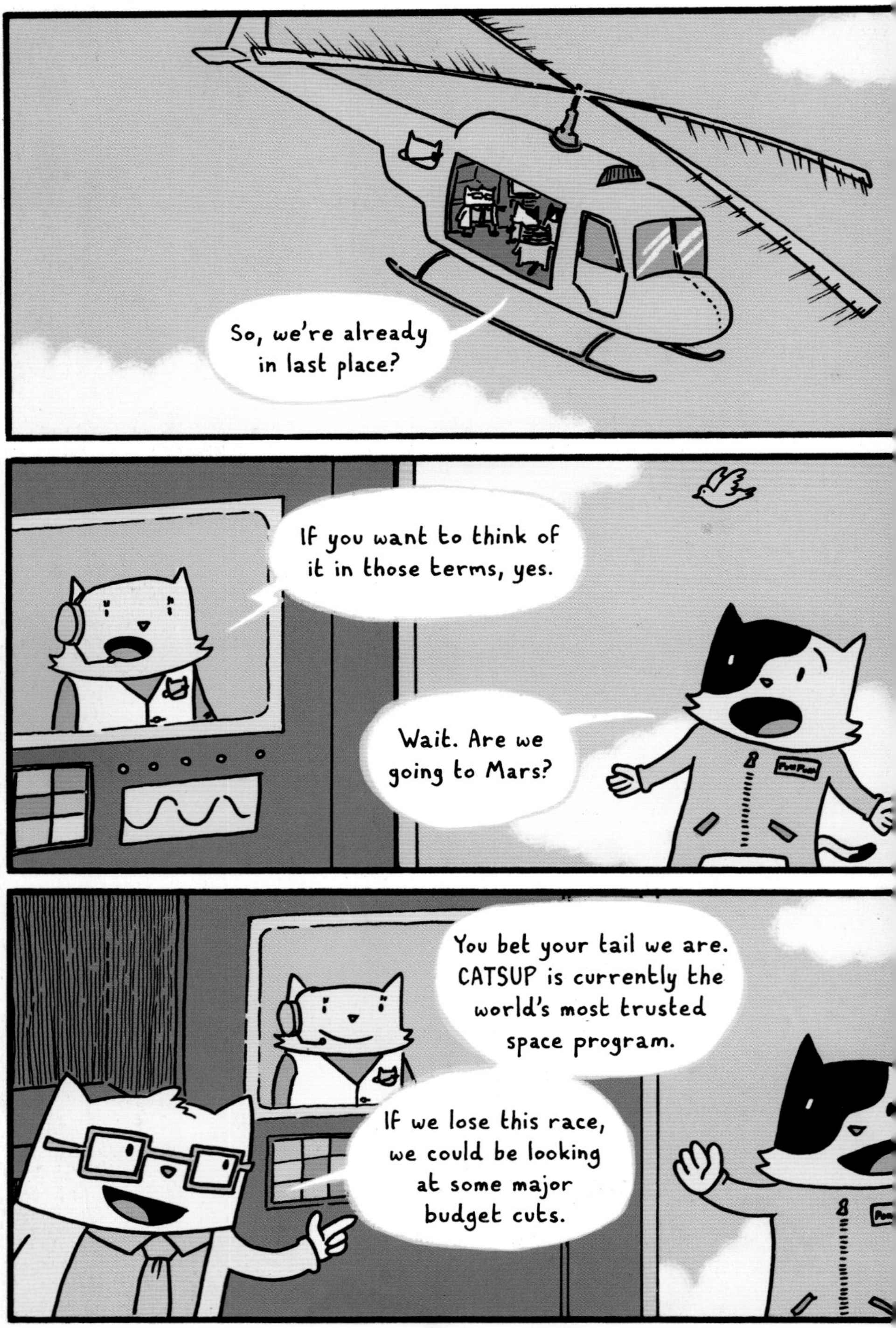

So, we're already in last place?
If you want to think of it in those terms, yes.
Wait. Are we going to Mars?
You bet your tail we are. CATSUP is currently the world's most trusted space program.
If we lose this race, we could be looking at some major budget cuts.

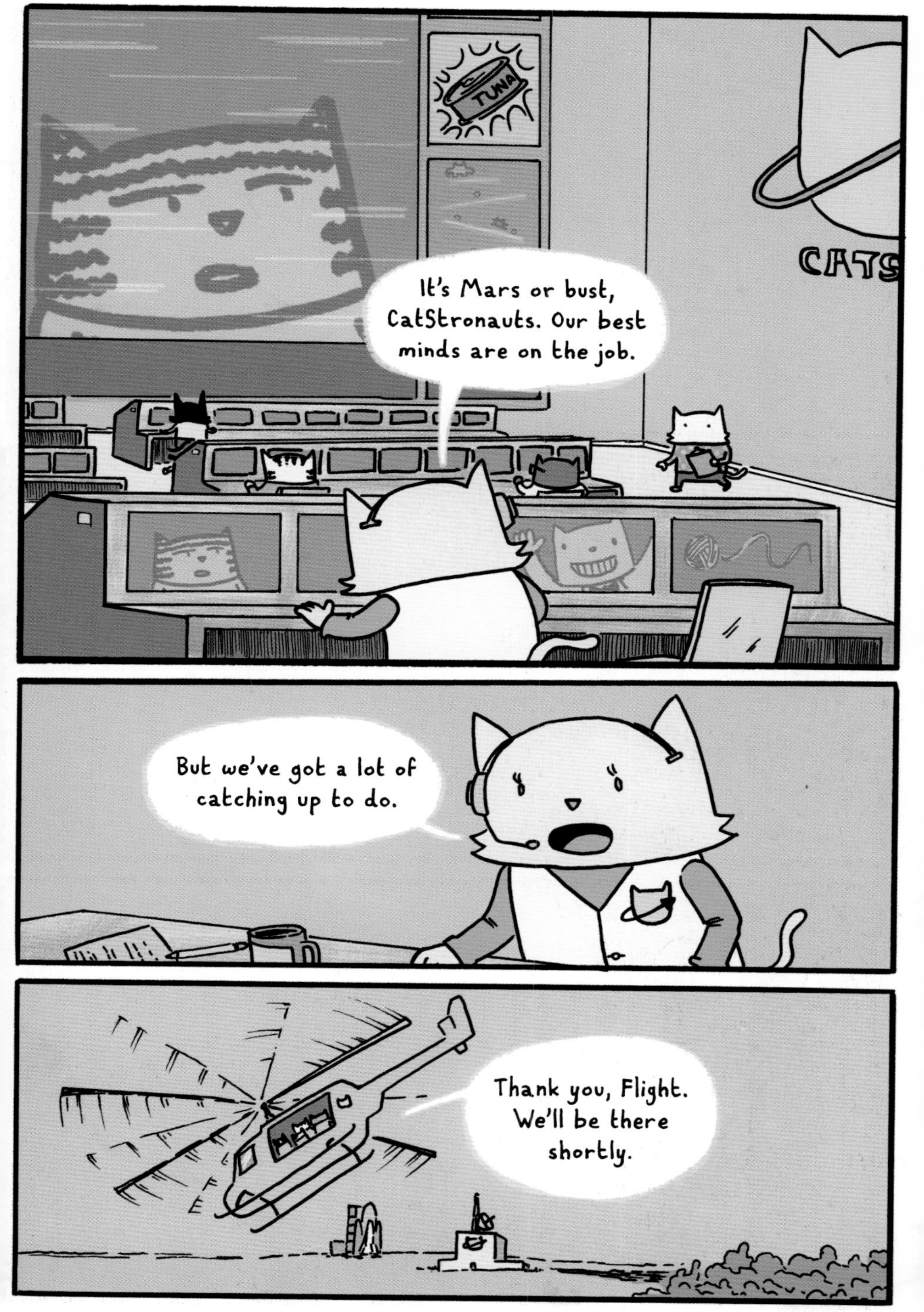
TUNA
CATS
It's Mars or bust, CatStronauts. Our best minds are on the job.
But we've got a lot of catching up to do.
Thank you, Flight. We'll be there shortly.

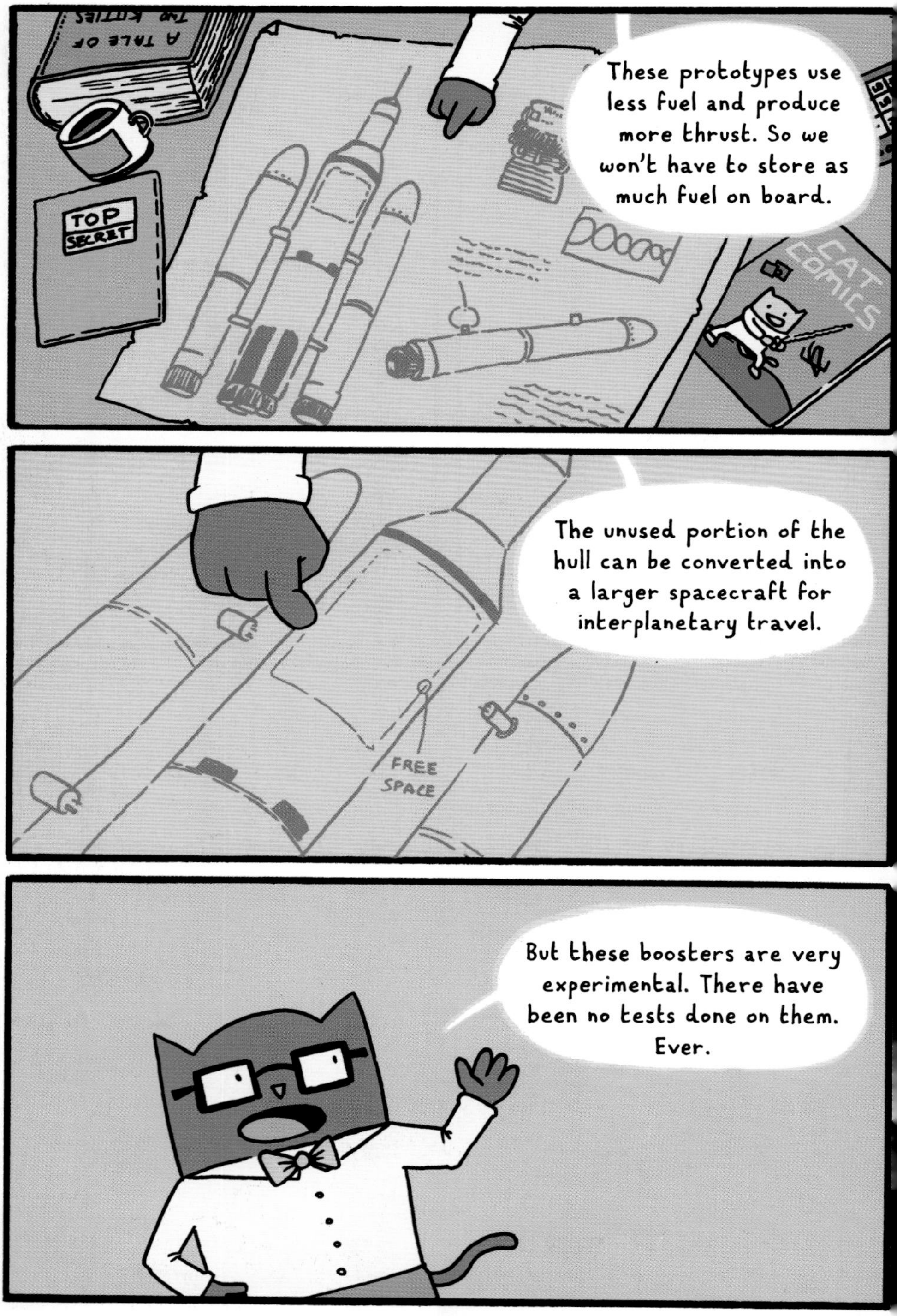
These prototypes use less fuel and produce more thrust. So we won't have to store as much fuel on board.
TOP SECRET
CAT COMICS
The unused portion of the hull can be converted into a larger spacecraft for interplanetary travel.
FREE SPACE
But these boosters are very experimental. There have been no tests done on them. Ever.

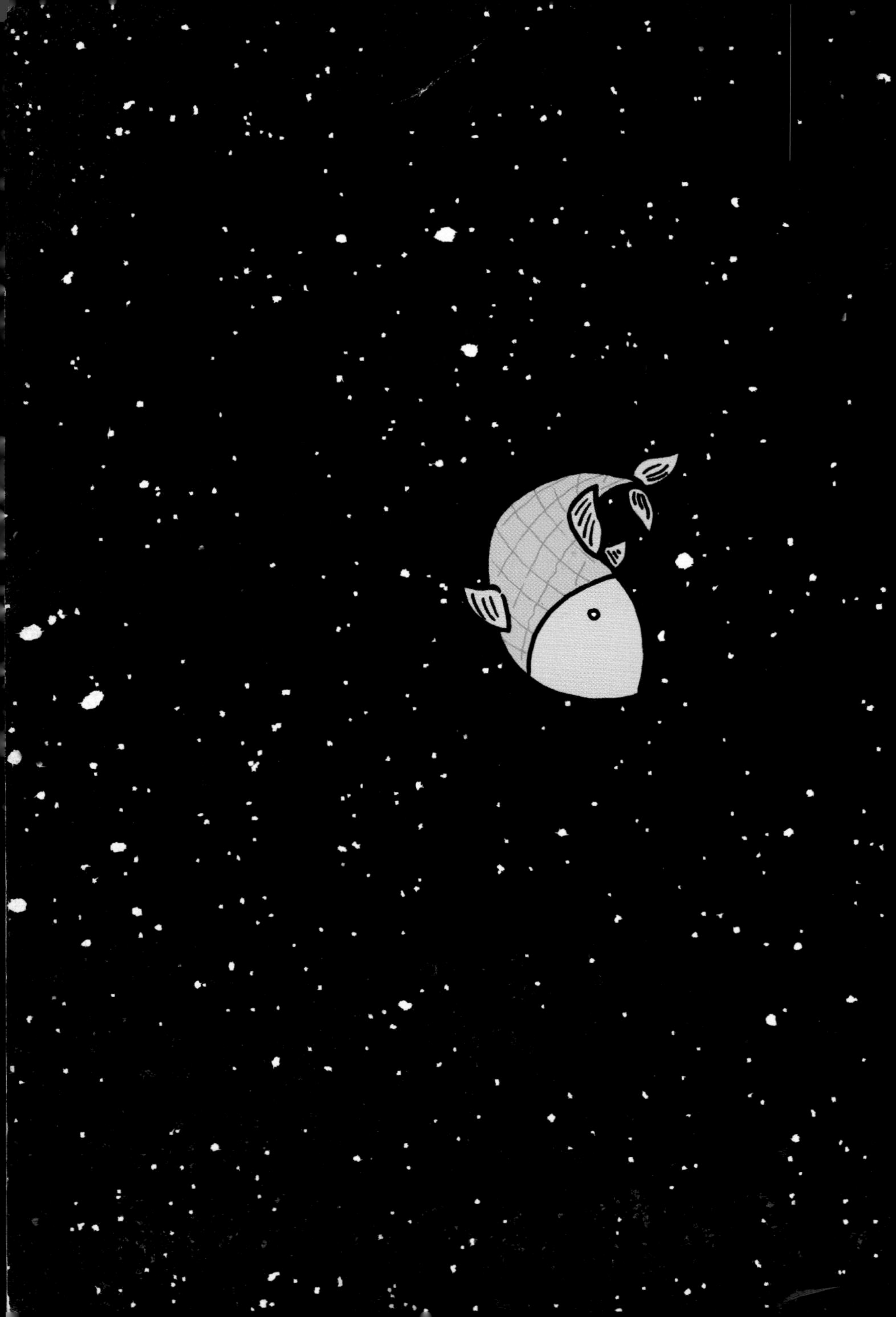

CHAPTER 4

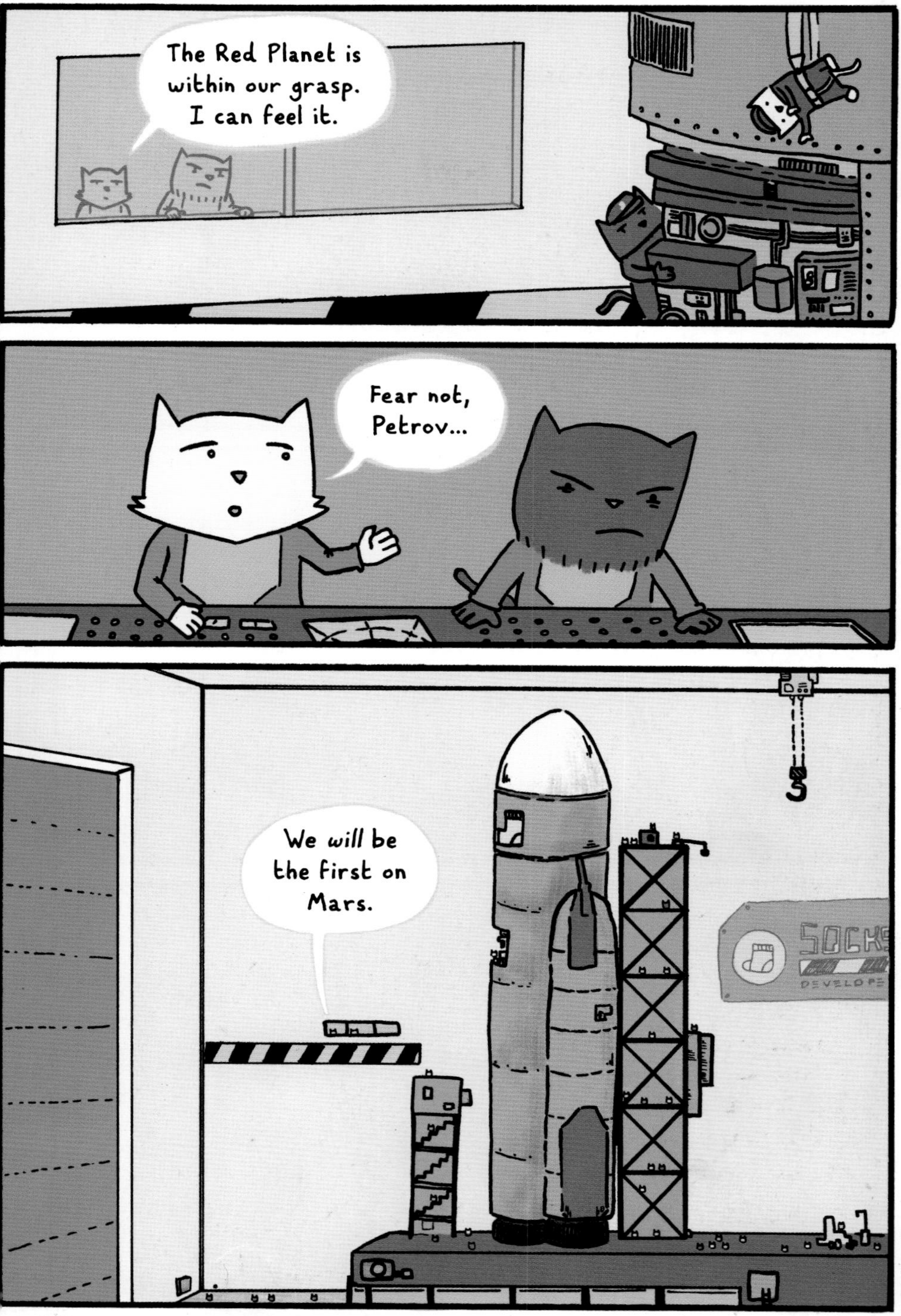
The Red Planet is within our grasp. I can feel it.
Fear not, Petrov...
We *will* be the first on Mars.

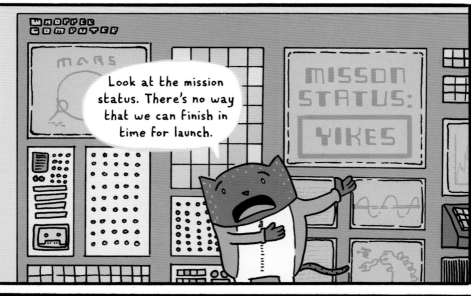

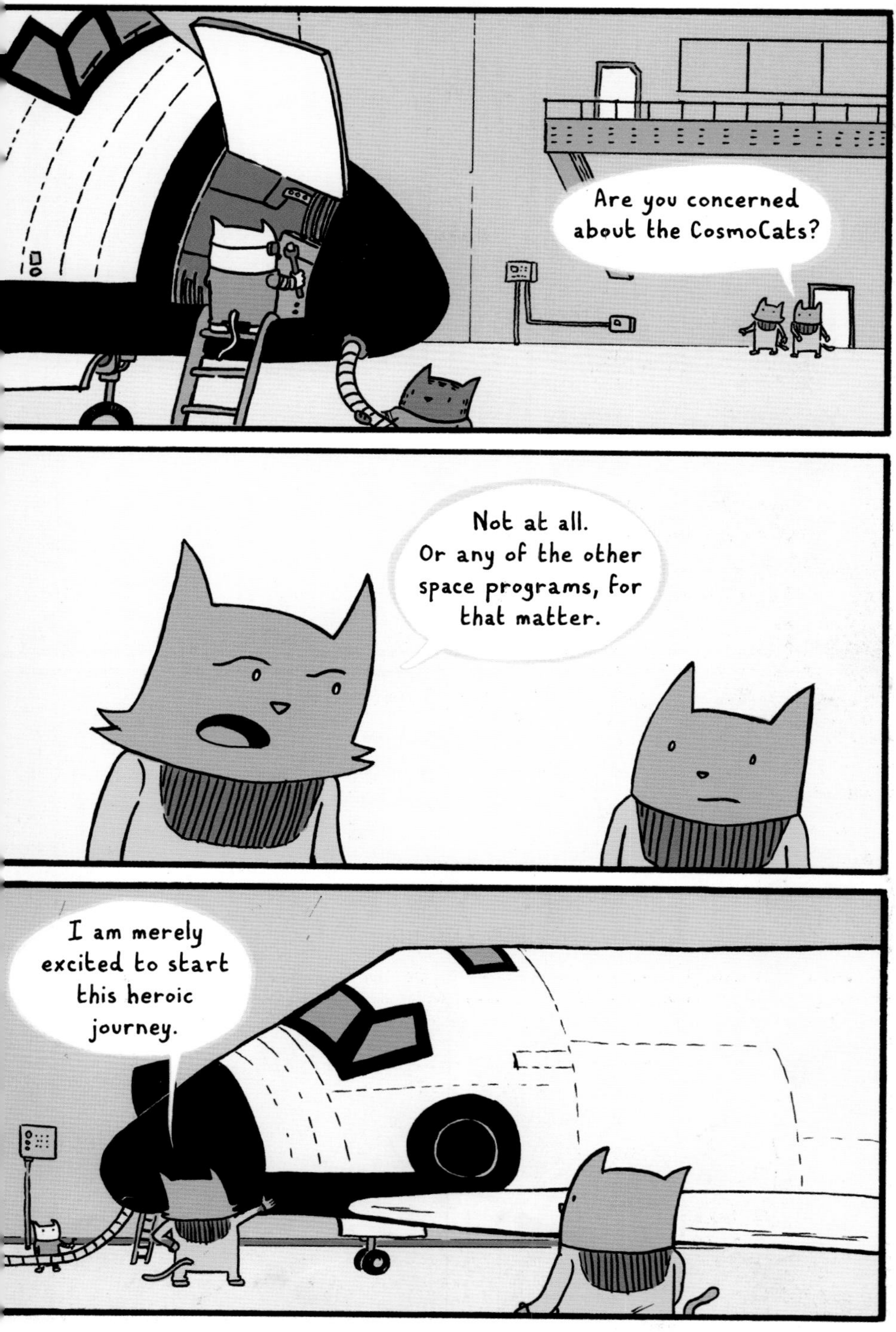
Are you concerned about the CosmoCats?
Not at all. Or any of the other space programs, for that matter.
I am merely excited to start this heroic journey.

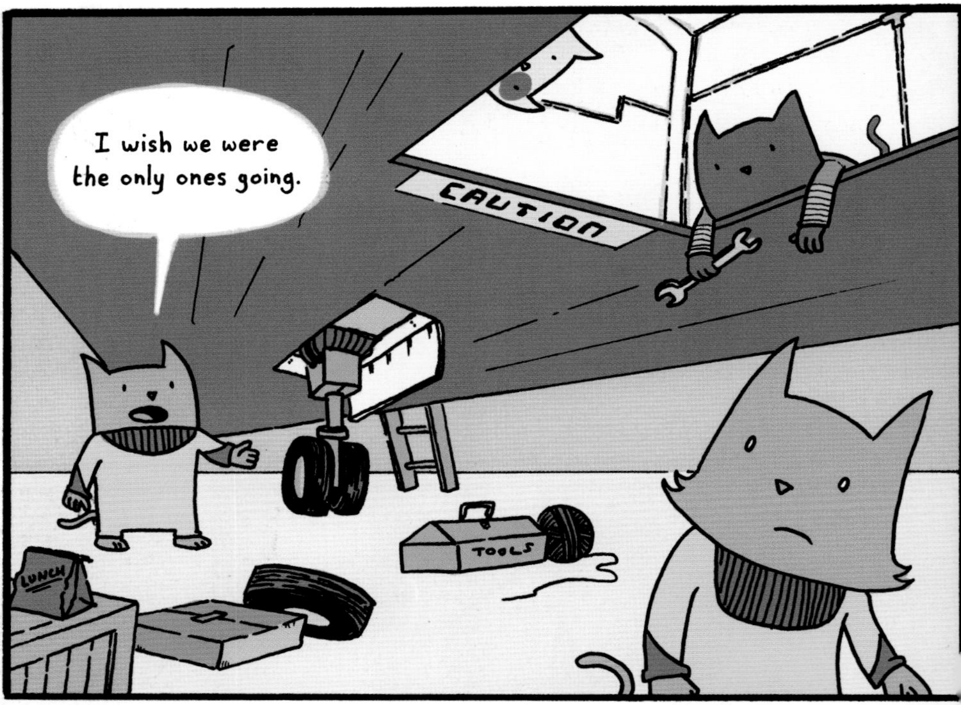
I wish we were the only ones going.
CAUTION
TOOLS
LUNCH

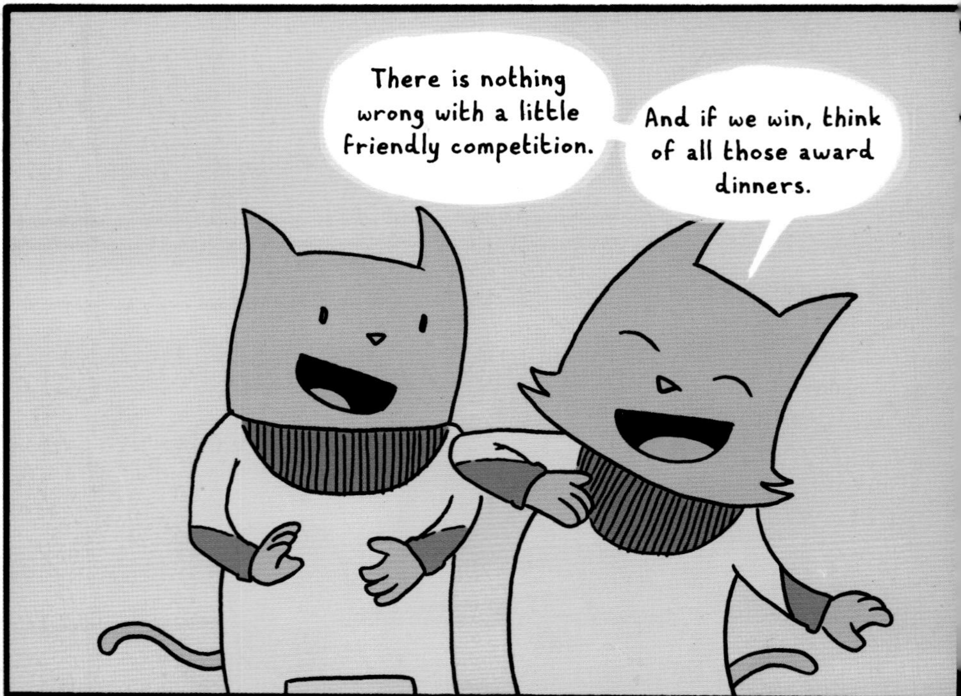
There is nothing wrong with a little friendly competition.
And if we win, think of all those award dinners.

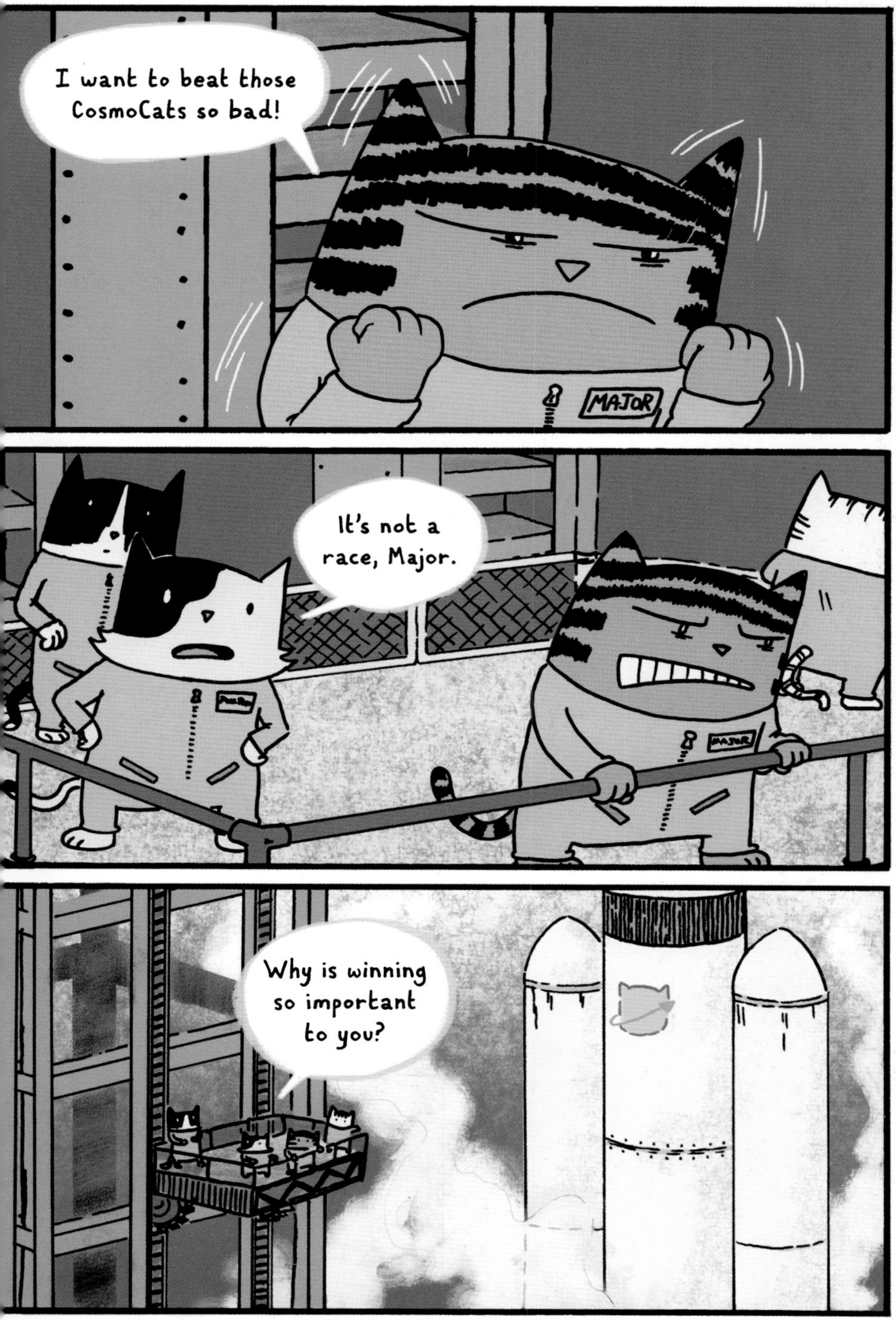
I want to beat those CosmoCats so bad!
MAJOR
It's not a race, Major.
MAJOR
Why is winning so important to you?

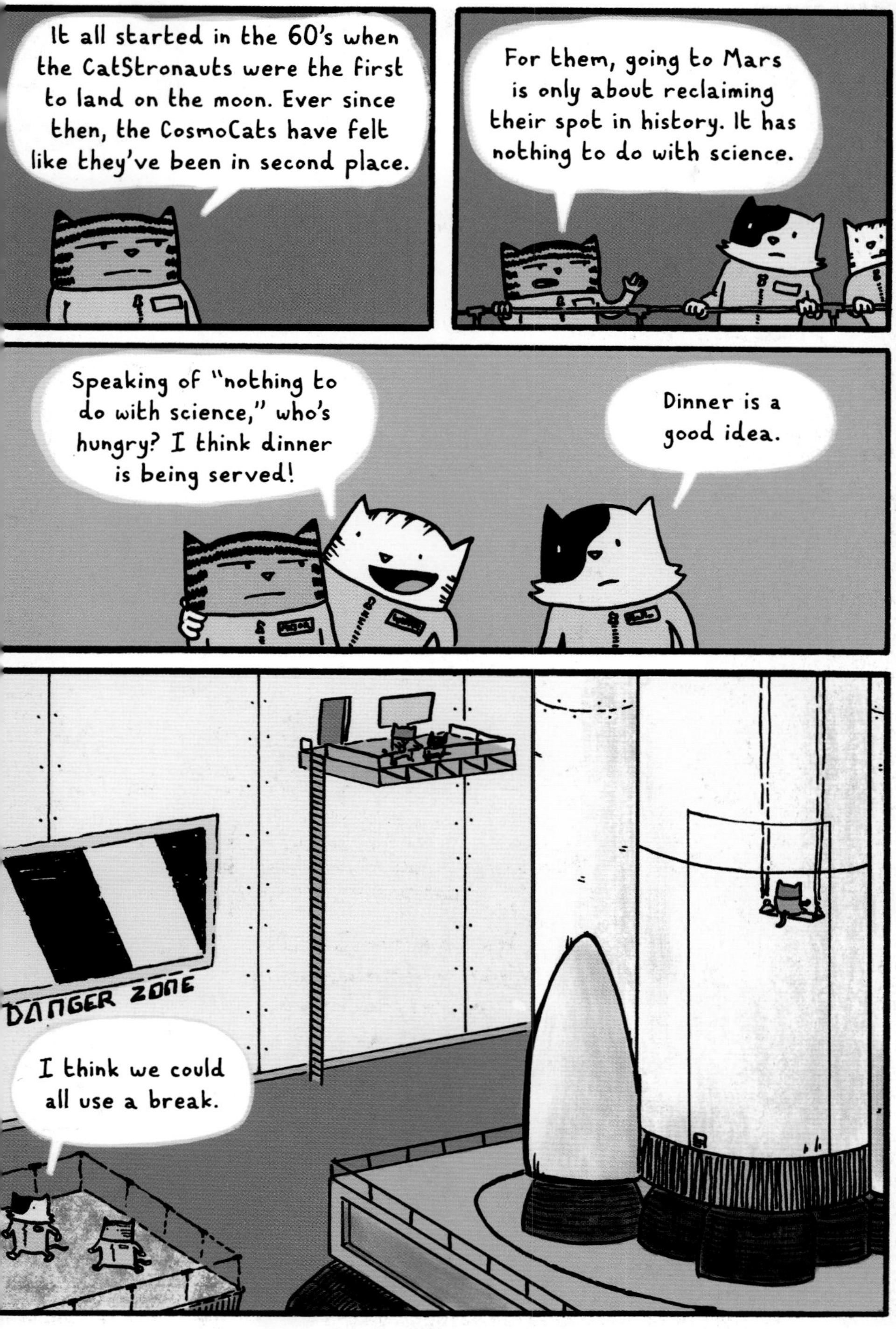

It all started in the 60's when the CatStronauts were the first to land on the moon. Ever since then, the CosmoCats have felt like they've been in second place.
For them, going to Mars is only about reclaiming their spot in history. It has nothing to do with science.
Speaking of "nothing to do with science," who's hungry? I think dinner is being served!
Dinner is a good idea.
DANGER ZONE
I think we could all use a break.

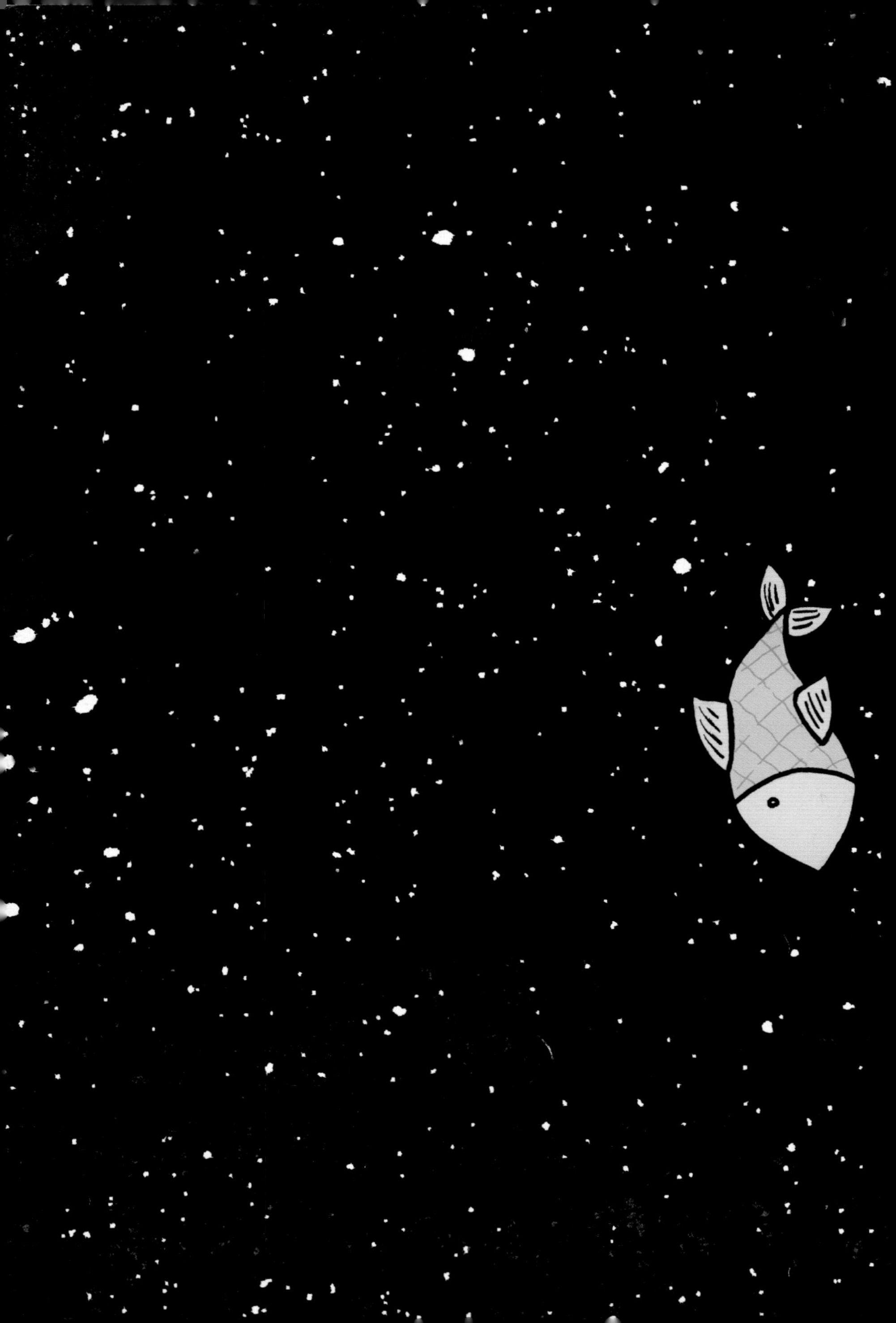

CHAPTER 5

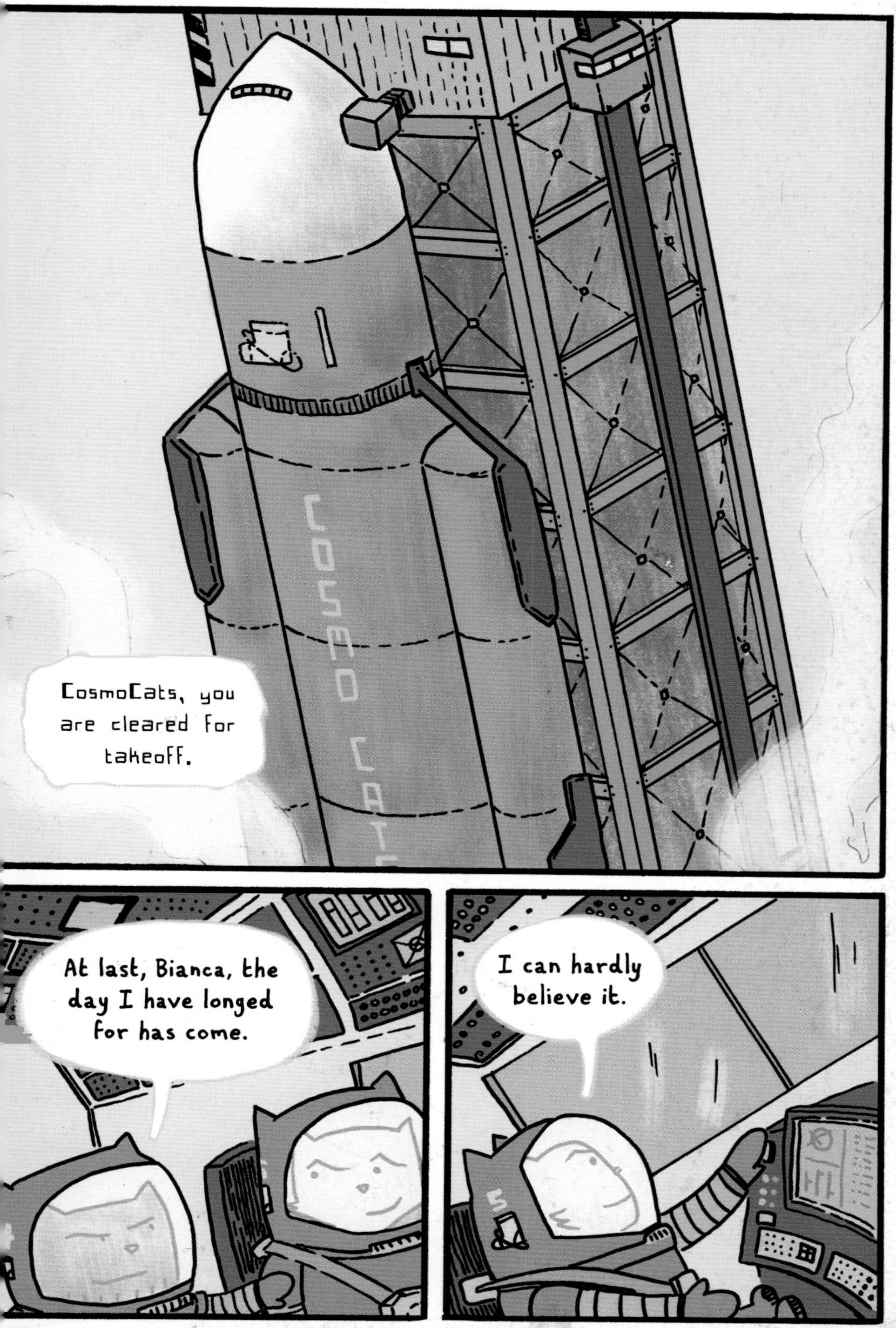
COSMO CATS
CosmoCats, you are cleared for takeoff.
At last, Bianca, the day I have longed for has come.
I can hardly believe it.

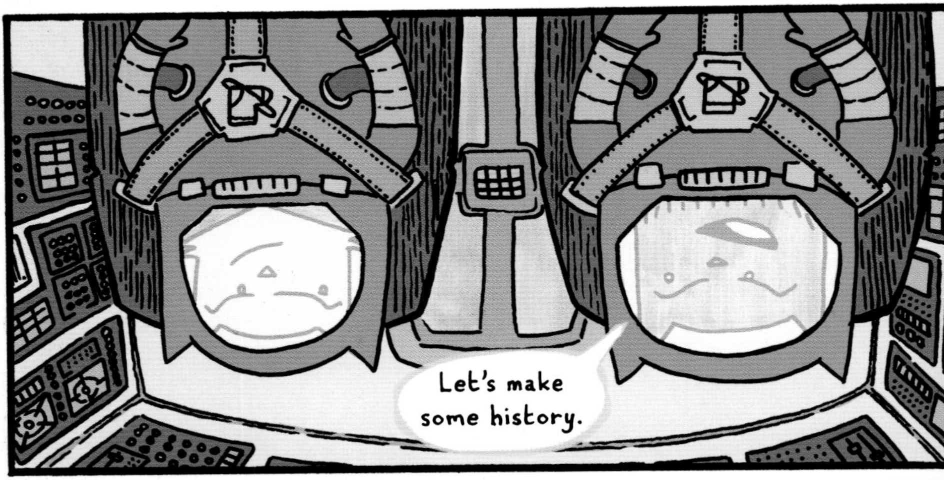
Let's make some history.

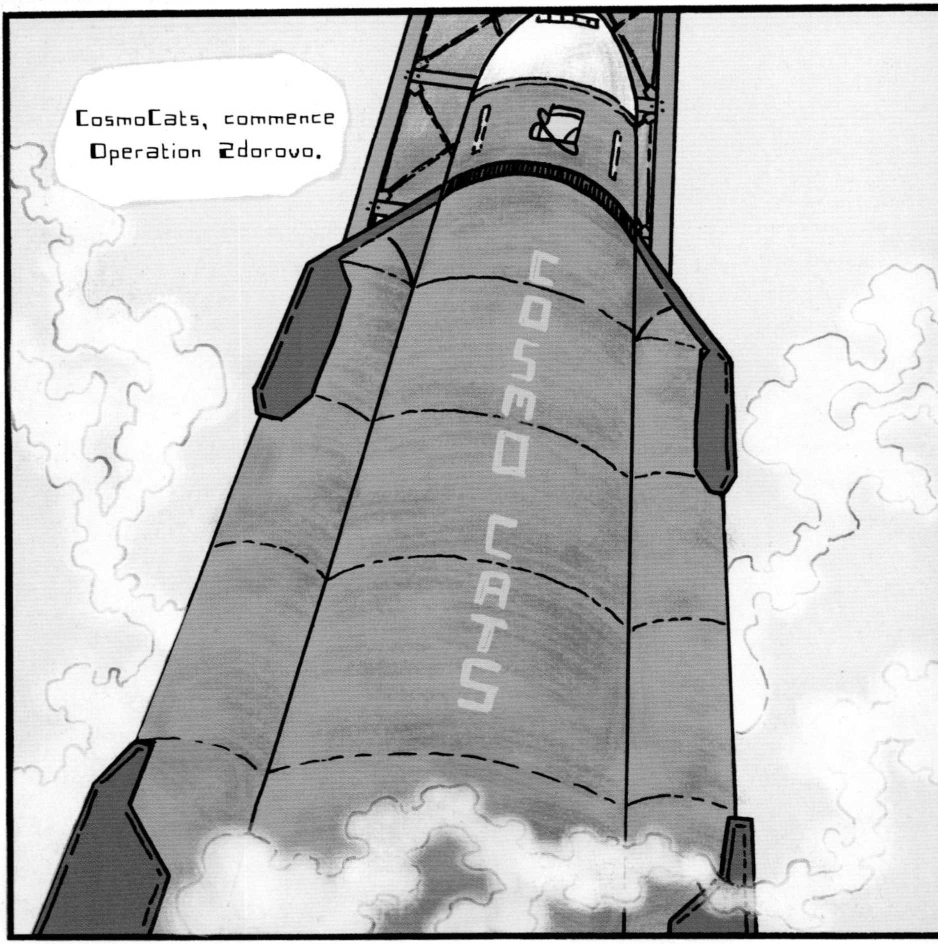
CosmoCats, commence Operation Zdorovo.
COSMO CATS

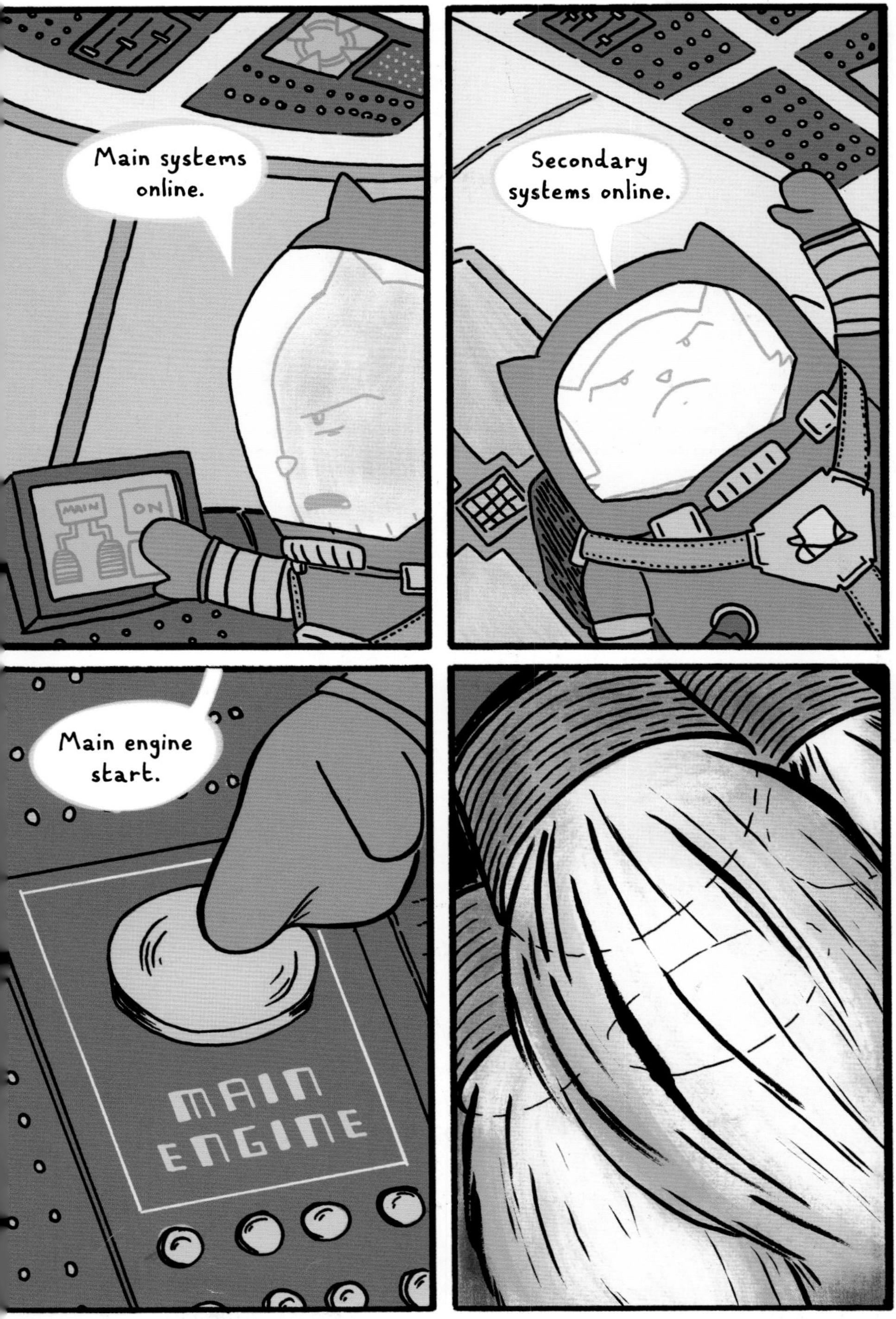
Main systems online.
MAIN
ON
Secondary systems online.
Main engine start.
MAIN ENGINE

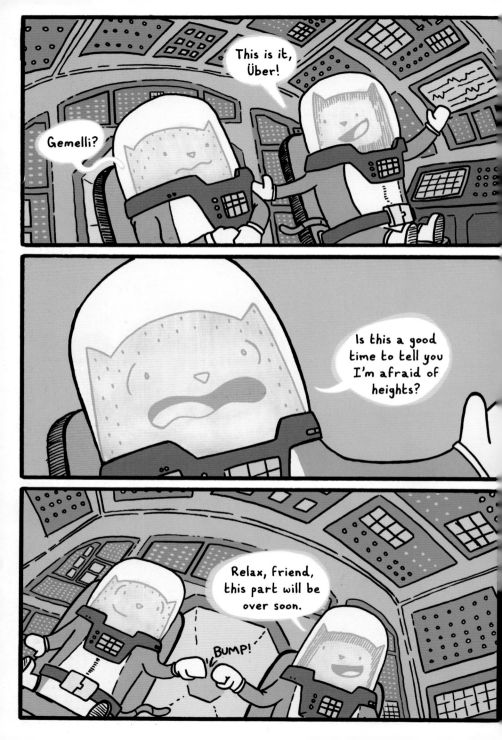

MEOW engines are now online.
Angle of thrust looks optimal.
Rockets will fire in 3, 2, 1.

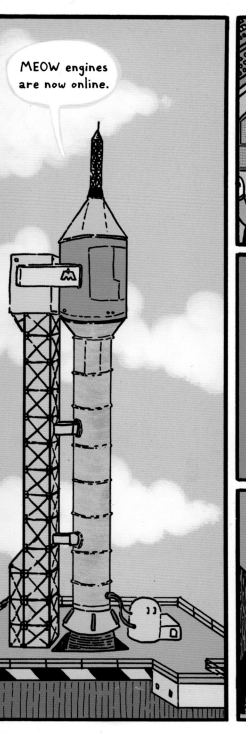

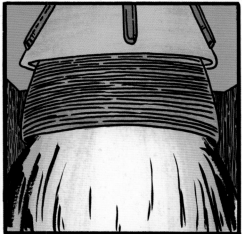

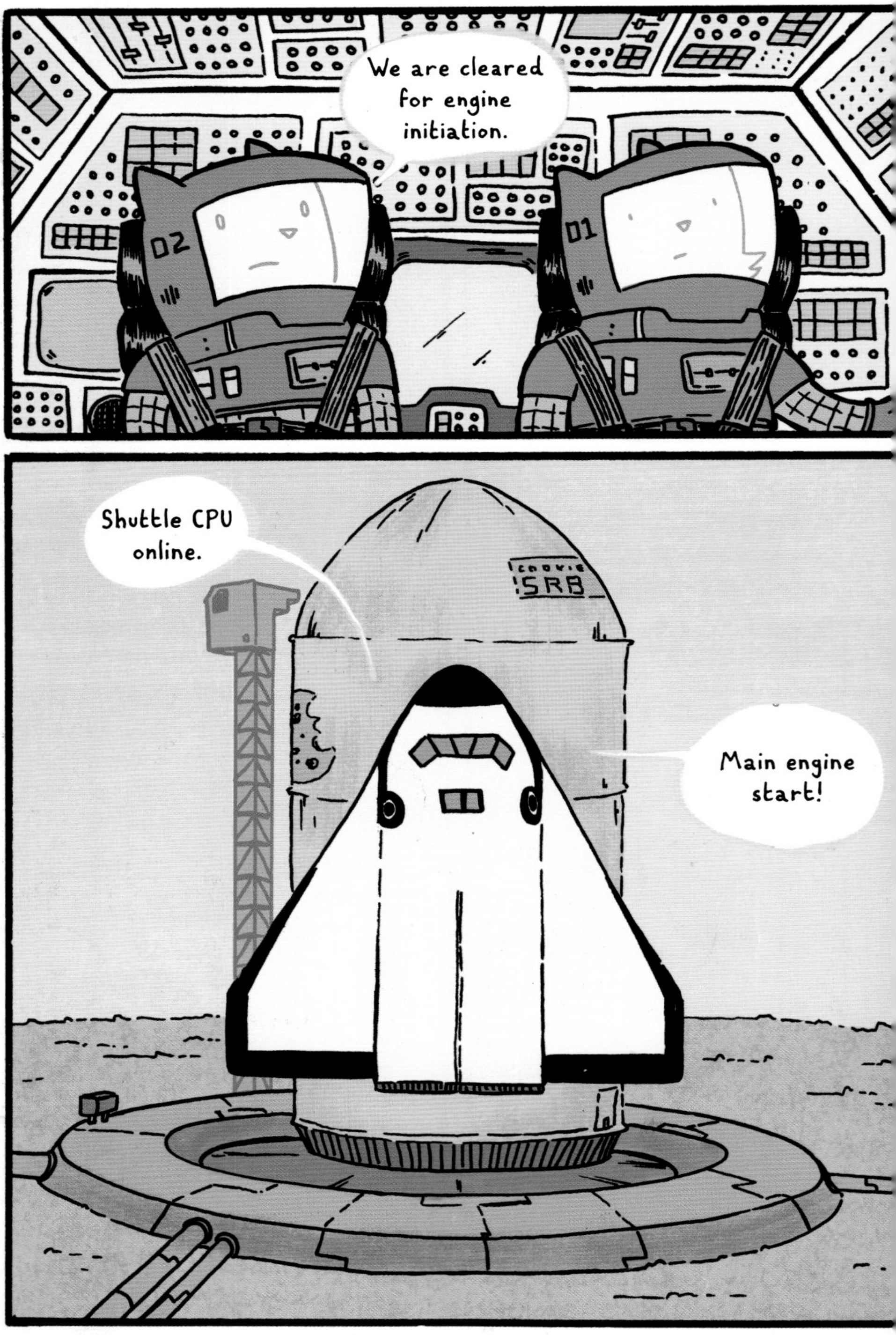
We are cleared for engine initiation.
D2
D1
Shuttle CPU online.
SRB
Main engine start!

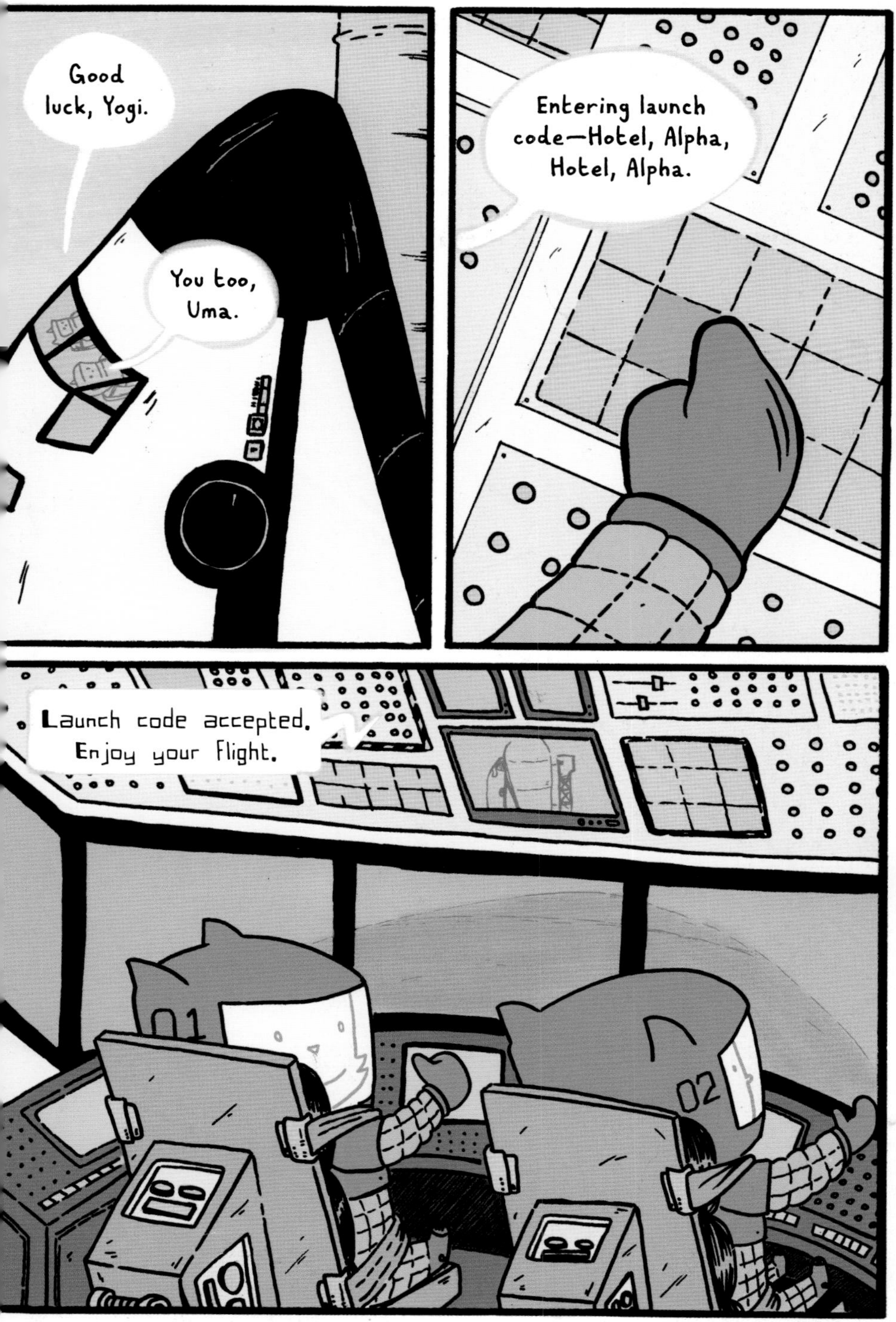
Good luck, Yogi.
You too, Uma.
Entering launch code—Hotel, Alpha, Hotel, Alpha.
Launch code accepted. Enjoy your flight.

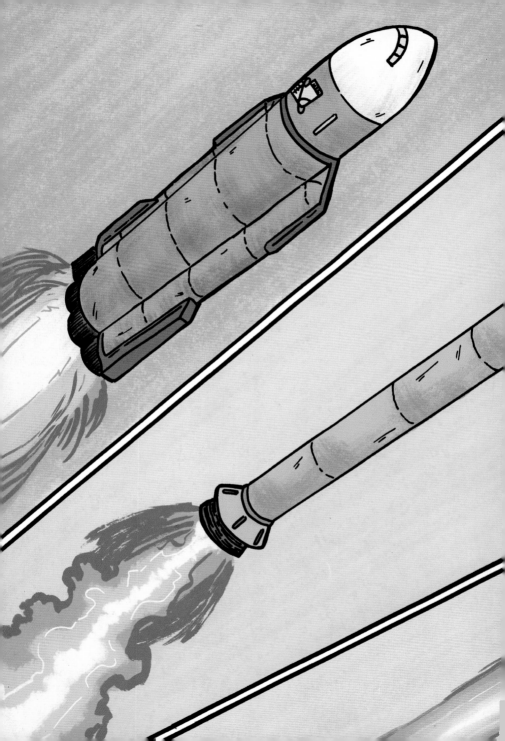

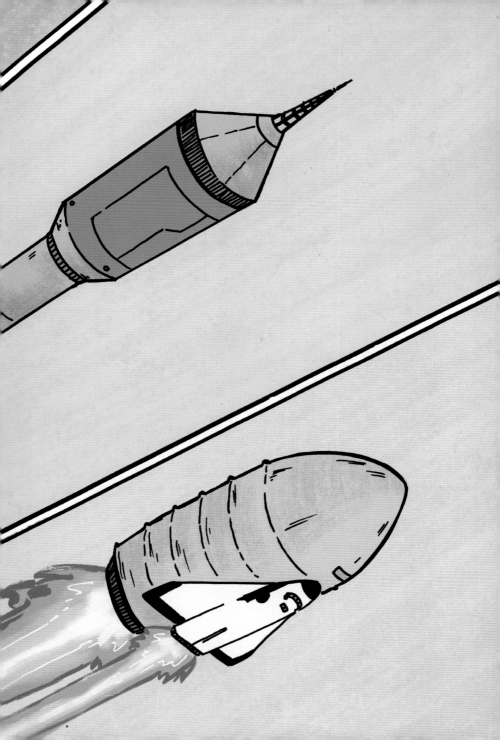

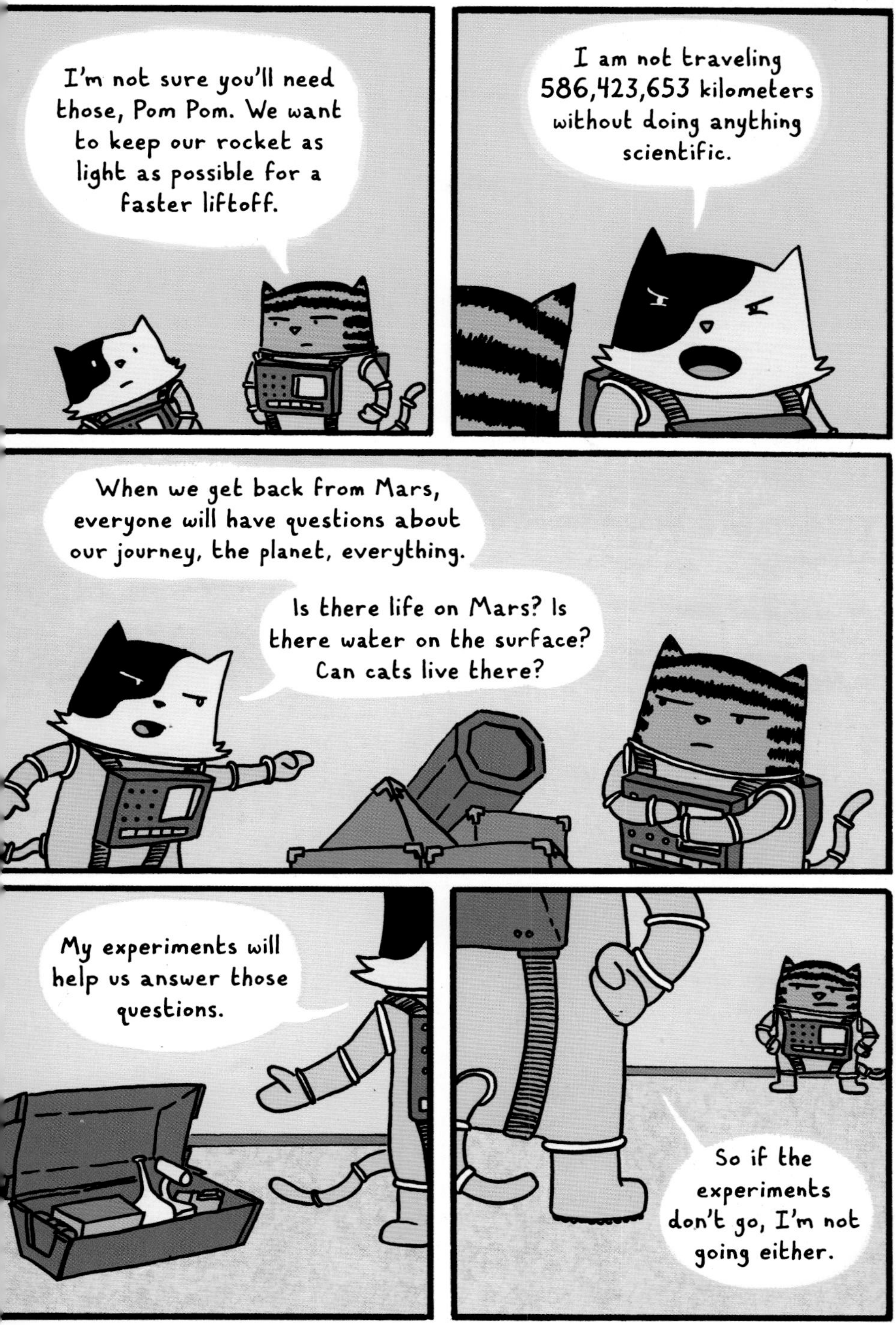
I'm not sure you'll need those, Pom Pom. We want to keep our rocket as light as possible for a faster liftoff.
I am not traveling 586,423,653 kilometers without doing anything scientific.
When we get back from Mars, everyone will have questions about our journey, the planet, everything.
Is there life on Mars? Is there water on the surface? Can cats live there?
My experiments will help us answer those questions.
So if the experiments don't go, I'm not going either.

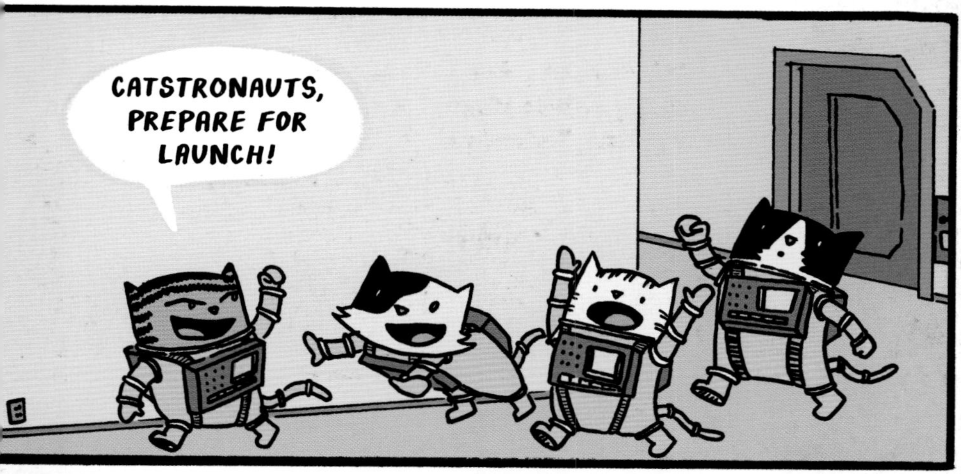
CATSTRONAUTS, PREPARE FOR LAUNCH!

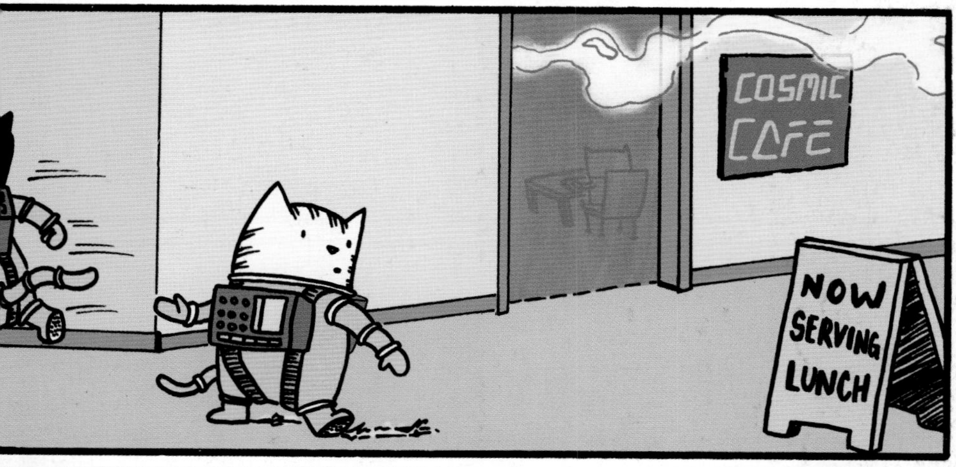
COSMIC CAFE
NOW SERVING LUNCH

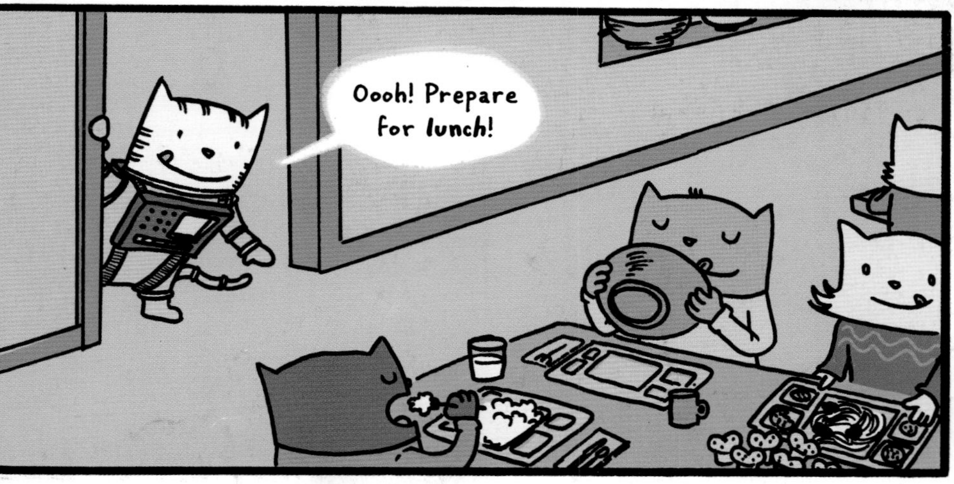
Oooh! Prepare for lunch!

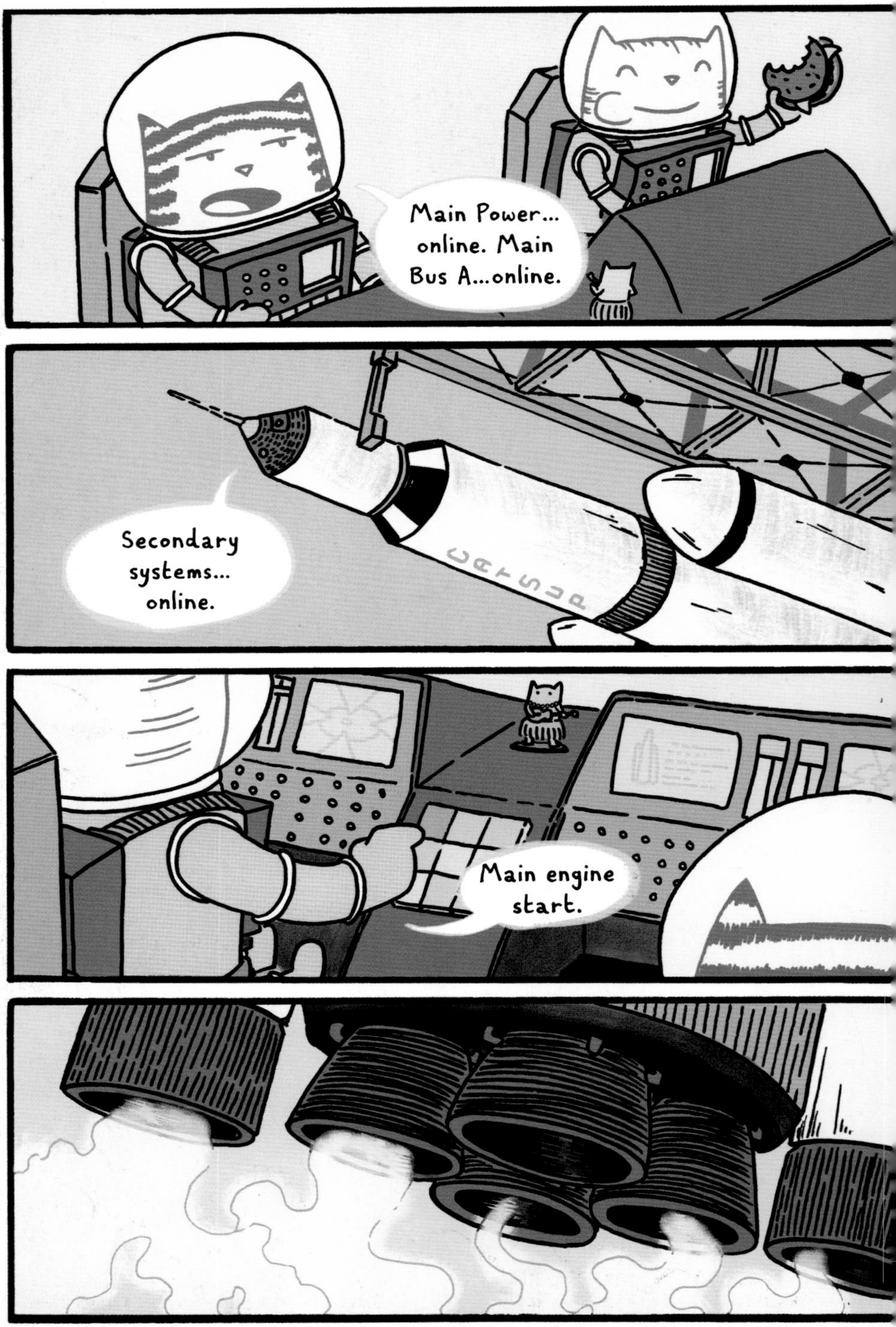
Main Power... online. Main Bus A...online.
Secondary systems... online.
CATSUP
Main engine start.

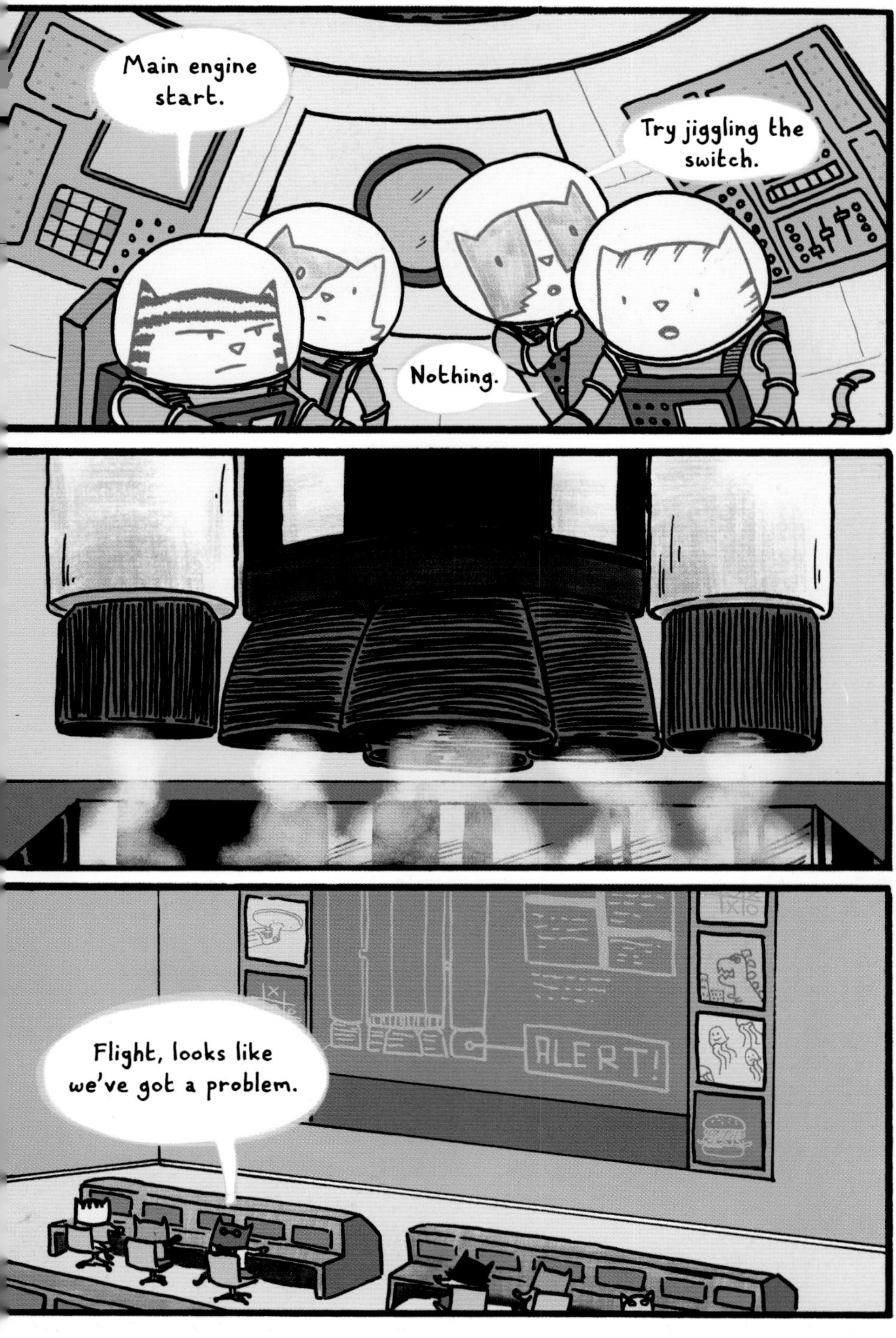
Main engine start.
Try jiggling the switch.
Nothing.
Flight, looks like we've got a problem.
ALERT!

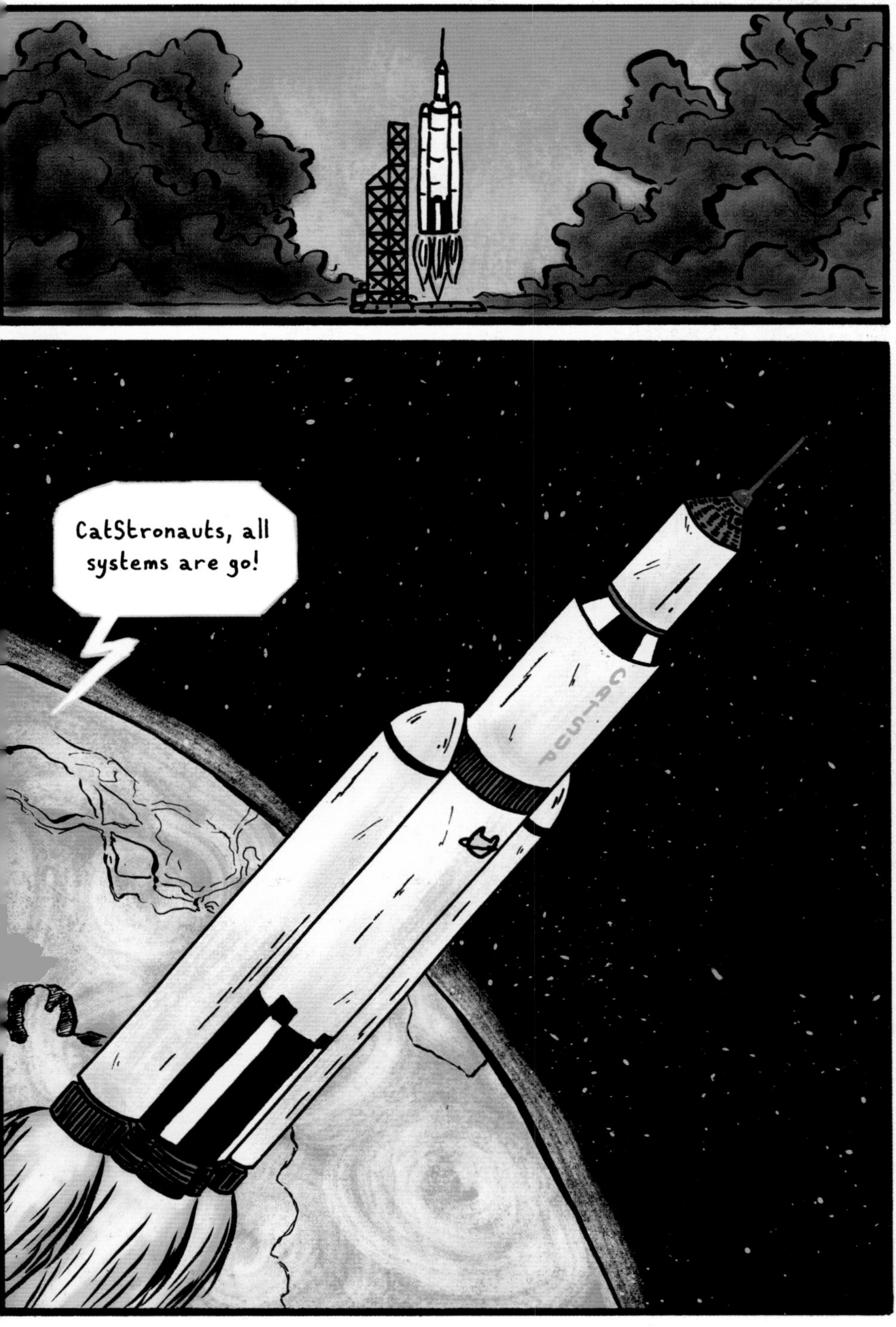
CatStronauts, all systems are go!
CATSUP

CHAPTER 6

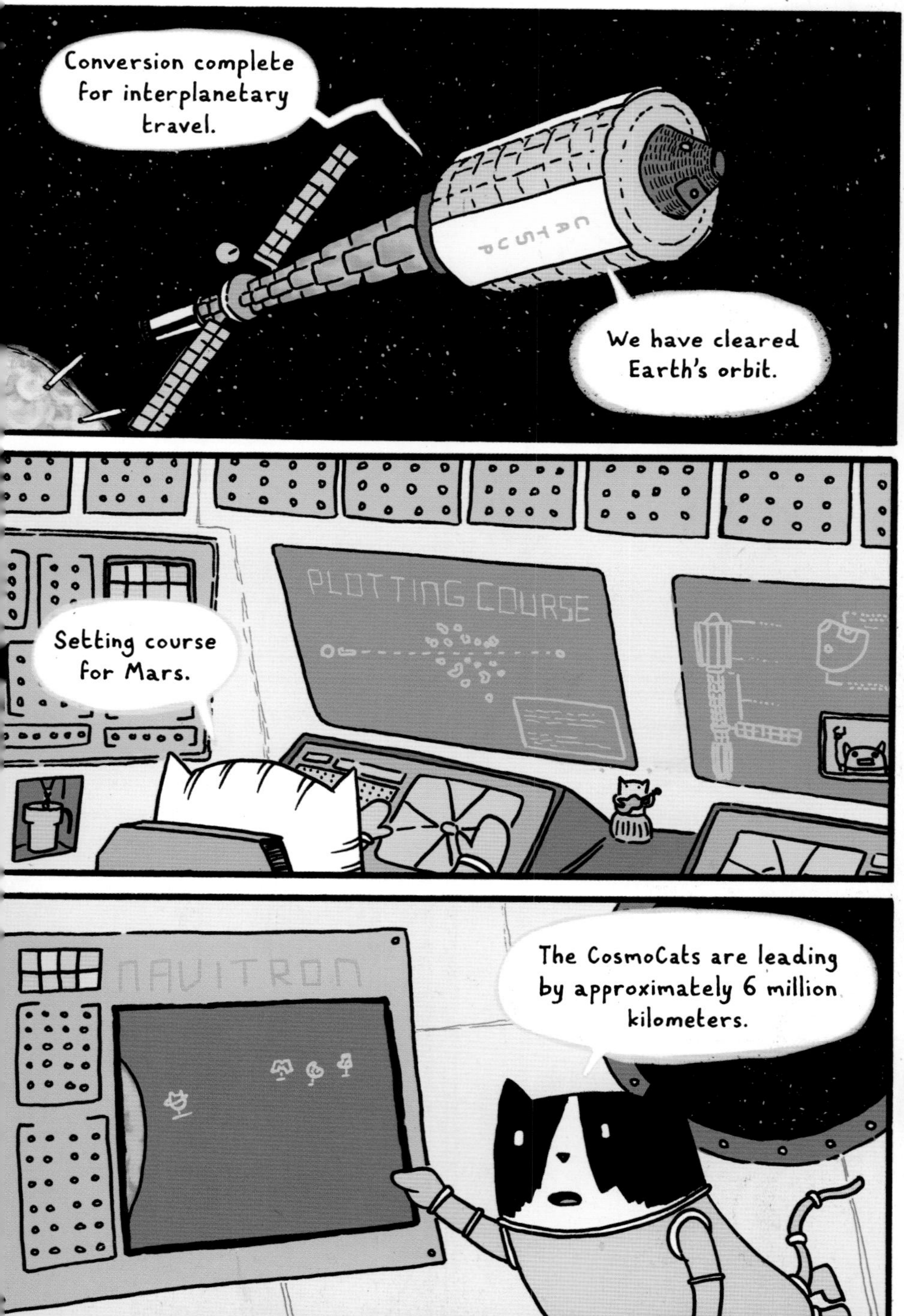
Conversion complete for interplanetary travel.
We have cleared Earth's orbit.
PLOTTING COURSE
Setting course for Mars.
NAVITRON
The CosmoCats are leading by approximately 6 million kilometers.

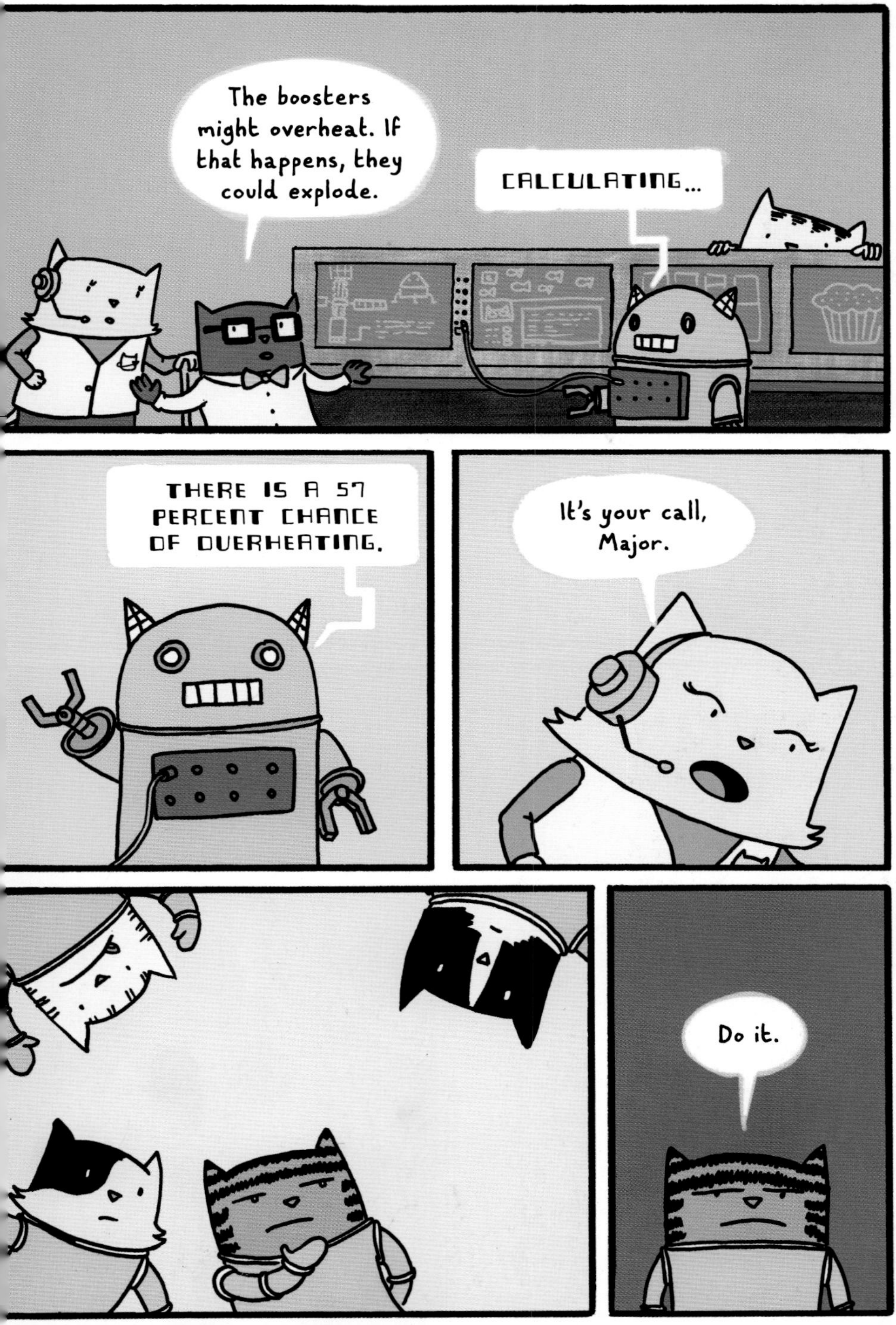
The boosters might overheat. If that happens, they could explode.
CALCULATING...
THERE IS A 57 PERCENT CHANCE OF OVERHEATING.
It's your call, Major.
Do it.

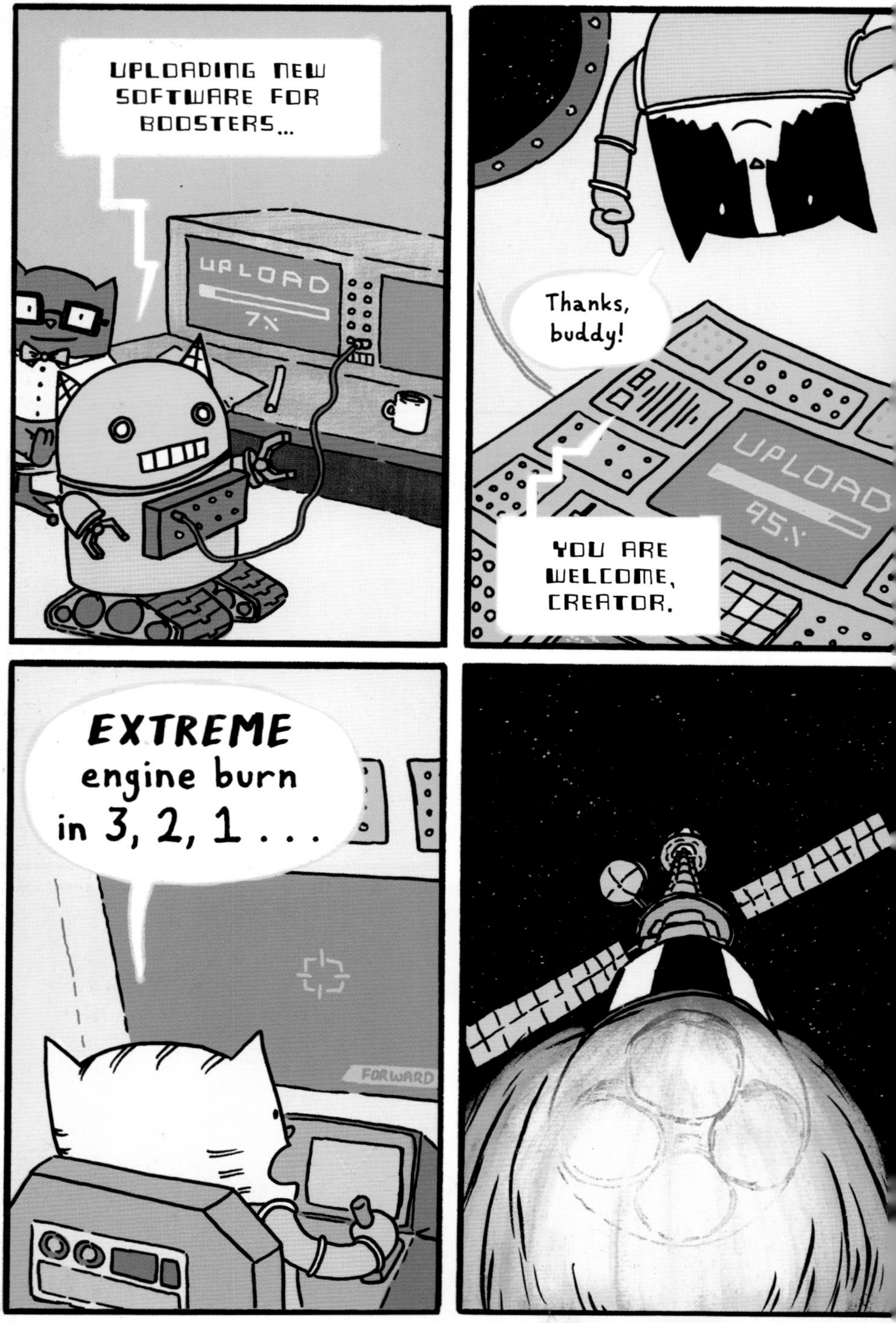
UPLOADING NEW SOFTWARE FOR BOOSTERS...
UPLOAD
7%
Thanks, buddy!
UPLOAD
95%
YOU ARE WELCOME, CREATOR.
EXTREME engine burn in 3, 2, 1 . . .
FORWARD

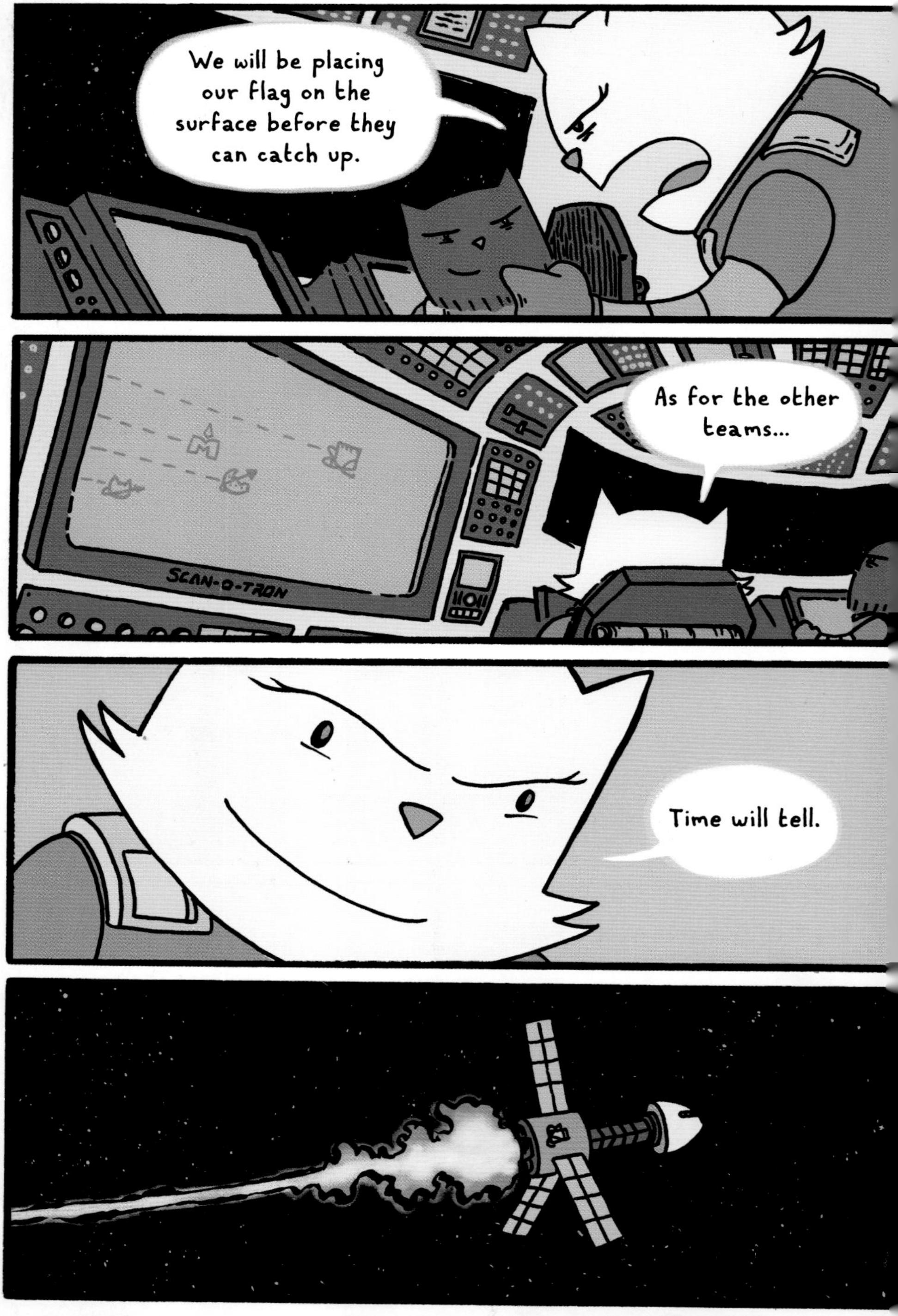

We will be placing our flag on the surface before they can catch up.
SCAN-O-TRON
As for the other teams...
Time will tell.

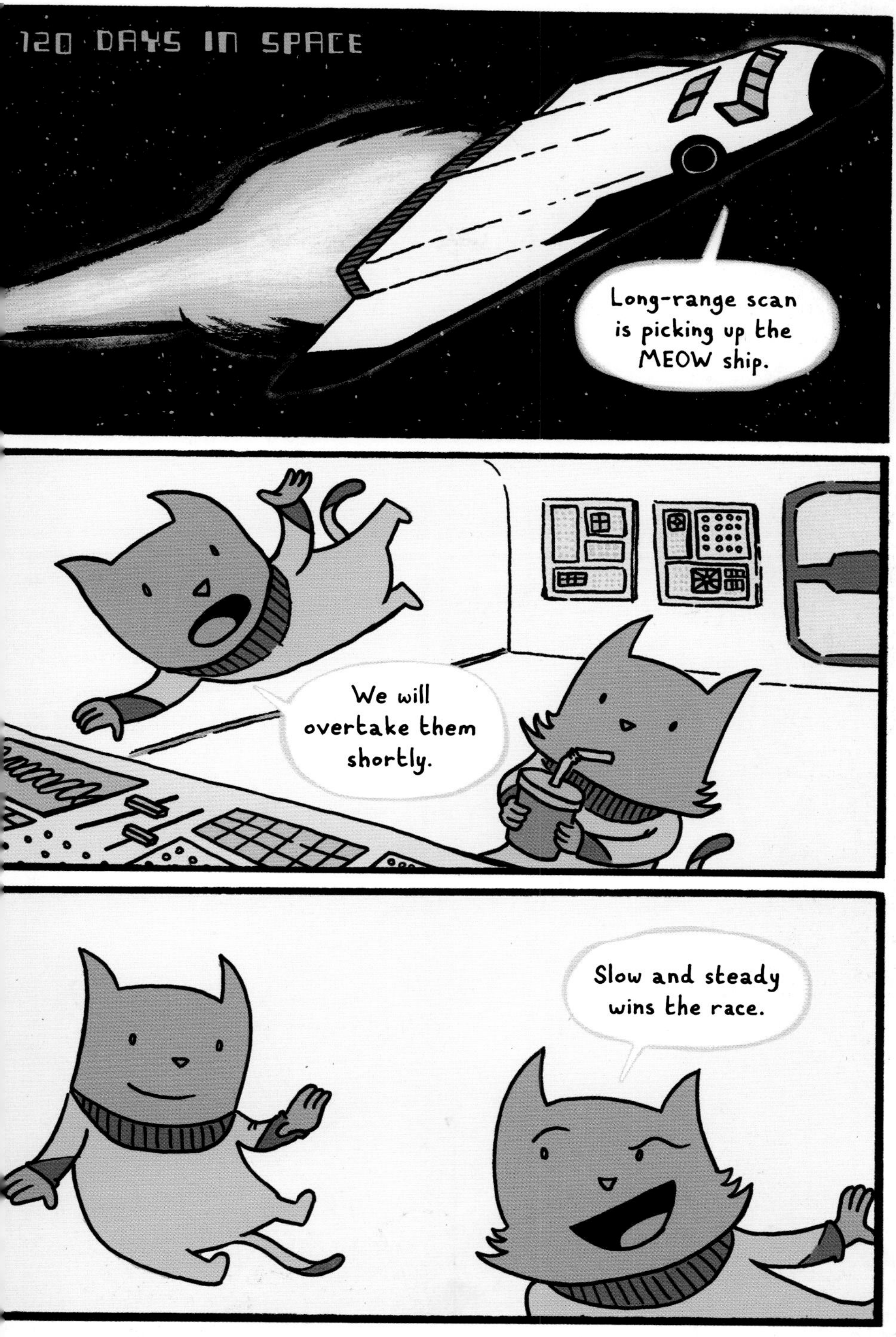
120 DAYS IN SPACE
Long-range scan is picking up the MEOW ship.
We will overtake them shortly.
Slow and steady wins the race.

Tails up, everyone! We are closing in on the others.

Let's see if I can sneak through....

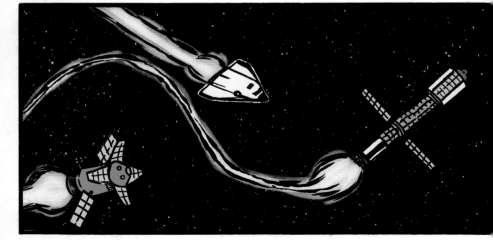

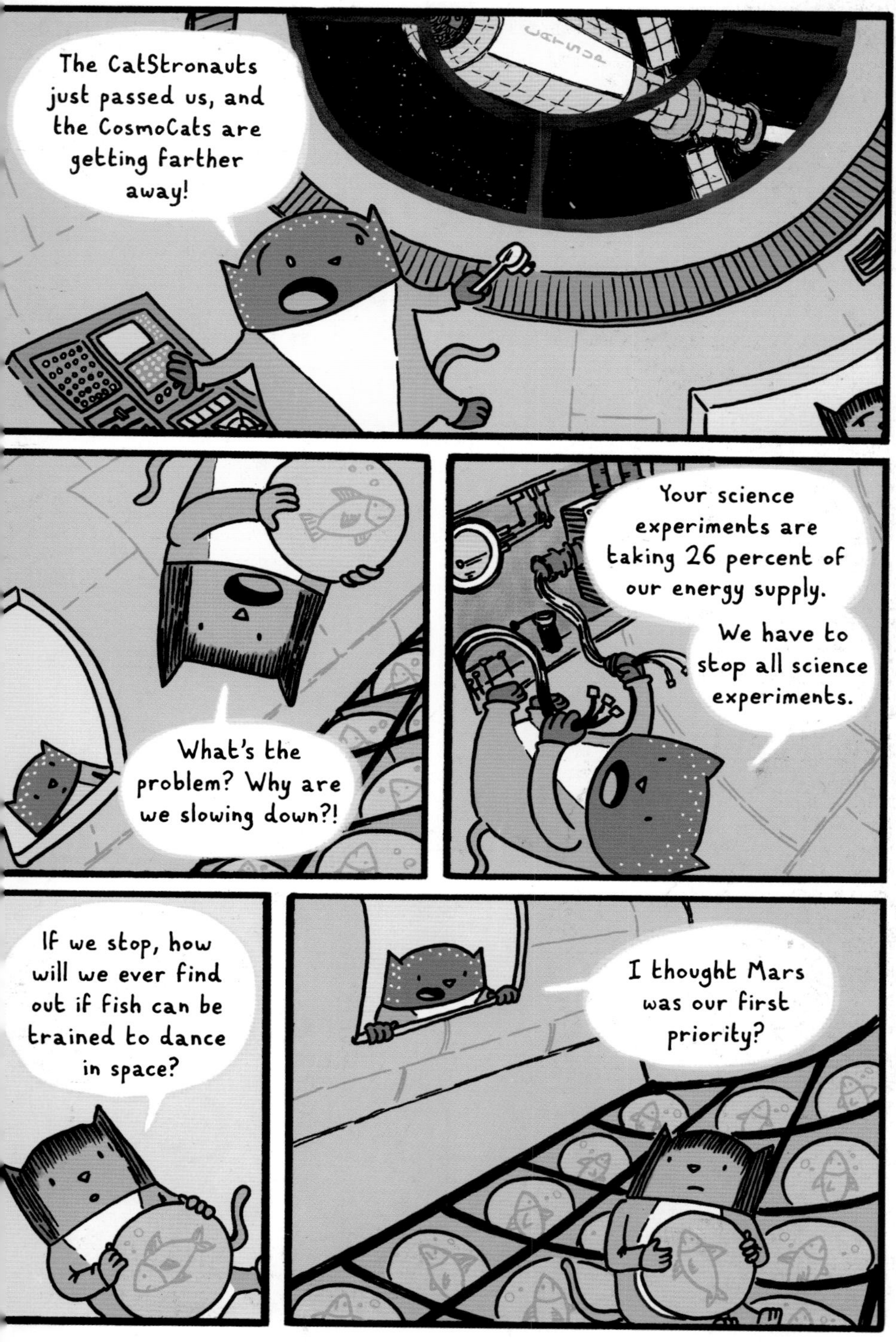
The CatStronauts just passed us, and the CosmoCats are getting farther away!
What's the problem? Why are we slowing down?!
Your science experiments are taking 26 percent of our energy supply.
We have to stop all science experiments.
If we stop, how will we ever find out if fish can be trained to dance in space?
I thought Mars was our first priority?

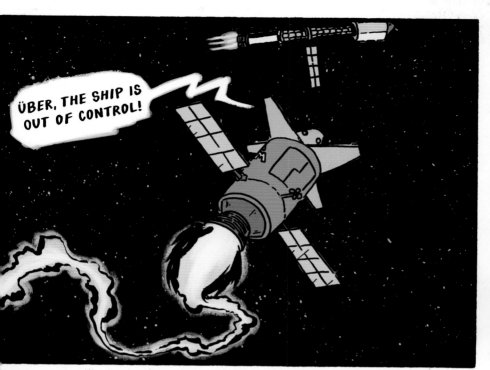

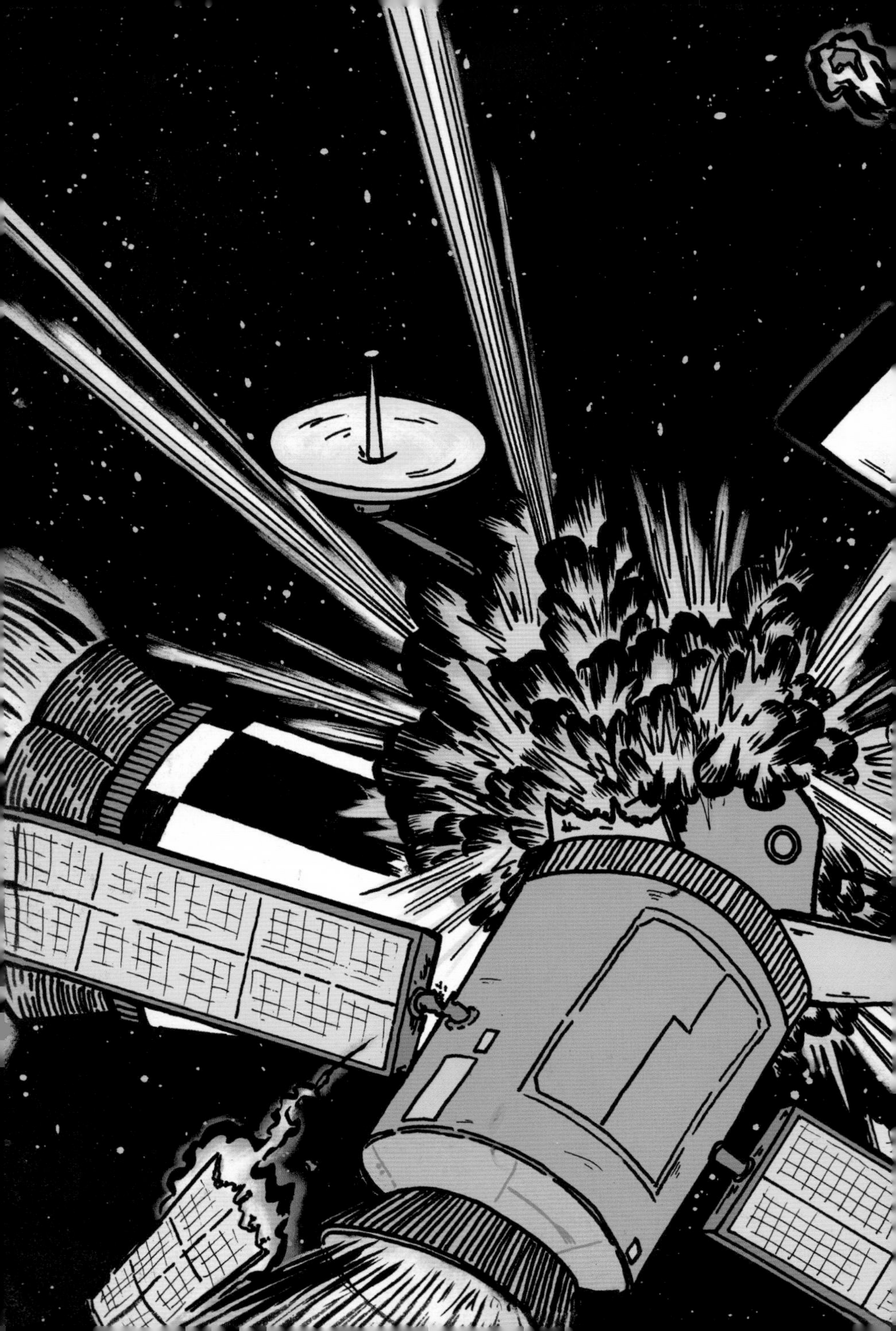

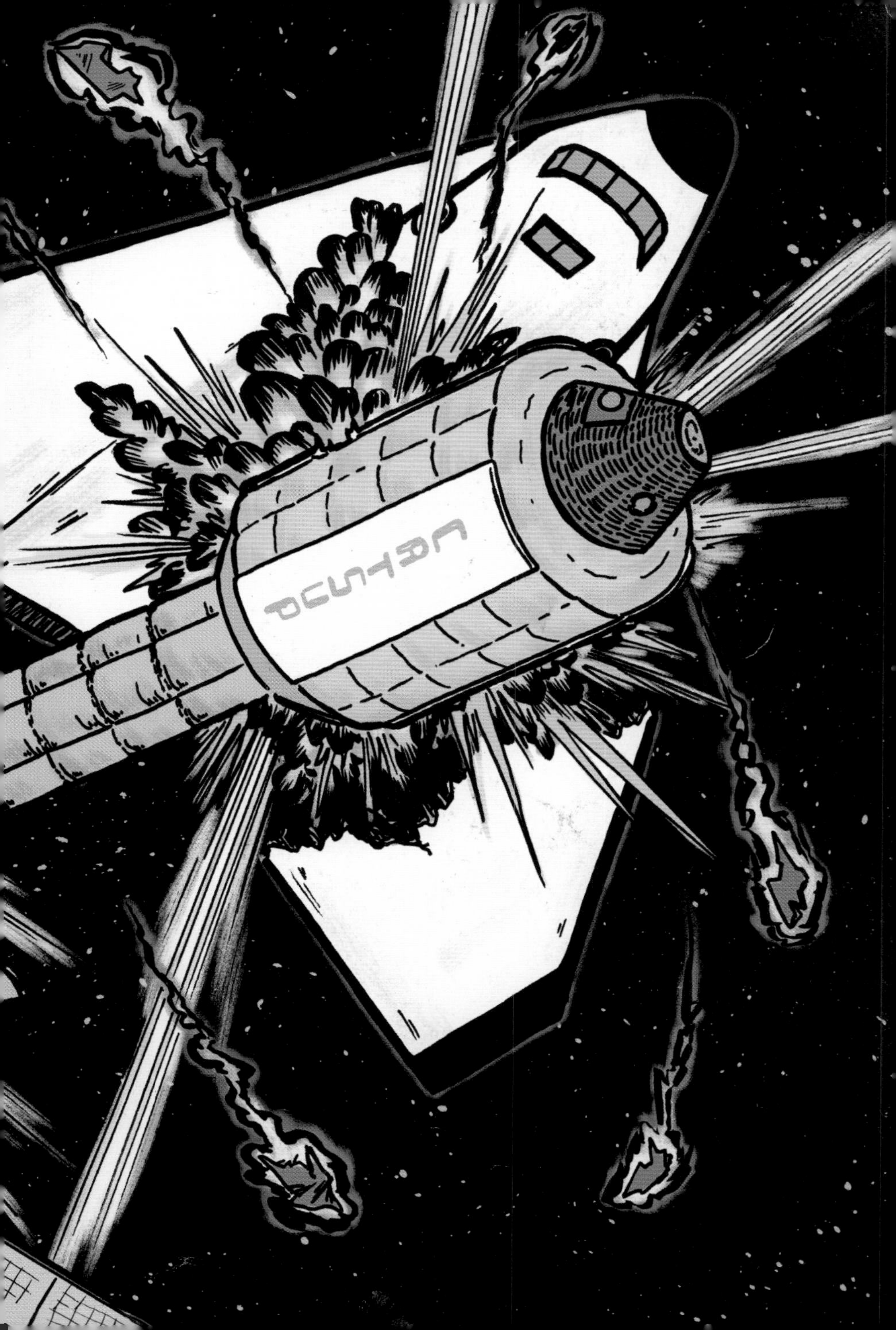

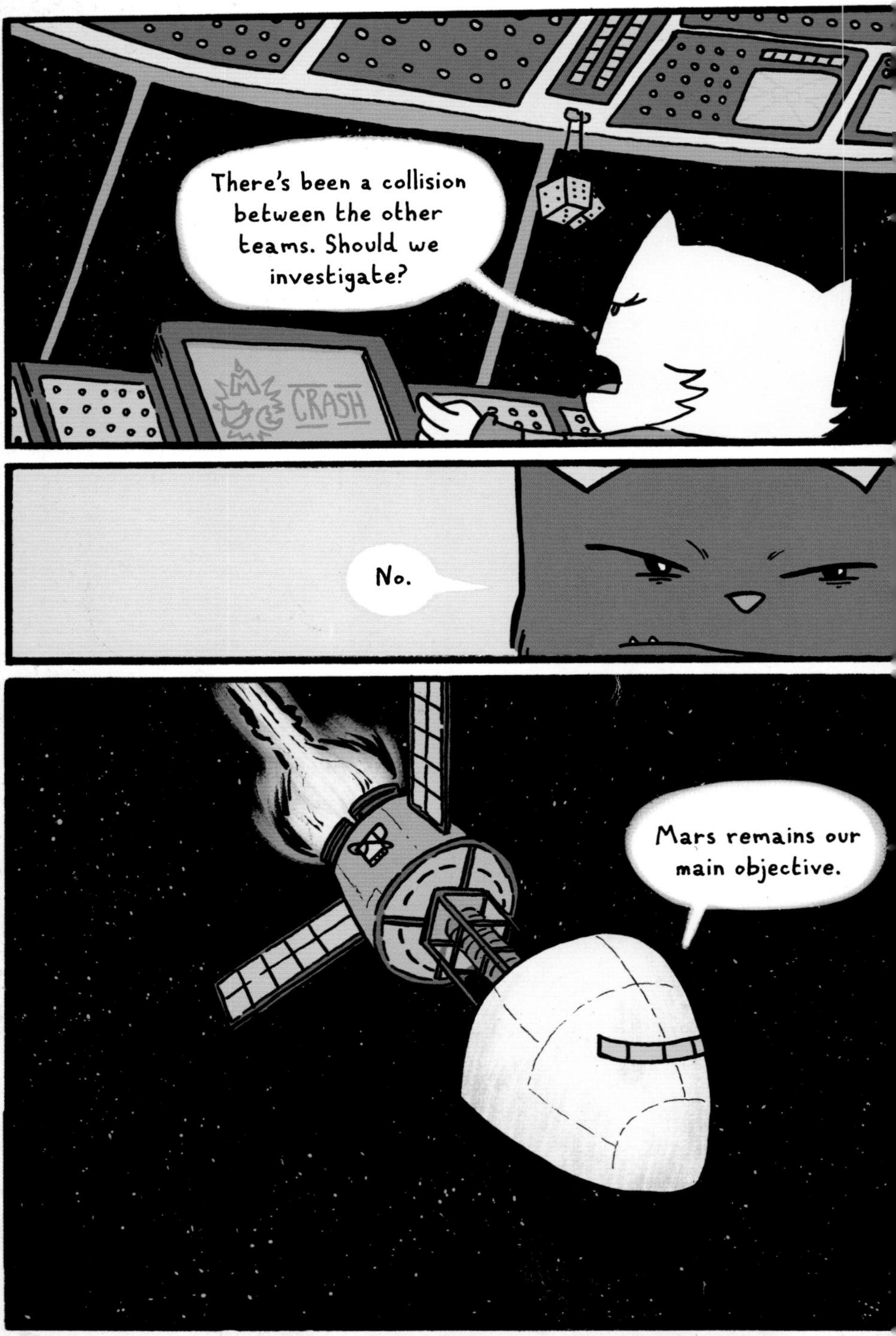
There's been a collision between the other teams. Should we investigate?
CRASH
No.
Mars remains our main objective.

CHAPTER 7

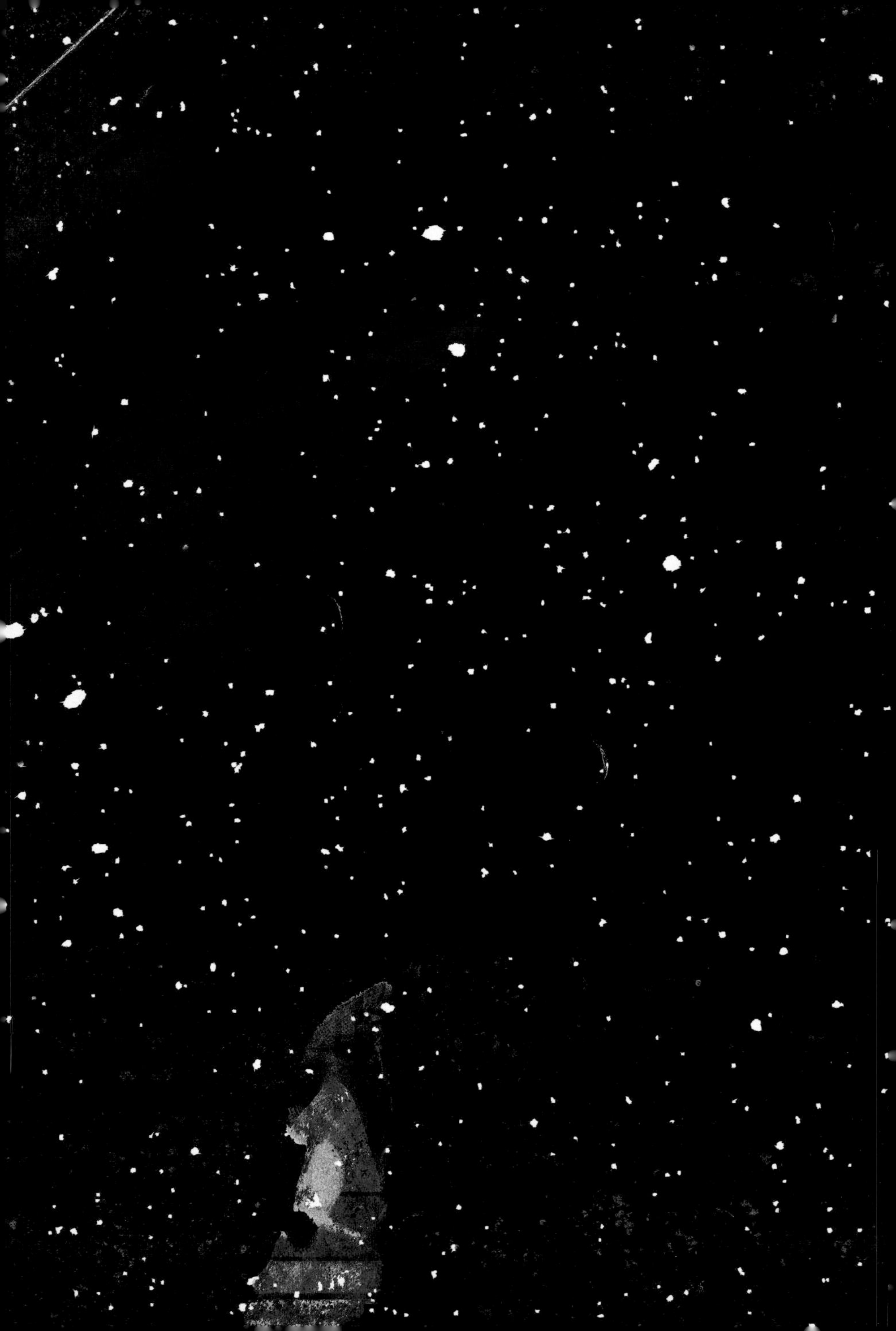

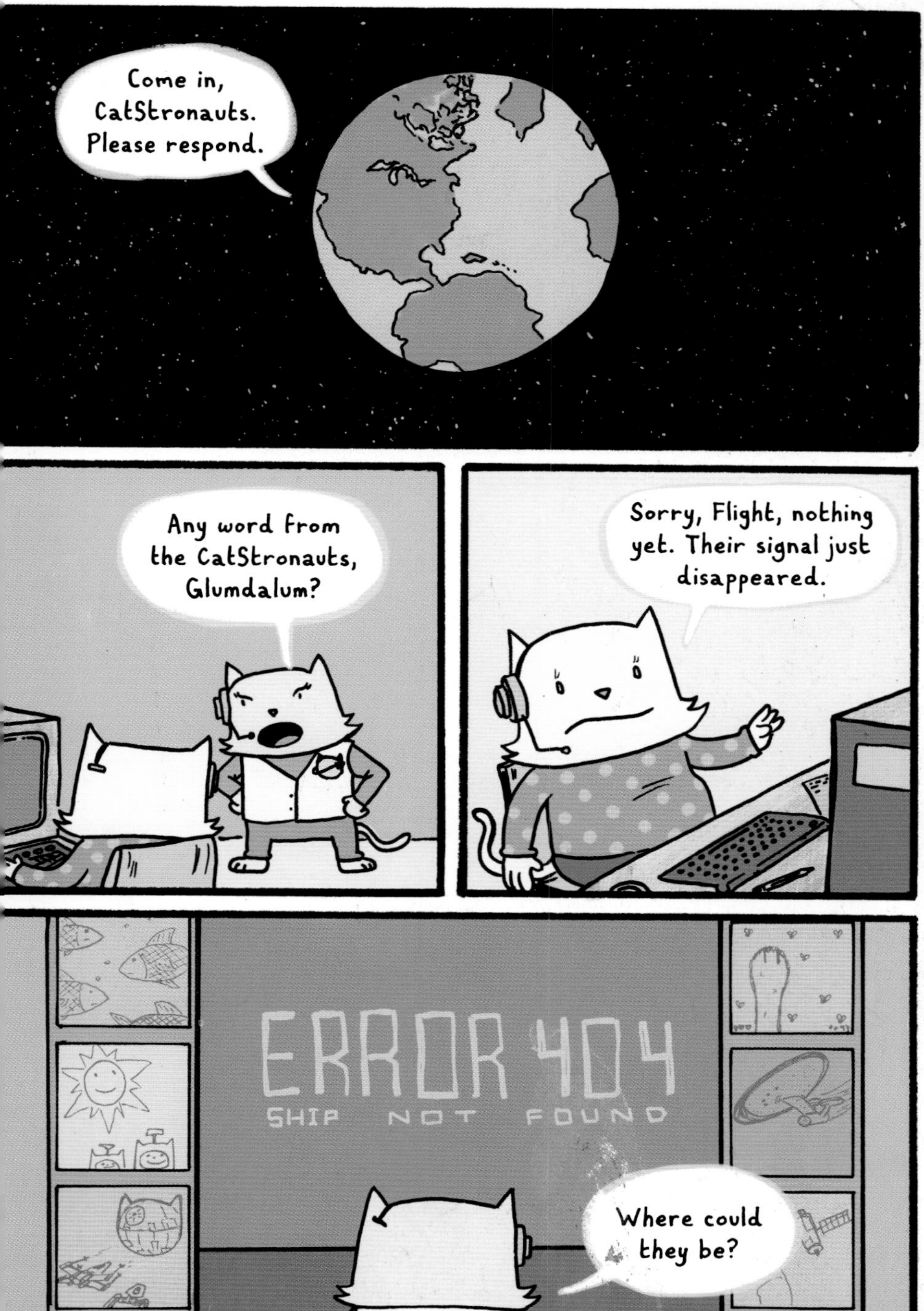
Come in, CatStronauts. Please respond.
Any word from the CatStronauts, Glumdalum?
Sorry, Flight, nothing yet. Their signal just disappeared.
ERROR 404
SHIP NOT FOUND
Where could they be?

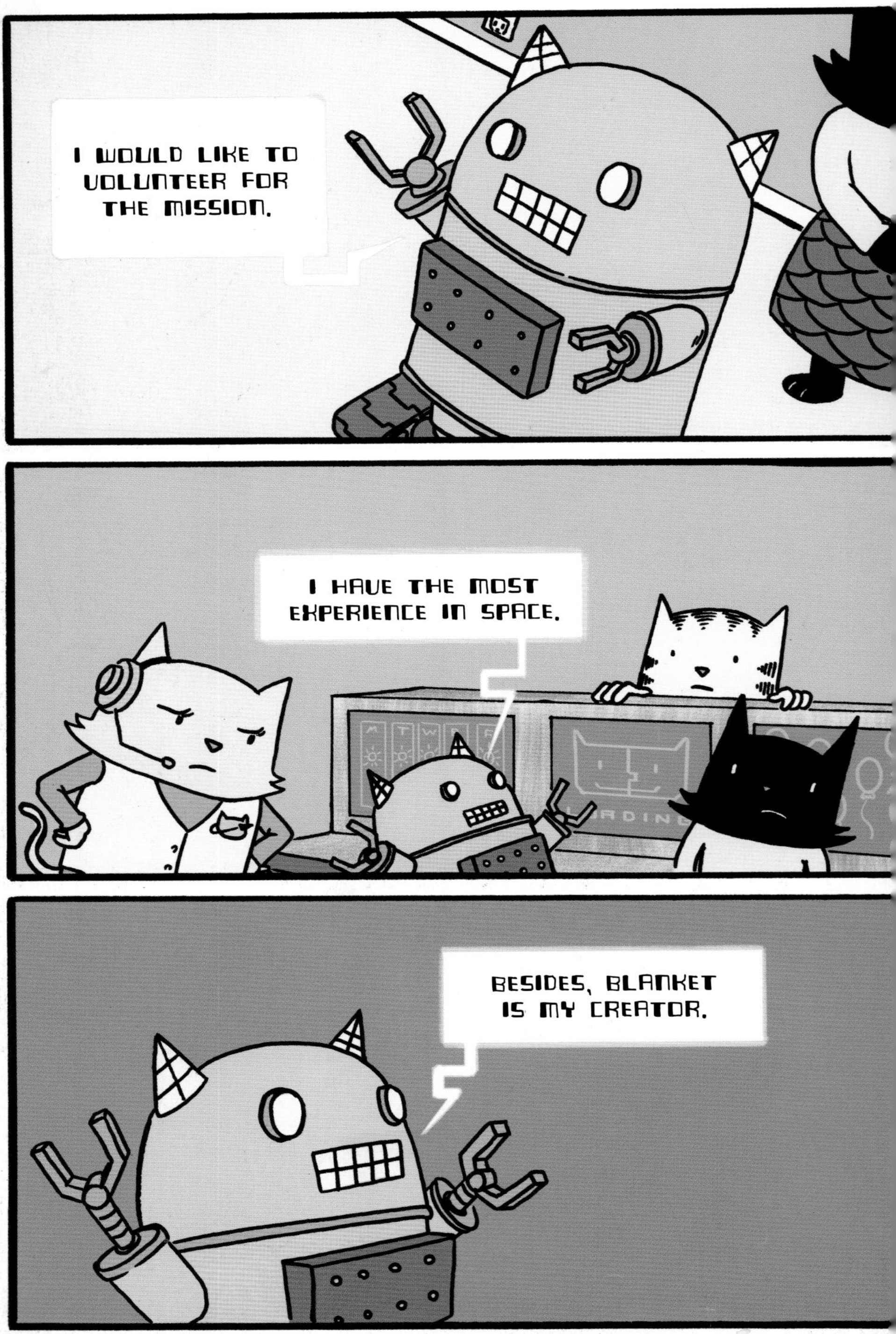
I WOULD LIKE TO VOLUNTEER FOR THE MISSION.
I HAVE THE MOST EXPERIENCE IN SPACE.
BESIDES, BLANKET IS MY CREATOR.

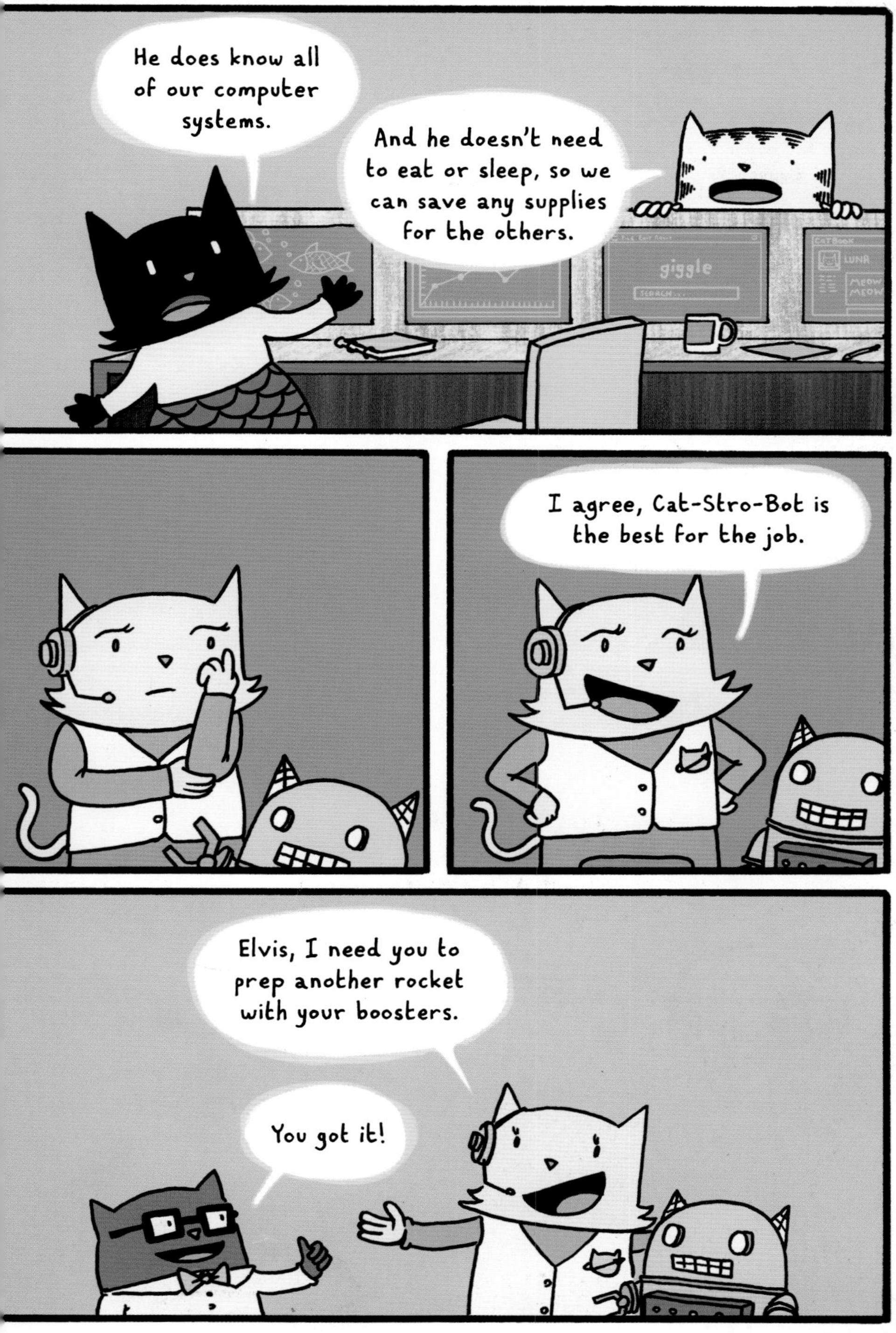
He does know all of our computer systems.
And he doesn't need to eat or sleep, so we can save any supplies for the others.
giggle
SEARCH...
LUNA
MEOW MEOW
I agree, Cat-Stro-Bot is the best for the job.
Elvis, I need you to prep another rocket with your boosters.
You got it!

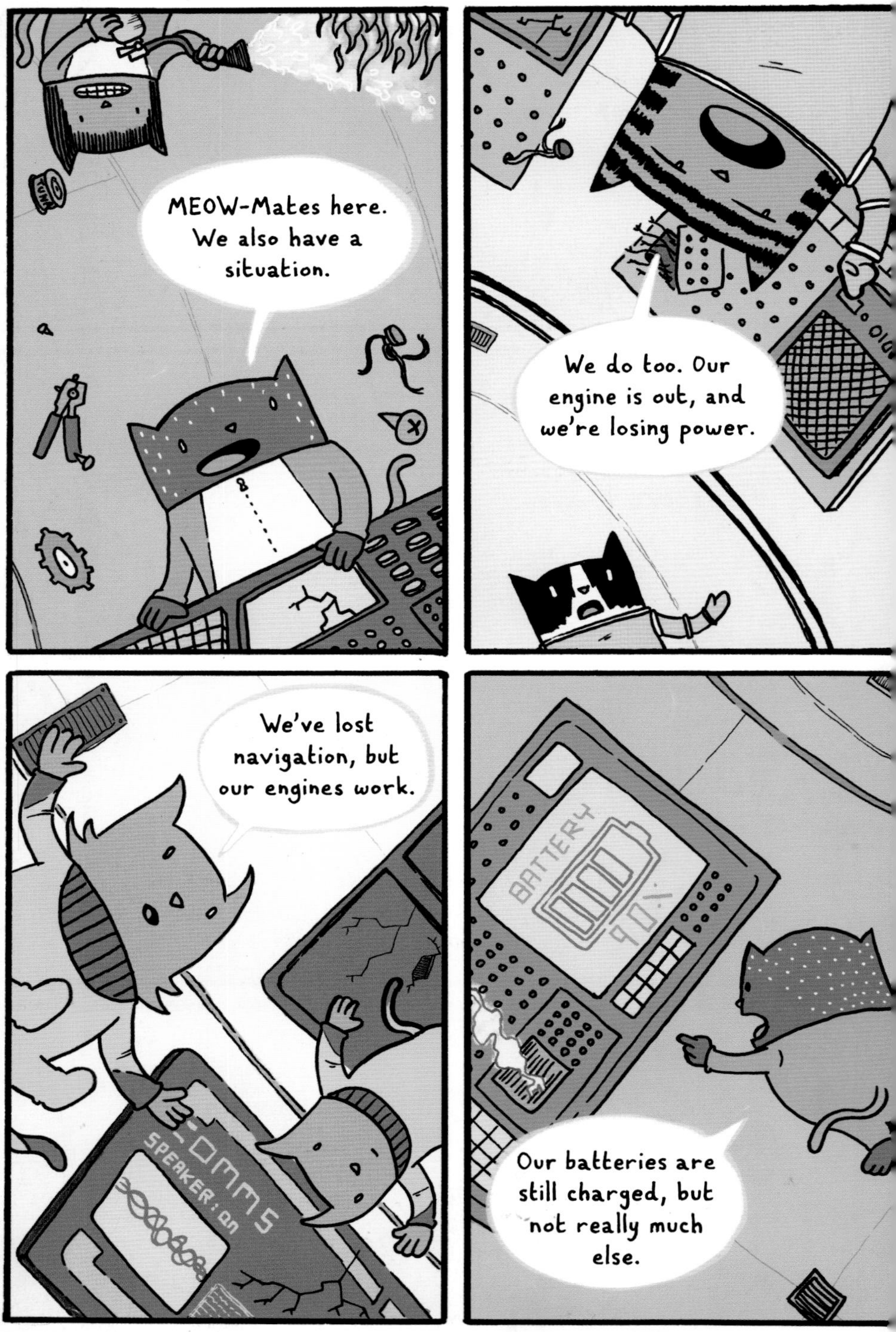
MEOW-Mates here. We also have a situation.
We do too. Our engine is out, and we're losing power.
We've lost navigation, but our engines work.
BATTERY
Our batteries are still charged, but not really much else.

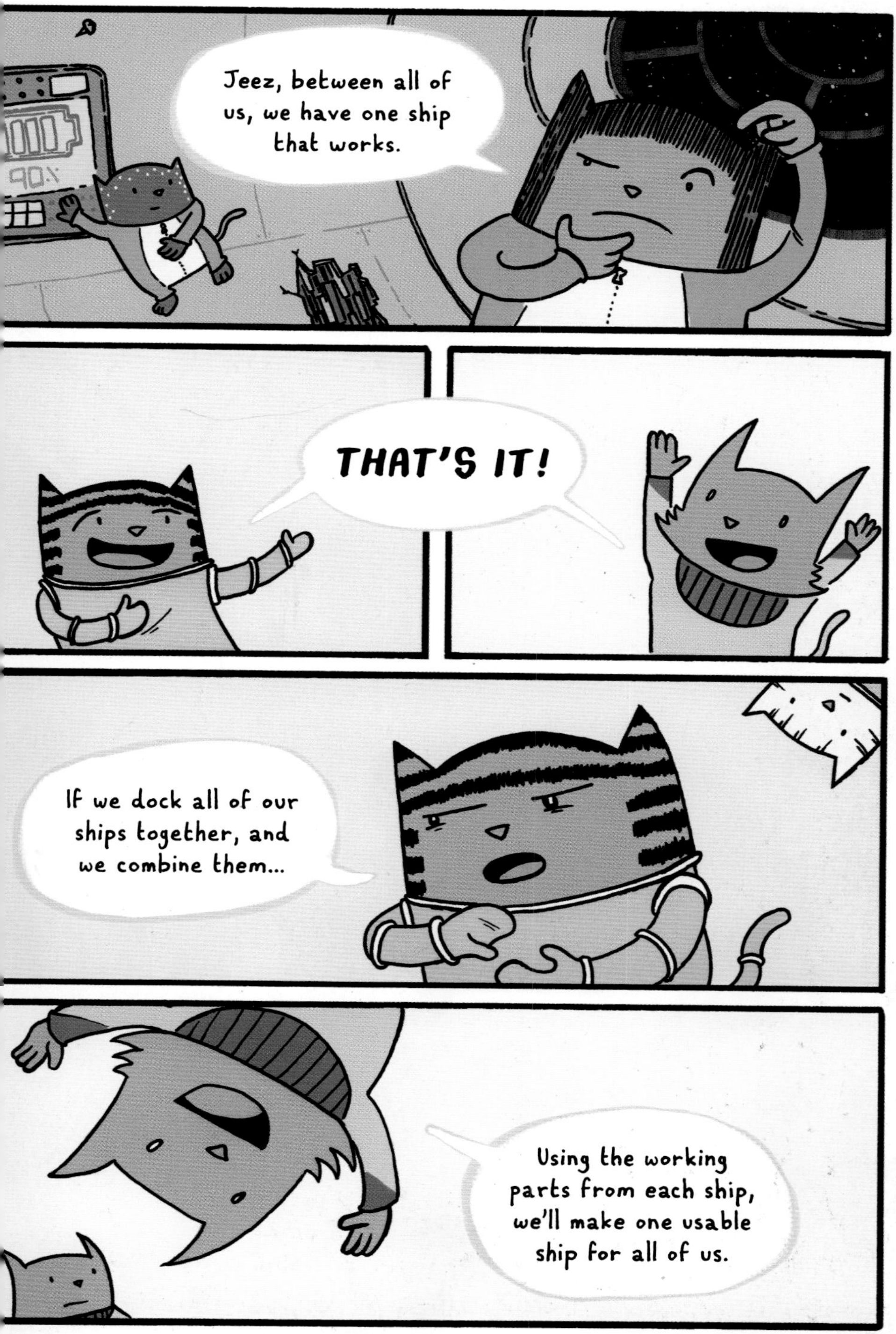
Jeez, between all of us, we have one ship that works.
THAT'S IT!
If we dock all of our ships together, and we combine them...
Using the working parts from each ship, we'll make one usable ship for all of us.

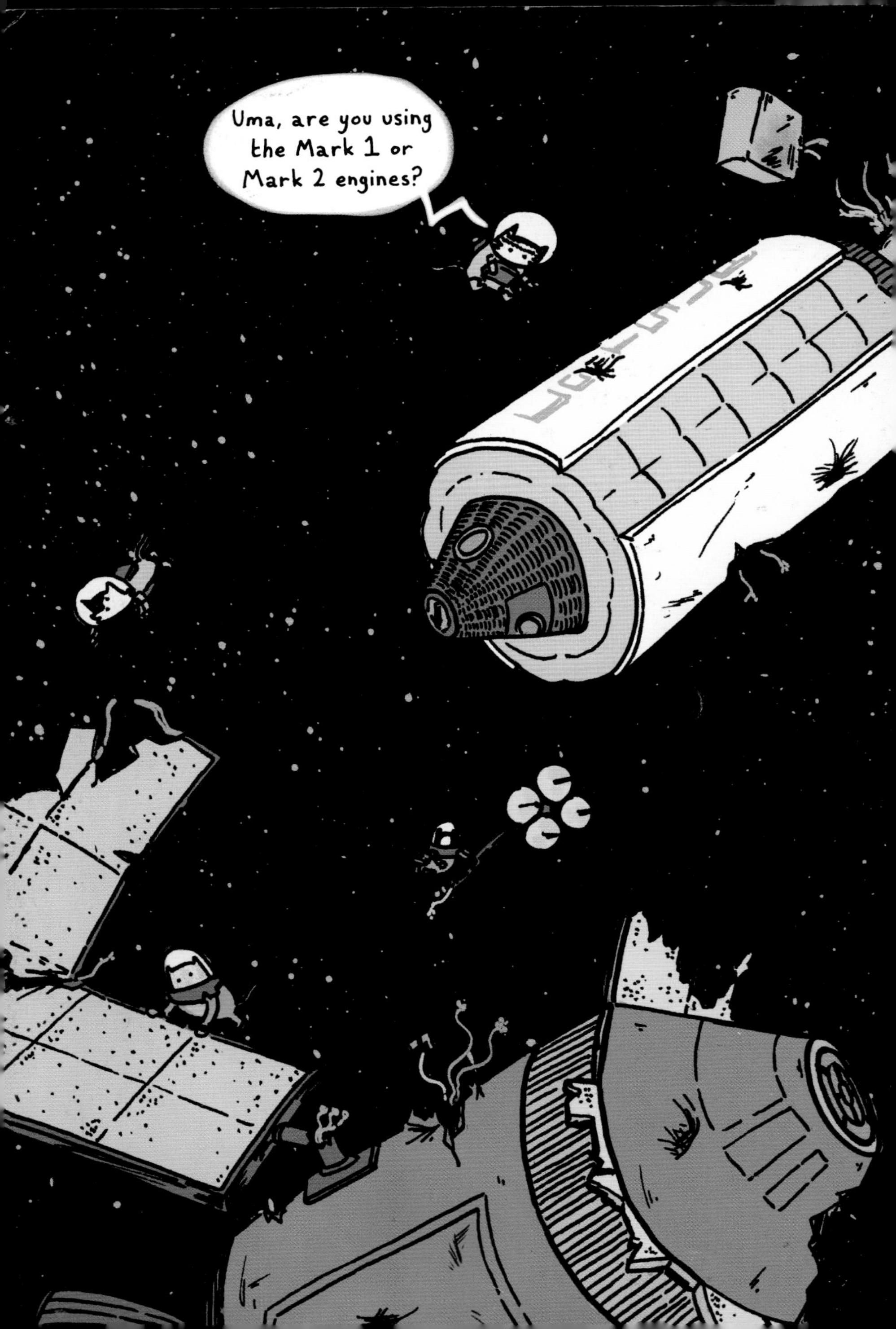
Uma, are you using the Mark 1 or Mark 2 engines?

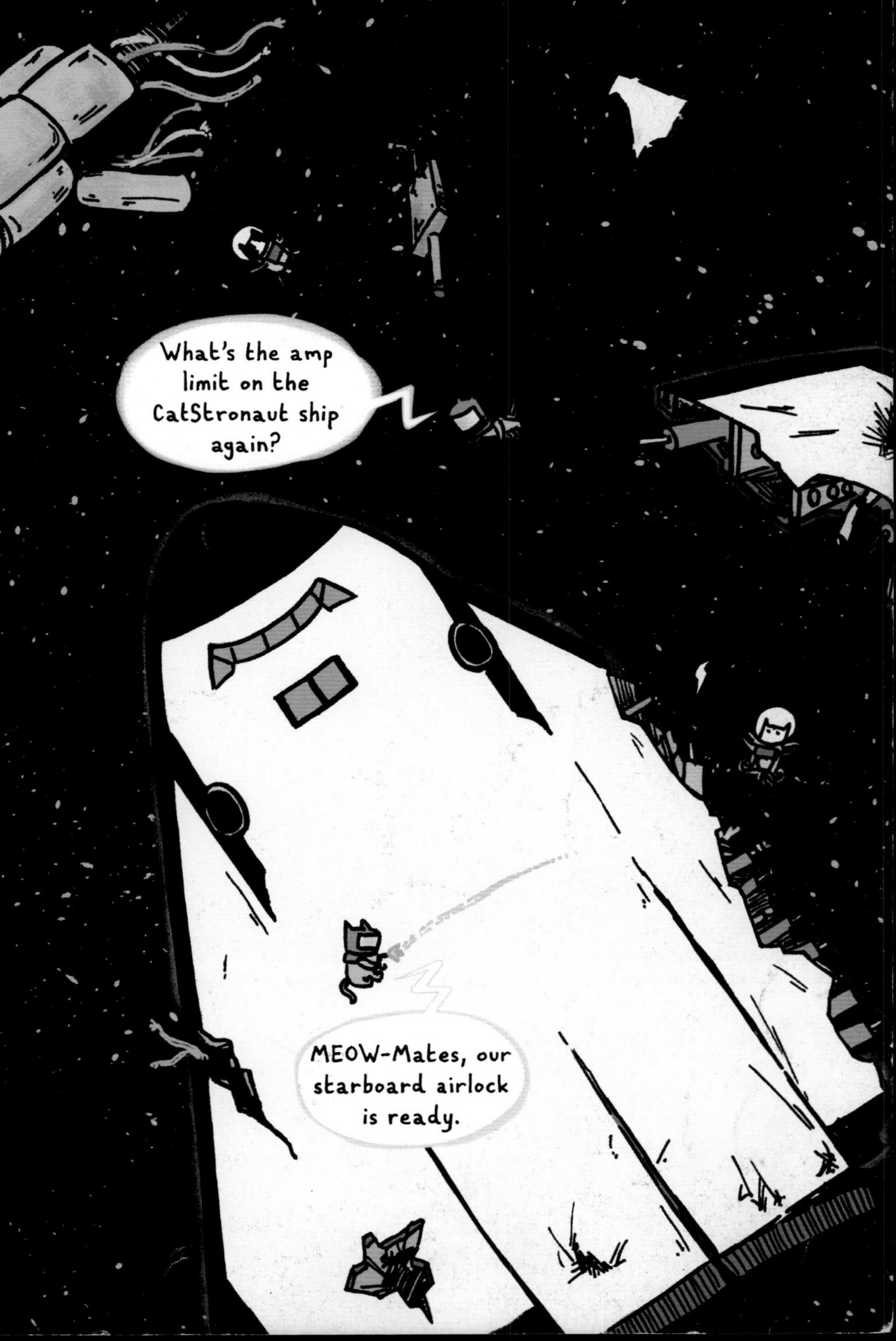
What's the amp limit on the CatStronaut ship again?
MEOW-Mates, our starboard airlock is ready.

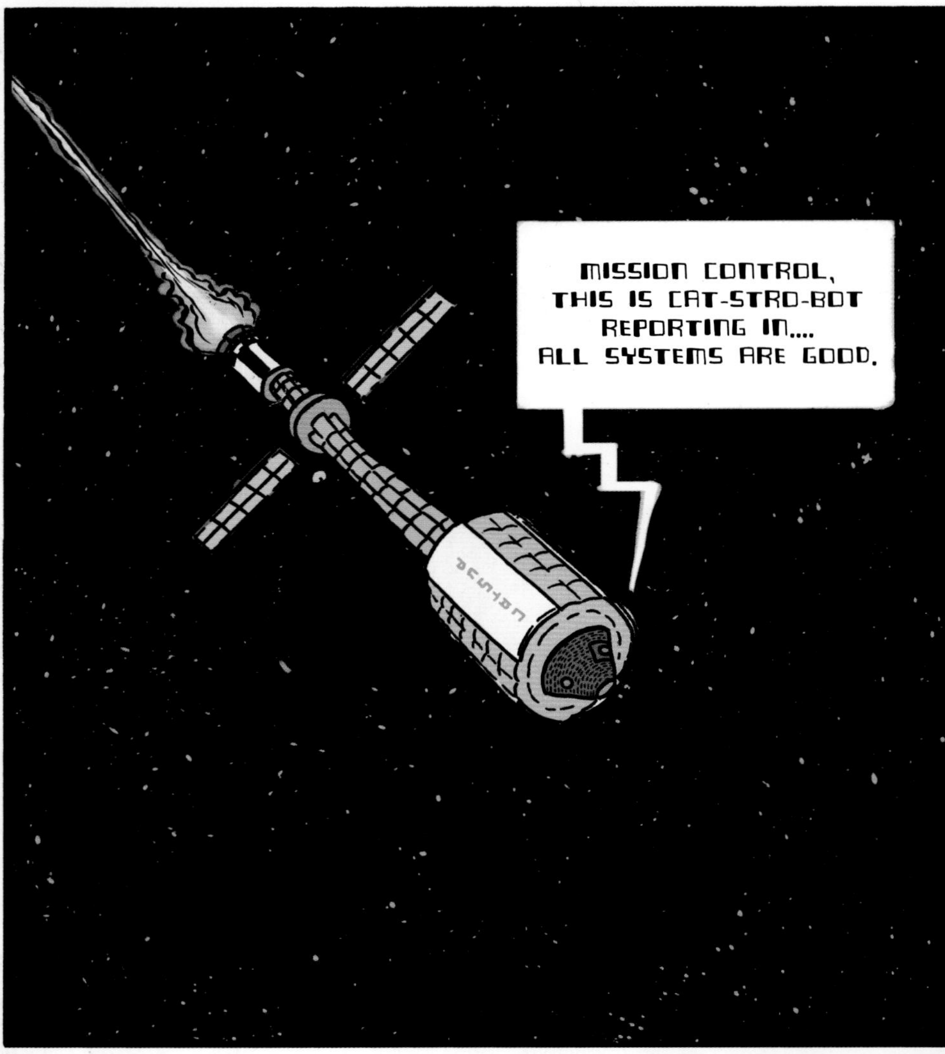
MISSION CONTROL,
THIS IS CAT-STRO-BOT
REPORTING IN....
ALL SYSTEMS ARE GOOD.

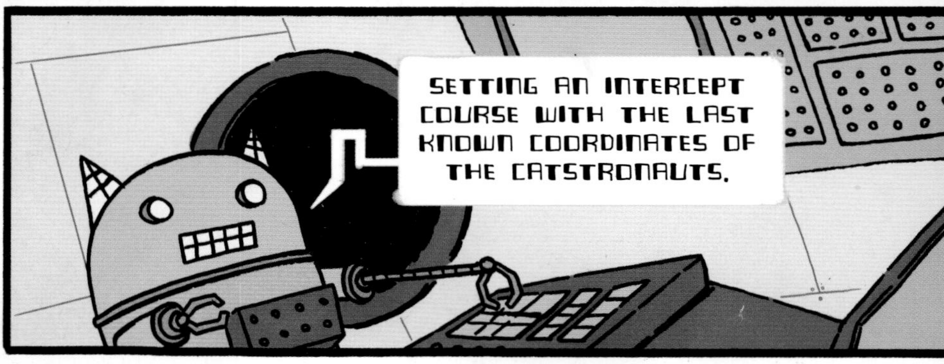
SETTING AN INTERCEPT
COURSE WITH THE LAST
KNOWN COORDINATES OF
THE CATSTRONAUTS.

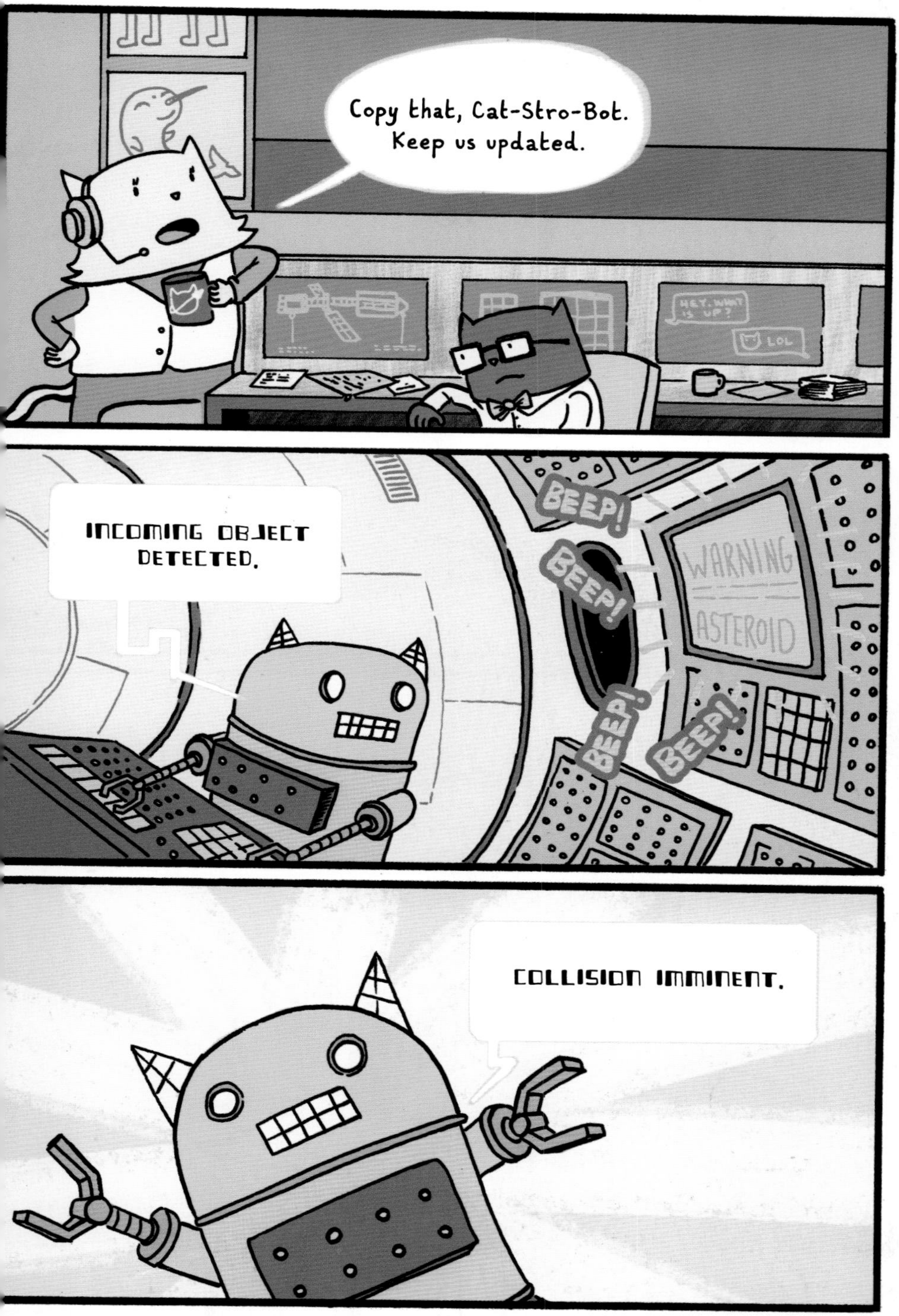
Copy that, Cat-Stro-Bot. Keep us updated.
HEY, WHAT IS UP?
LOL
INCOMING OBJECT DETECTED.
BEEP!
BEEP!
WARNING
ASTEROID
BEEP!
BEEP!
COLLISION IMMINENT.

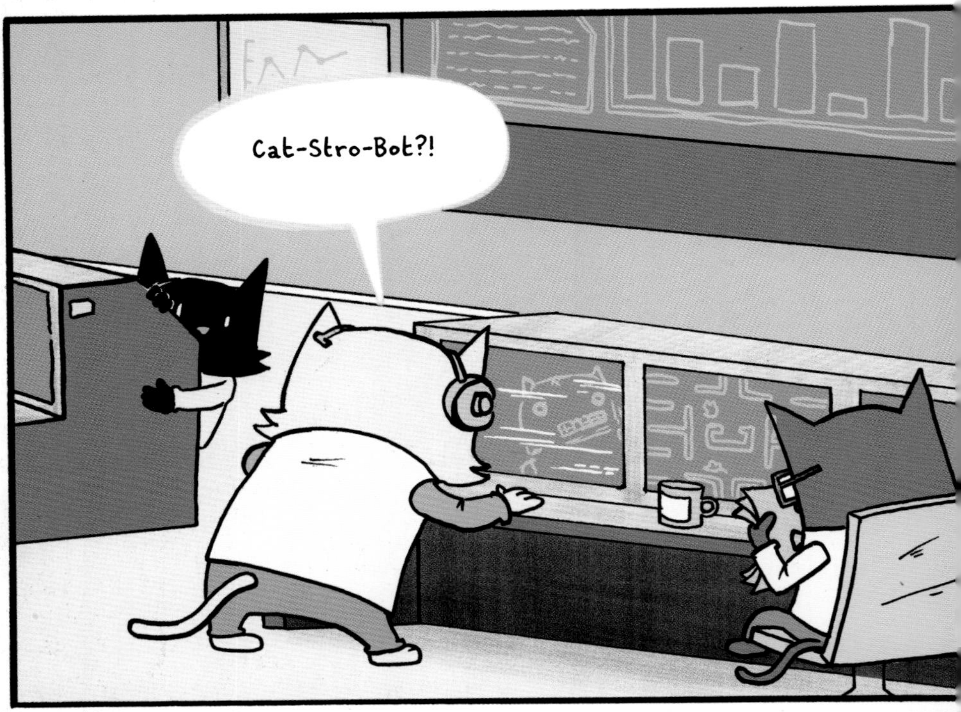
Cat-Stro-Bot?!

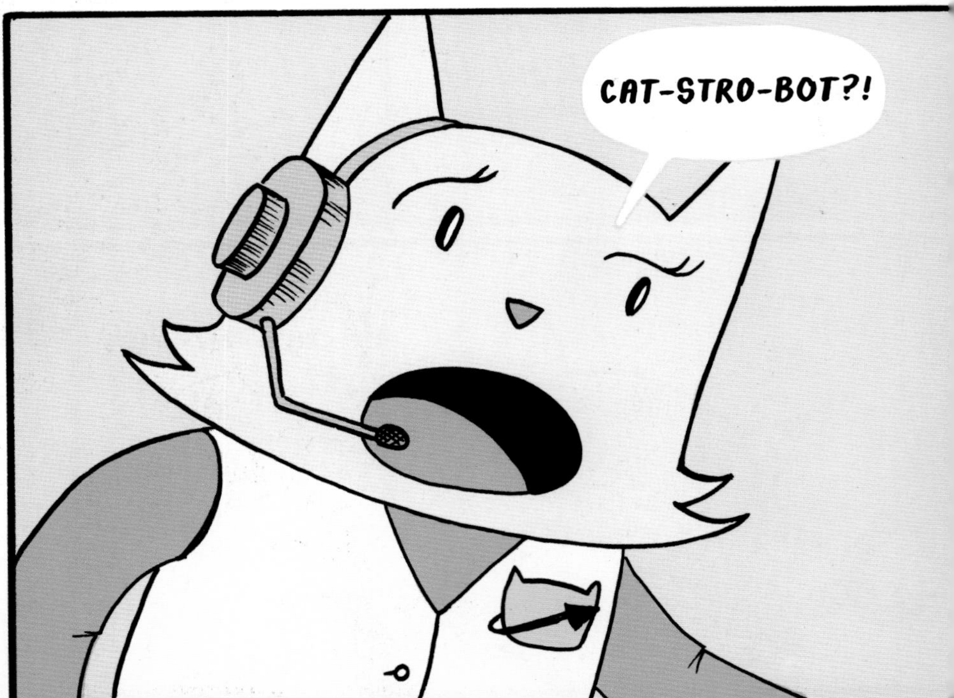
CAT-STRO-BOT?!

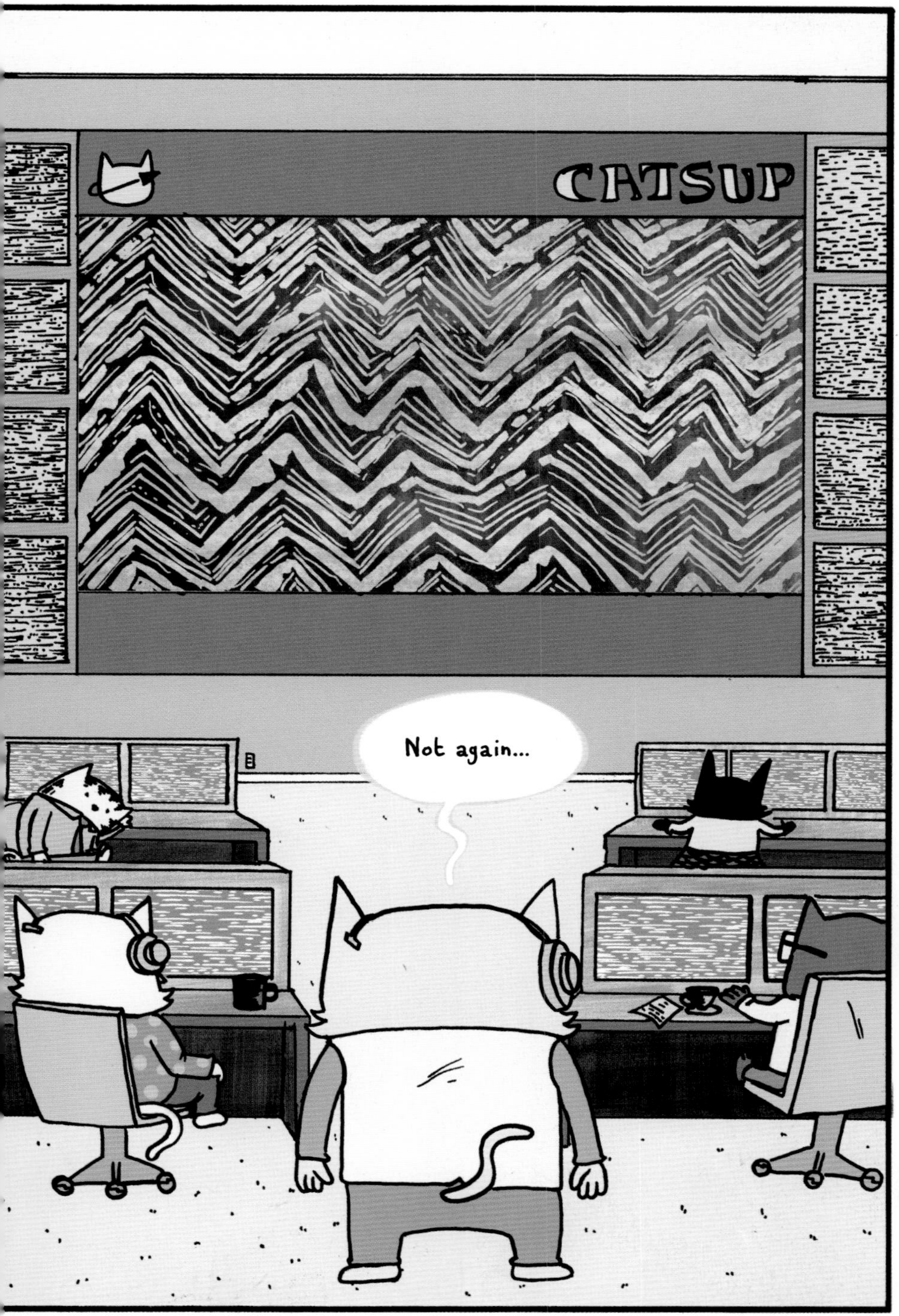
CATSUP
Not again...

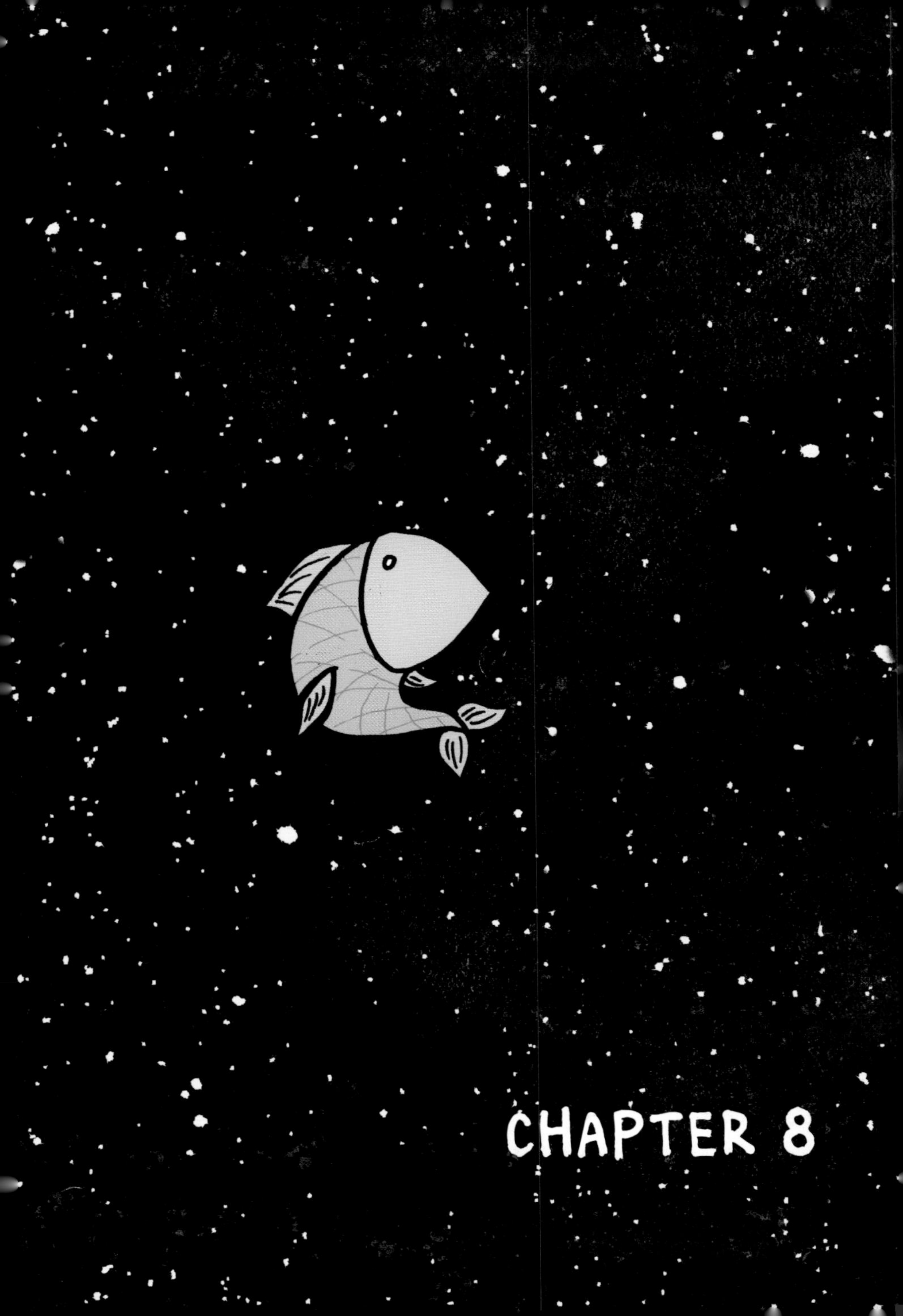
CHAPTER 8

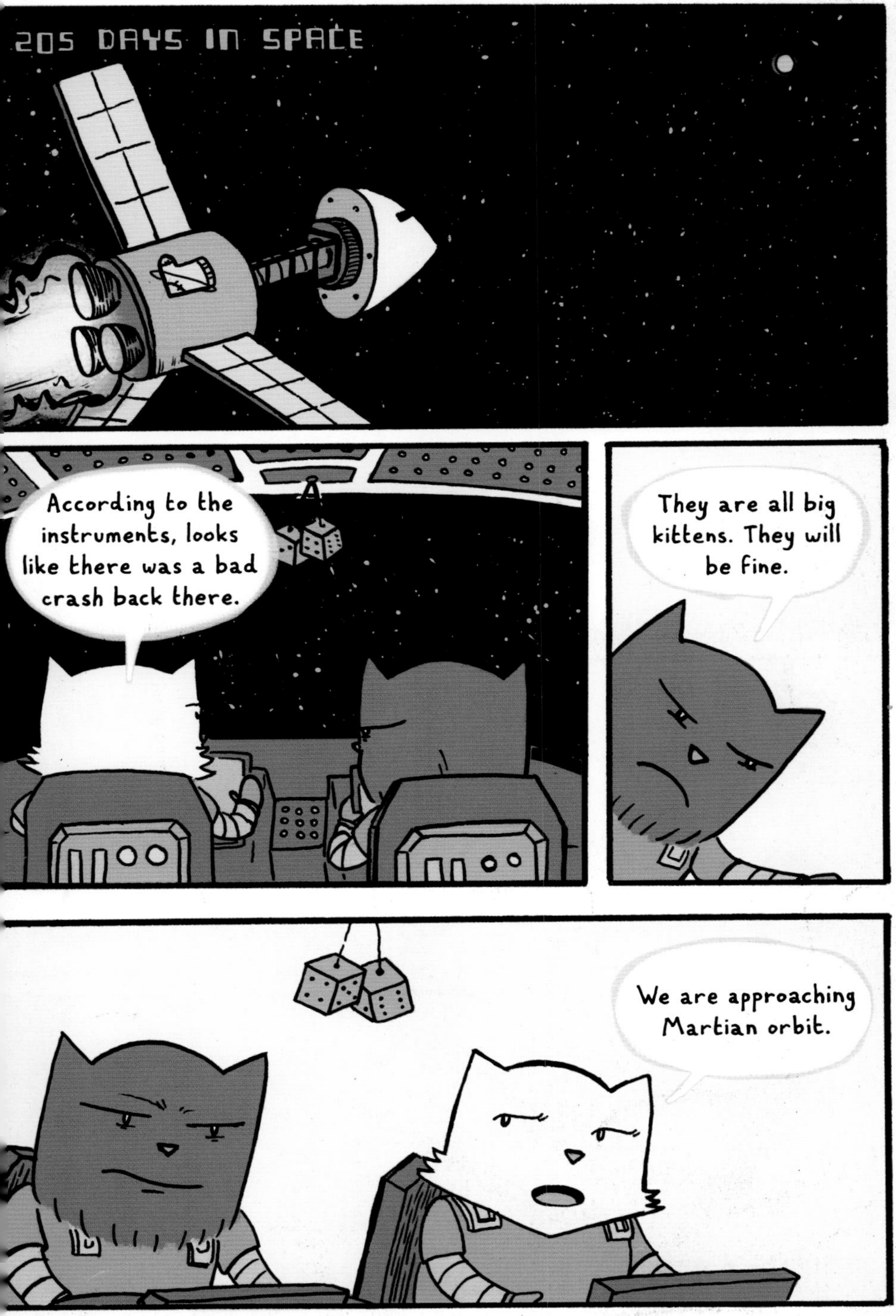

205 DAYS IN SPACE
According to the instruments, looks like there was a bad crash back there.
They are all big kittens. They will be fine.
We are approaching Martian orbit.

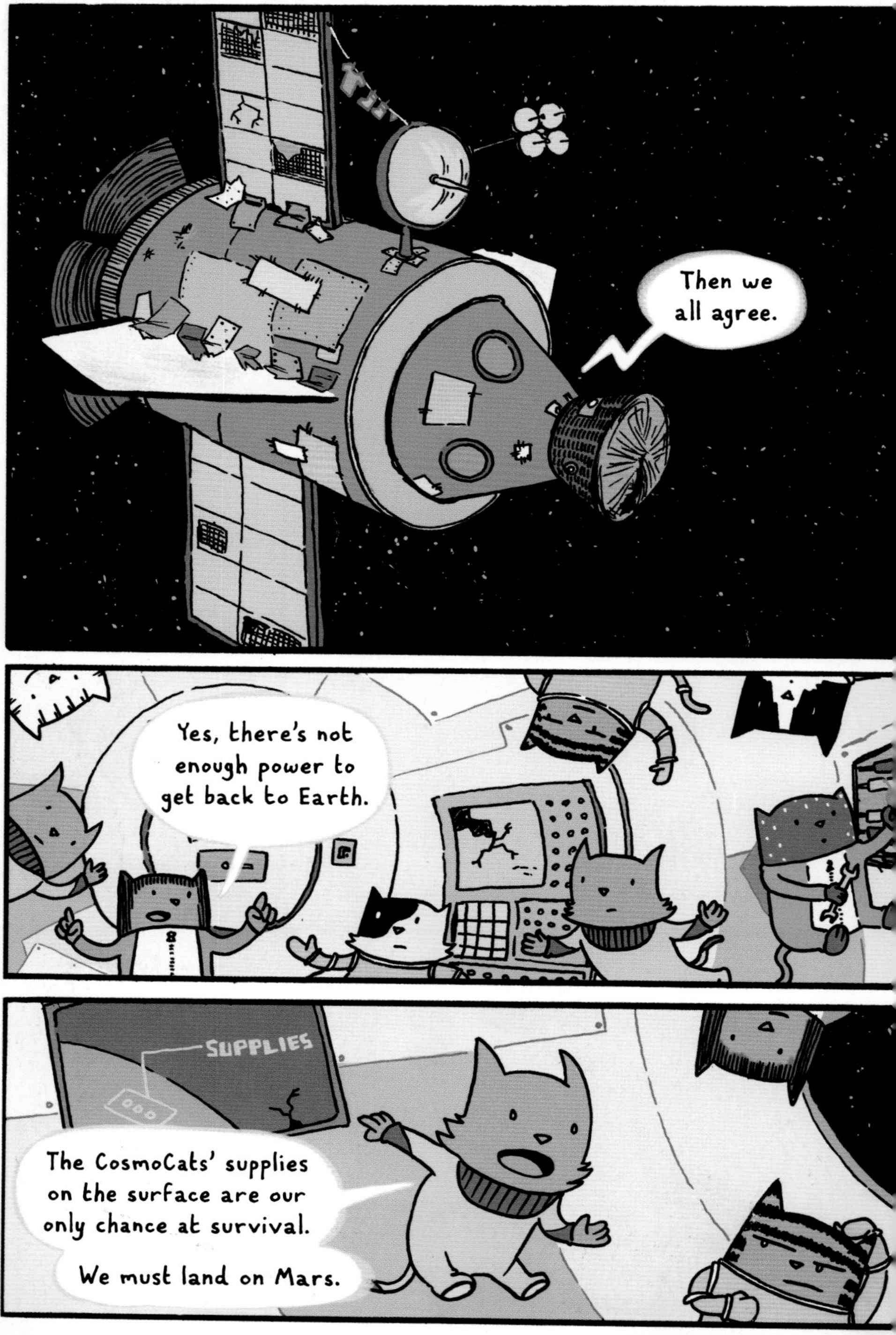
Then we all agree.
Yes, there's not enough power to get back to Earth.
SUPPLIES
The CosmoCats' supplies on the surface are our only chance at survival.
We must land on Mars.

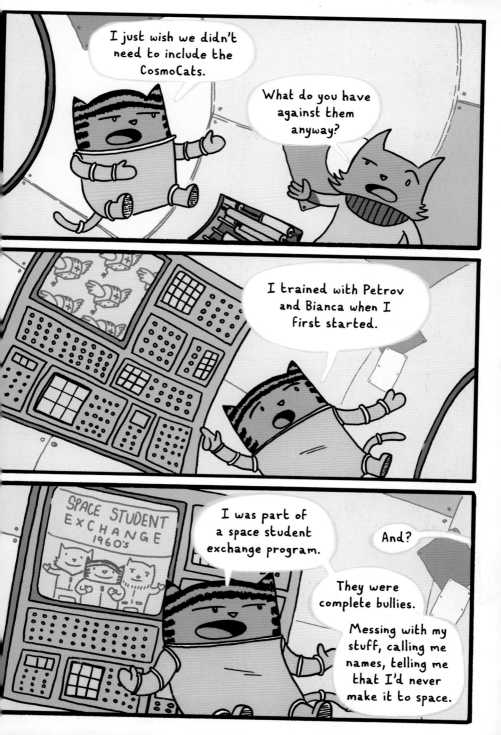

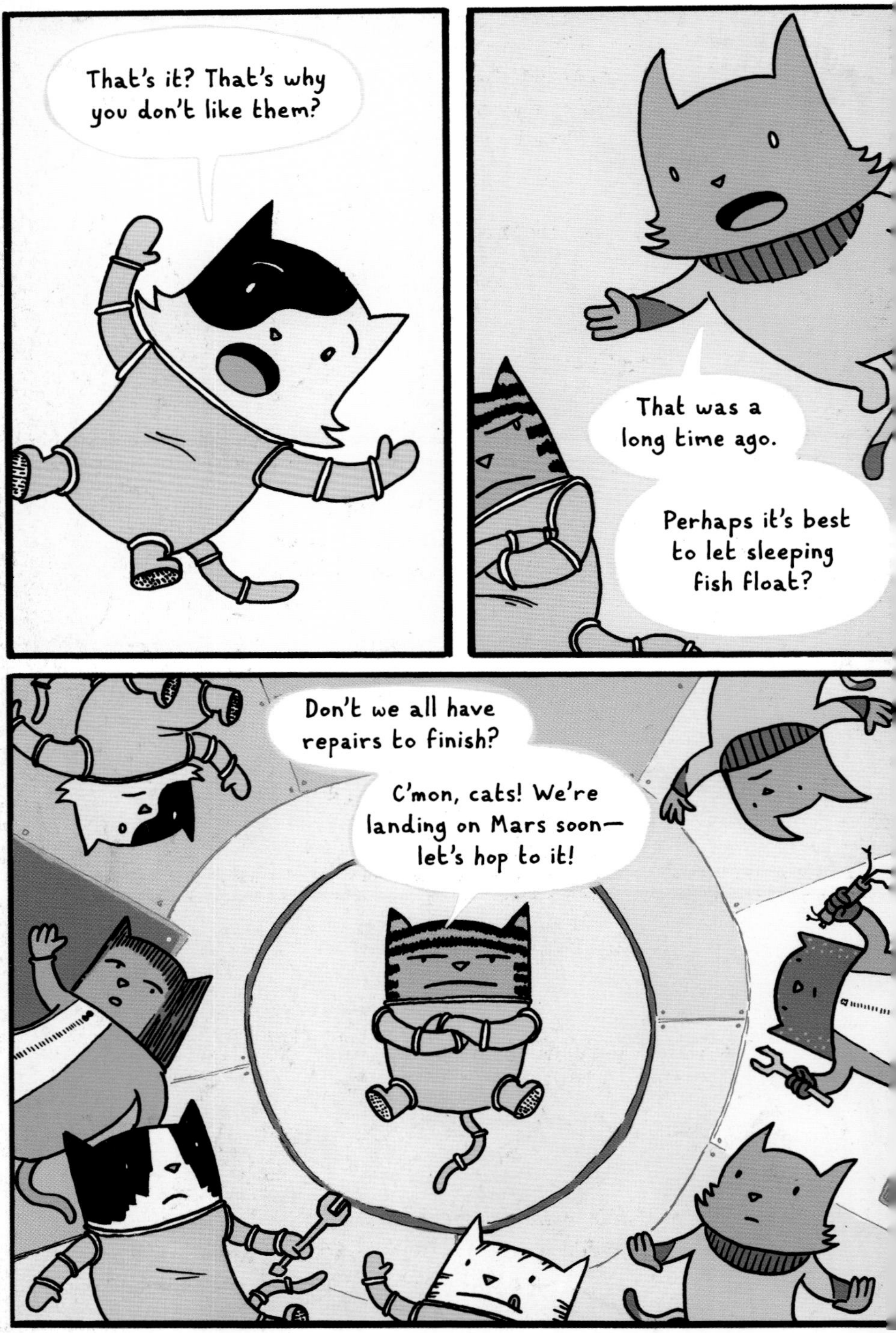
That's it? That's why you don't like them?
That was a long time ago.
Perhaps it's best to let sleeping fish float?
Don't we all have repairs to finish?
C'mon, cats! We're landing on Mars soon—let's hop to it!

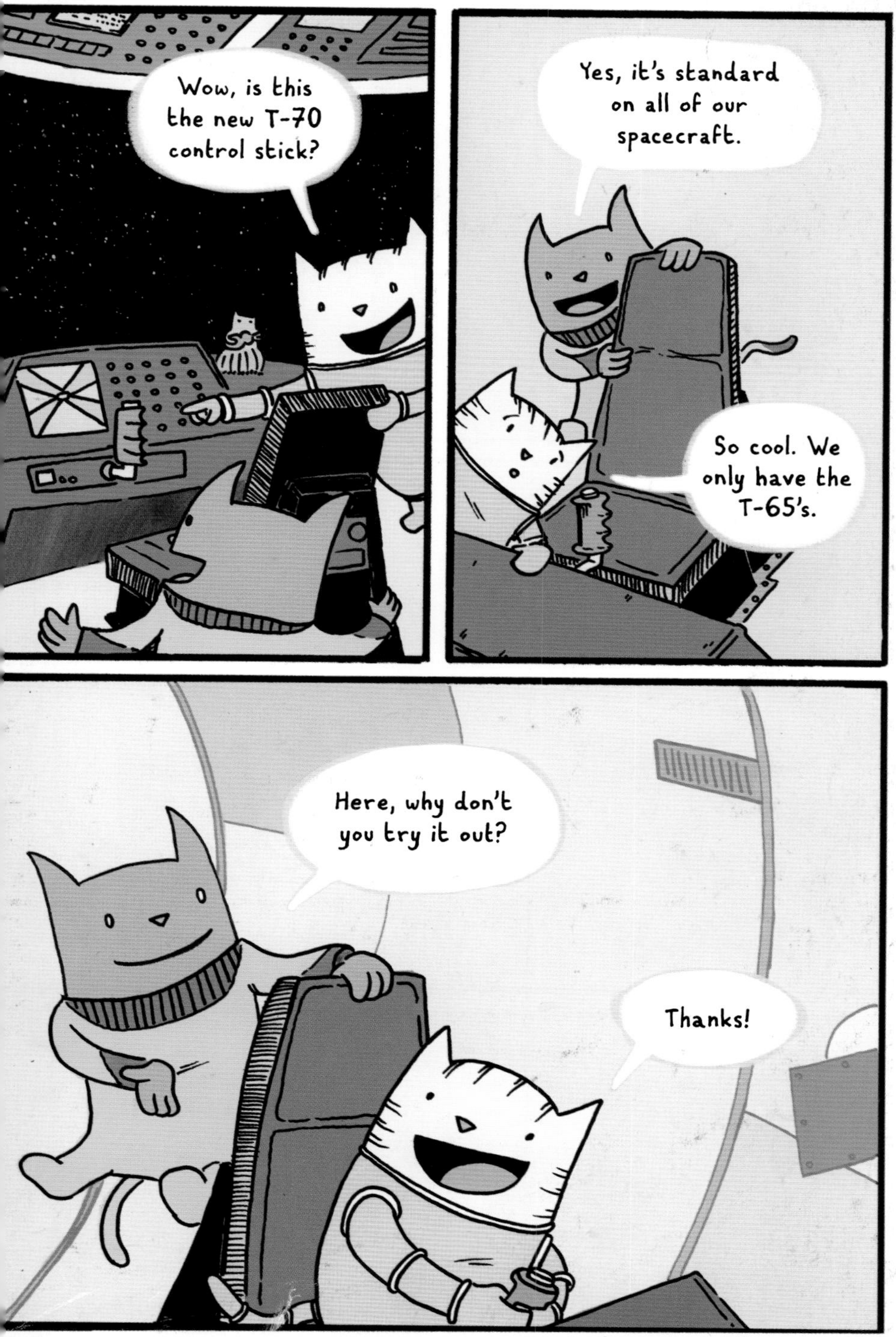
Wow, is this the new T-70 control stick?
Yes, it's standard on all of our spacecraft.
So cool. We only have the T-65's.
Here, why don't you try it out?
Thanks!

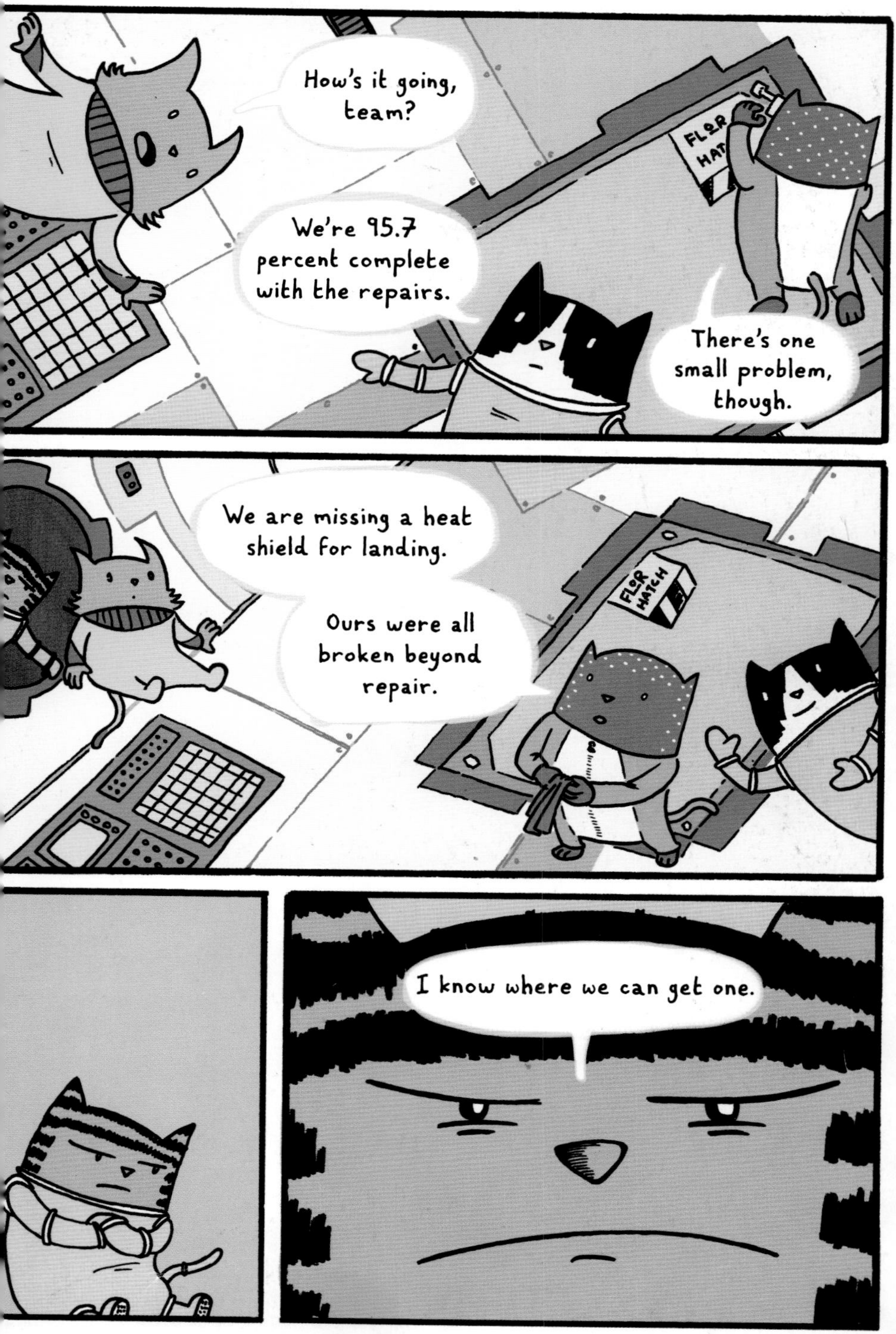
How's it going, team?
We're 95.7 percent complete with the repairs.
There's one small problem, though.
FLOOR HATCH
We are missing a heat shield for landing.
Ours were all broken beyond repair.
FLOOR HATCH
I know where we can get one.

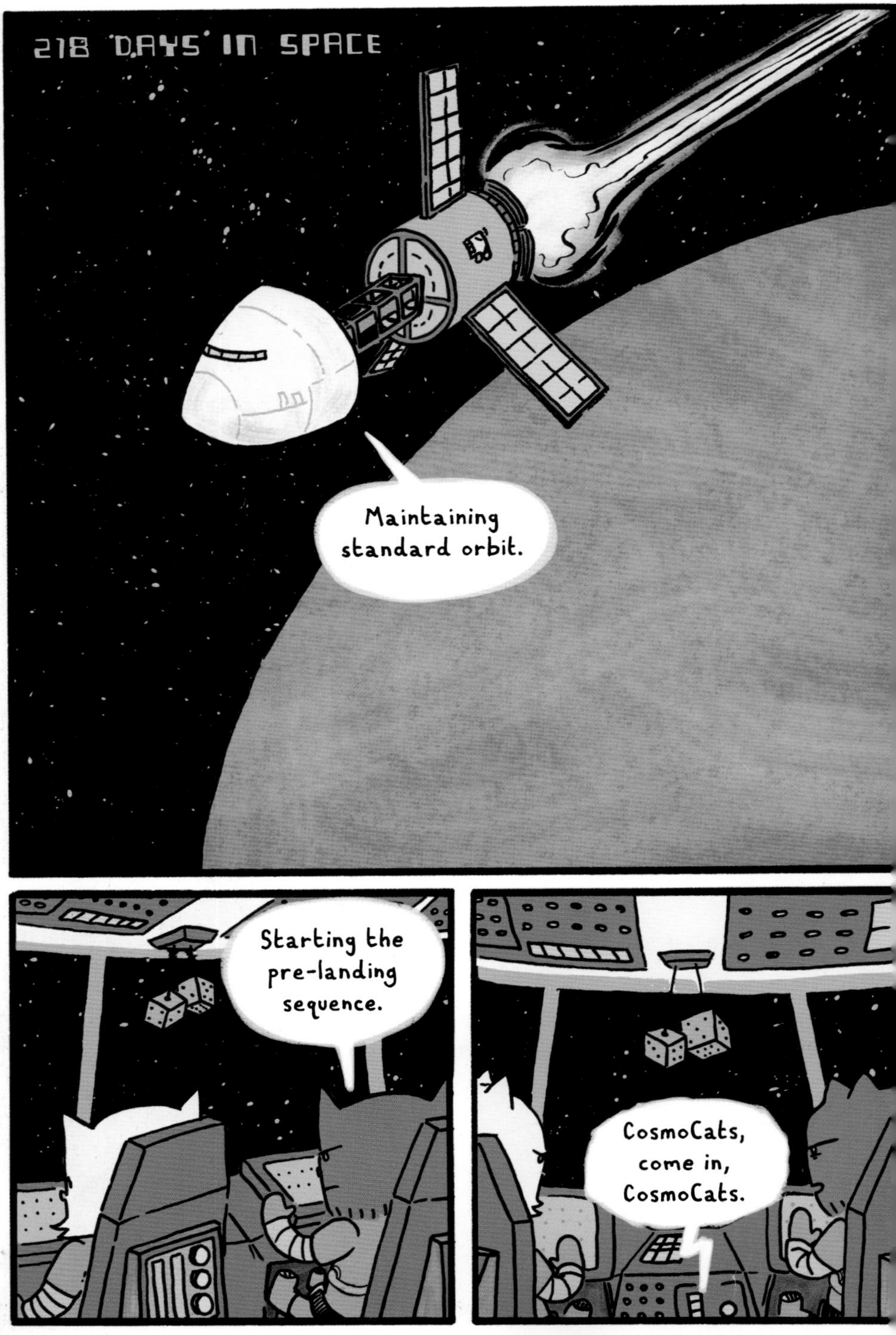
218 DAYS IN SPACE
Maintaining standard orbit.
Starting the pre-landing sequence.
CosmoCats, come in, CosmoCats.

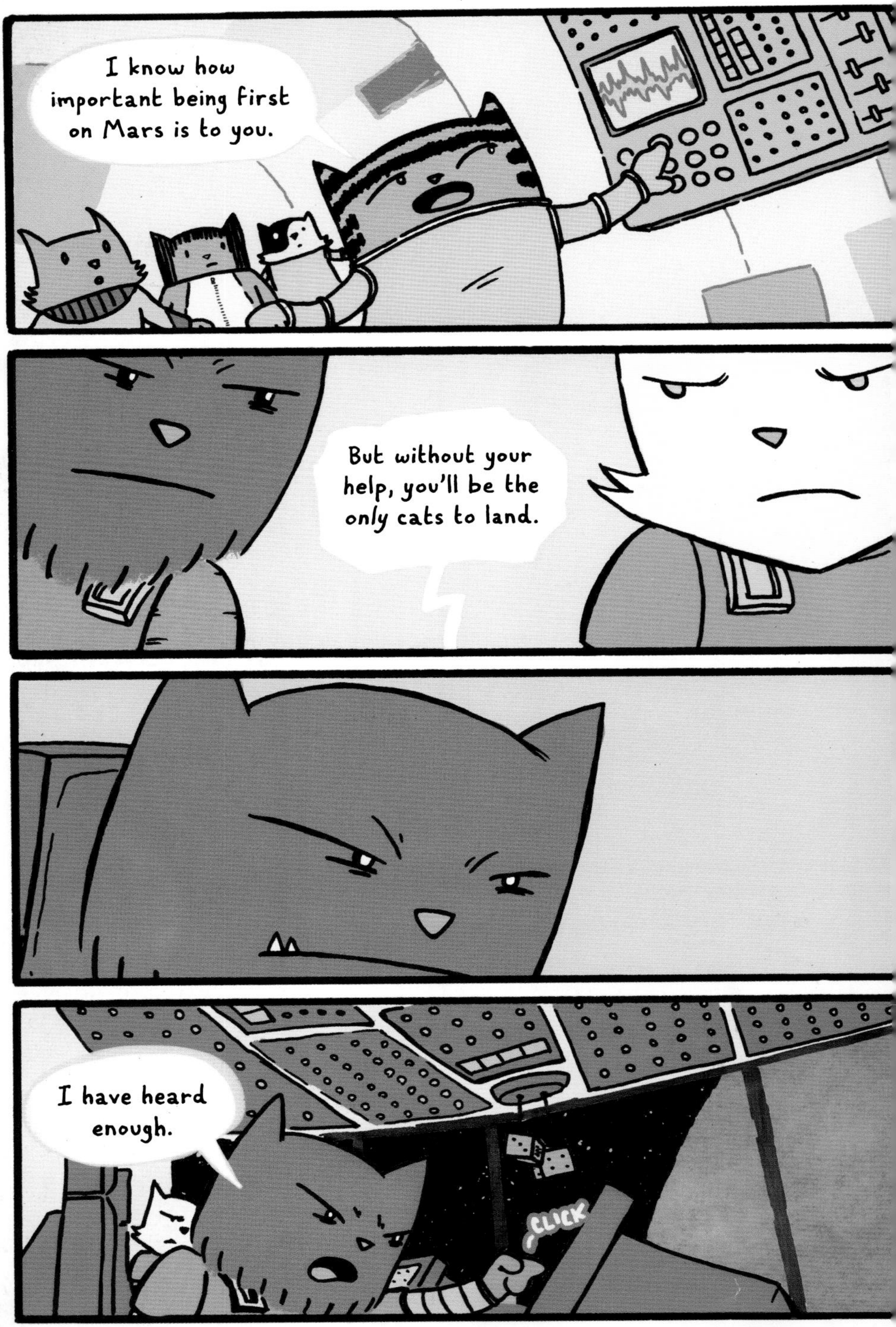
I know how important being first on Mars is to you.
But without your help, you'll be the only cats to land.
I have heard enough.
CLICK

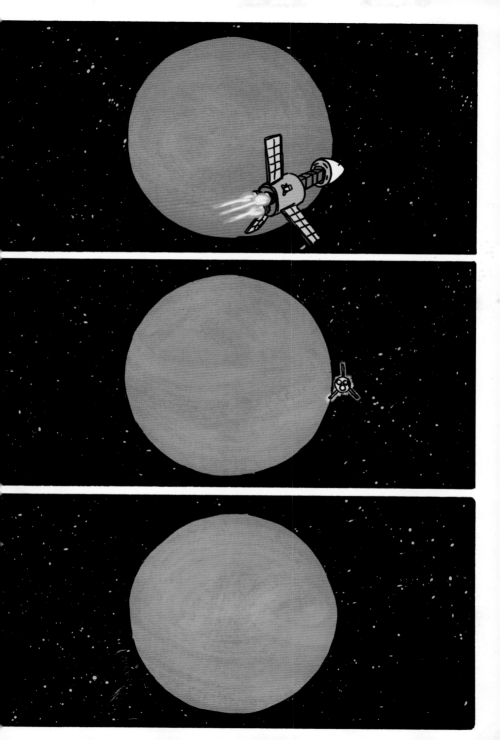

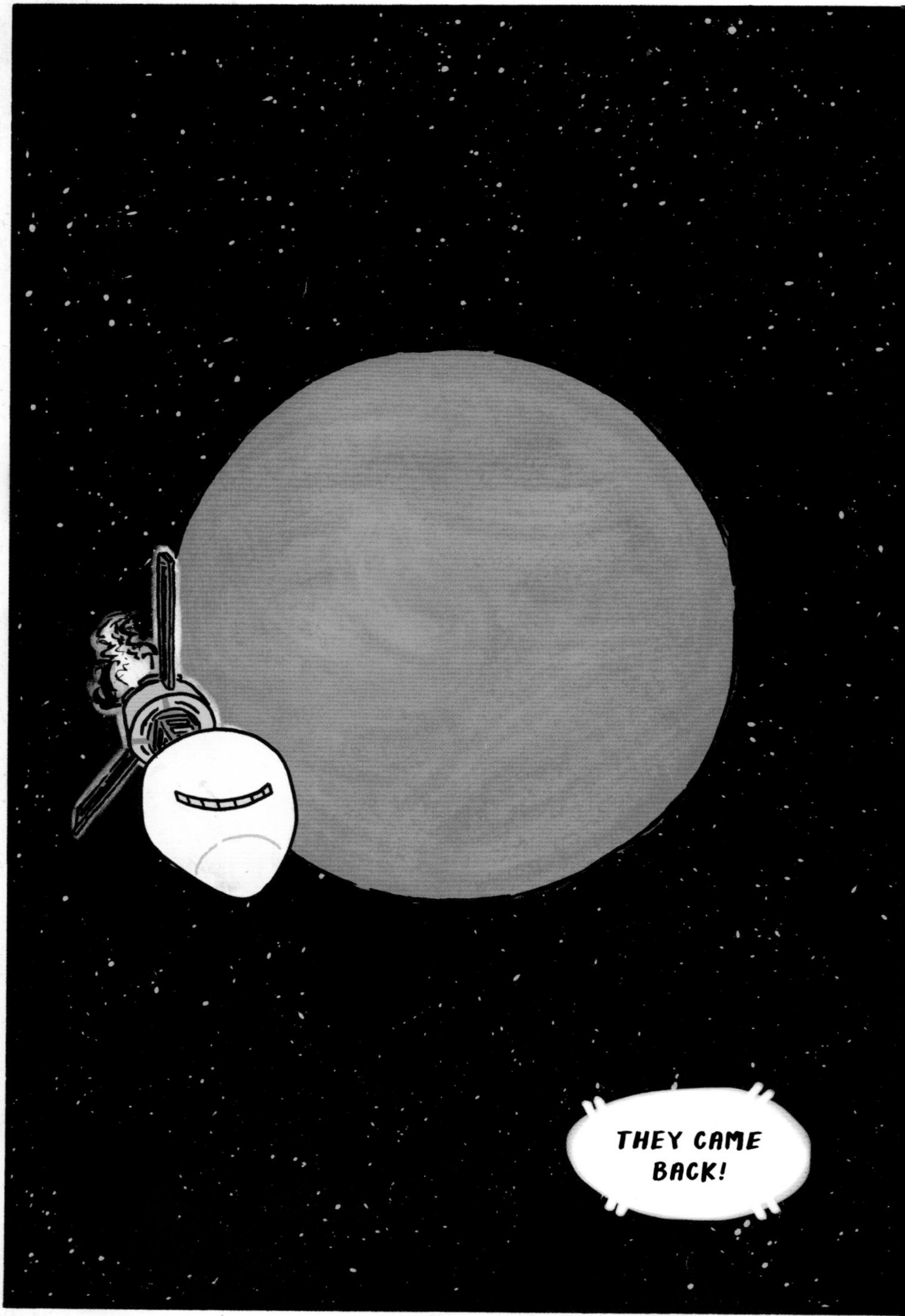
THEY CAME BACK!

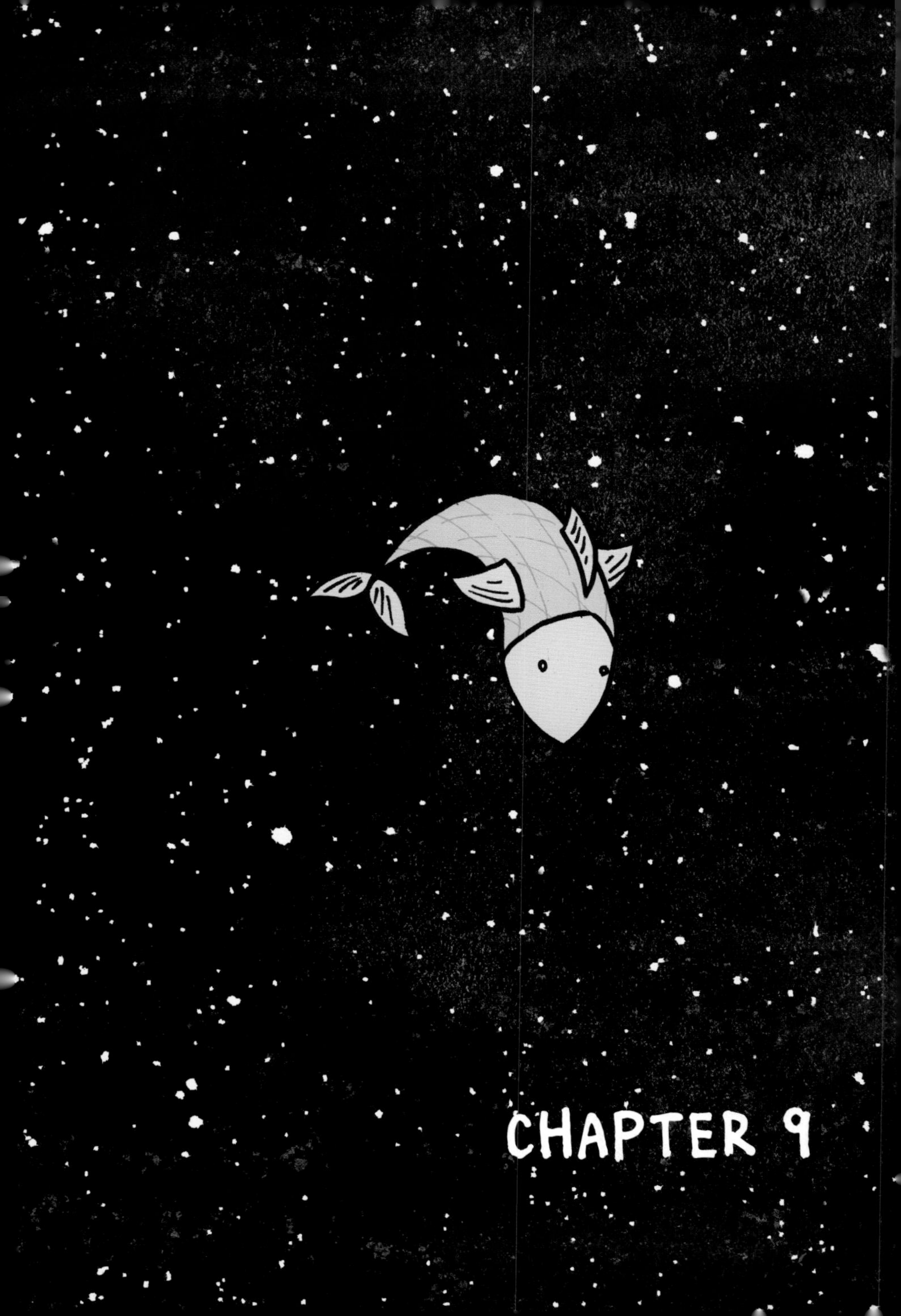
CHAPTER 9

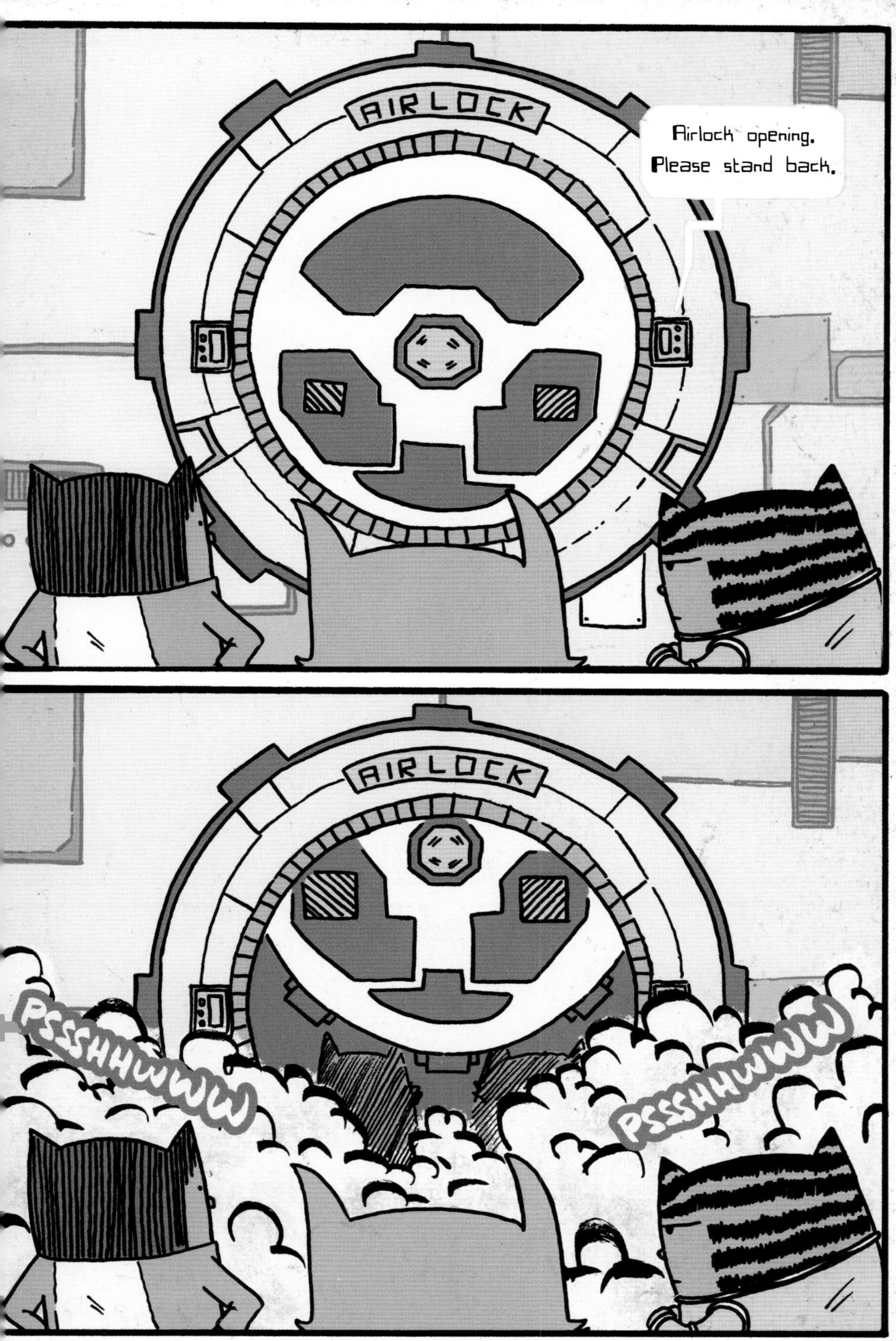
AIRLOCK
Airlock opening.
Please stand back.
AIRLOCK
PSSSHHWWWW
PSSSHHWWWW

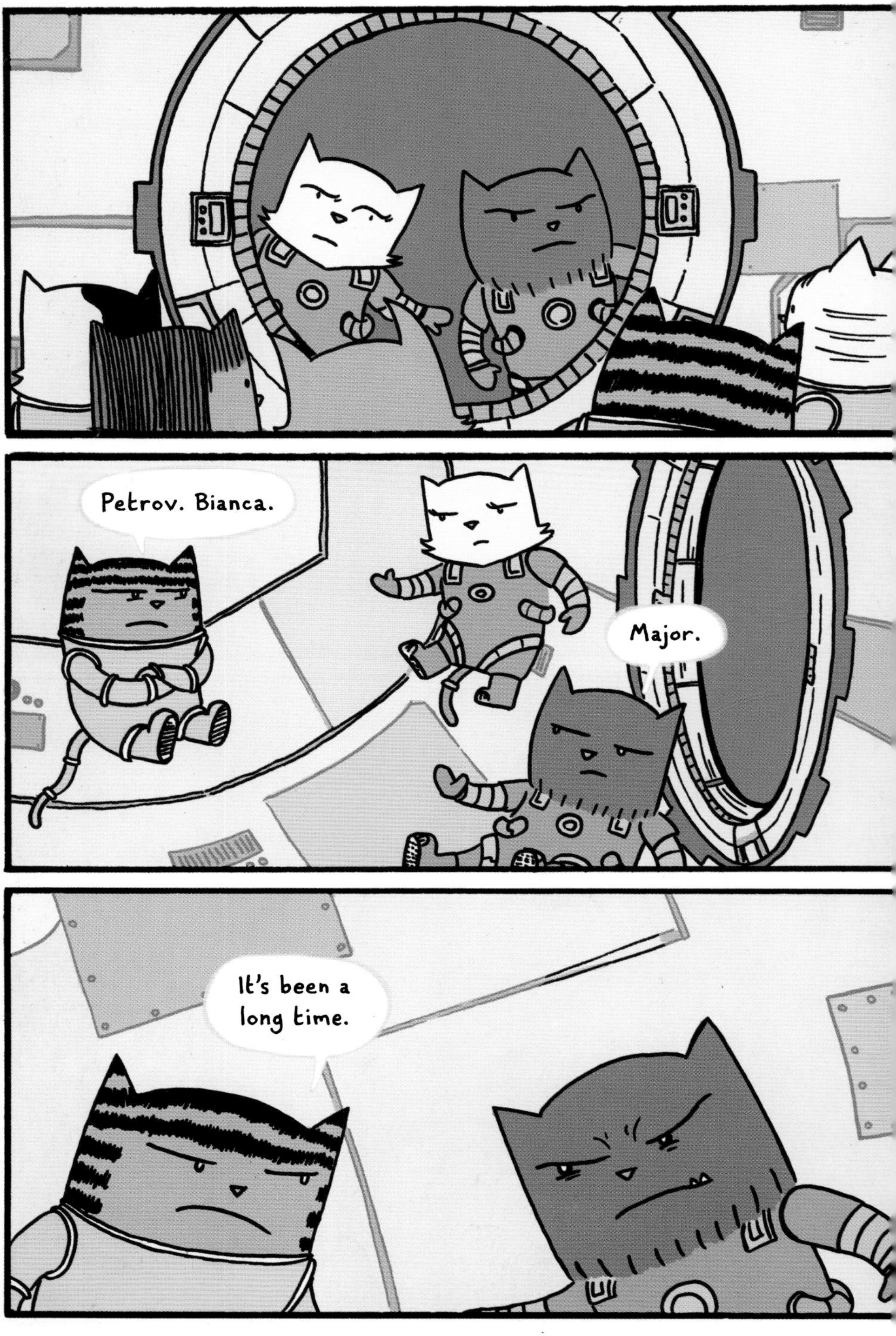
Petrov. Bianca.
Major.
It's been a long time.

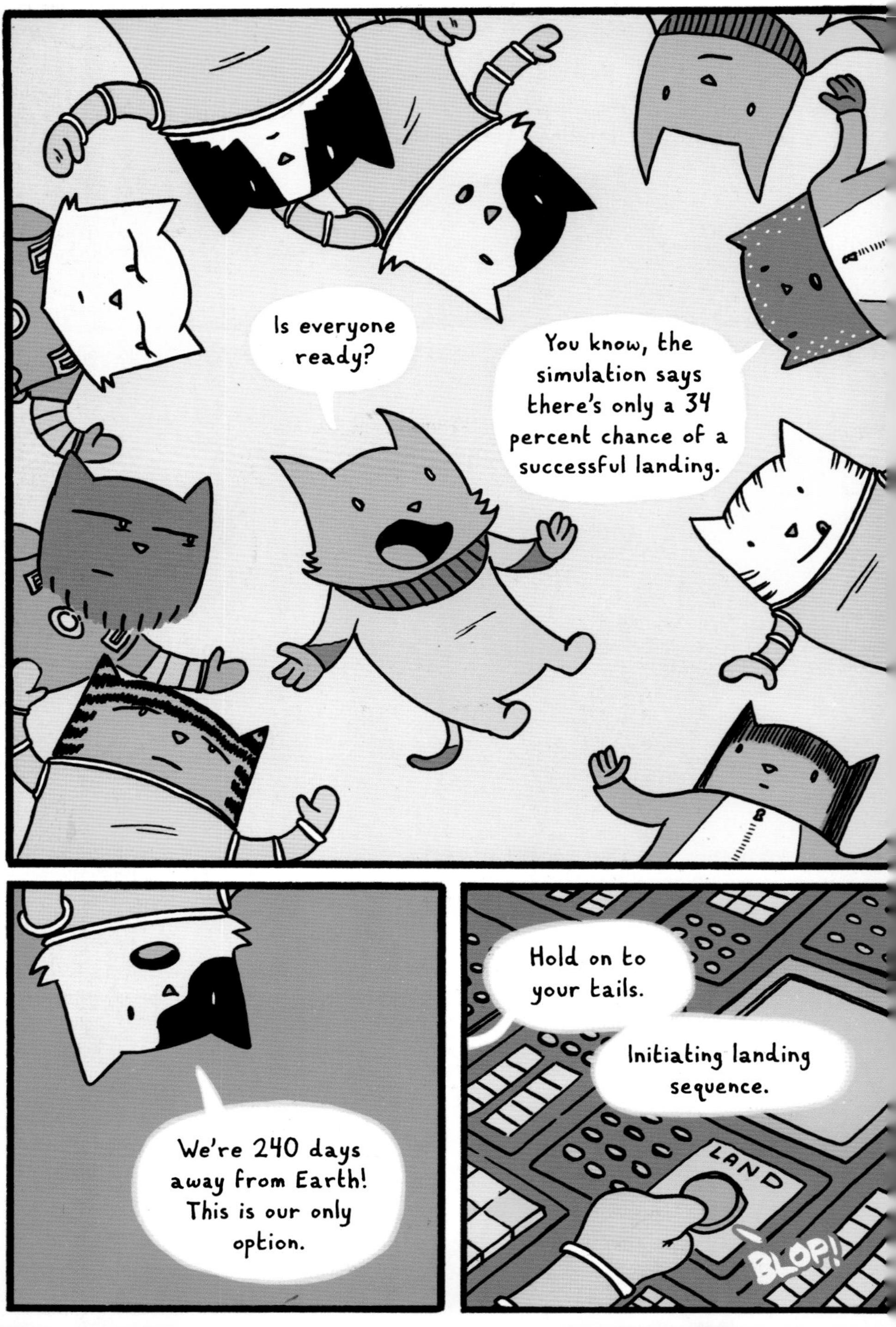
Is everyone ready?
You know, the simulation says there's only a 34 percent chance of a successful landing.
We're 240 days away from Earth! This is our only option.
Hold on to your tails.
Initiating landing sequence.
LAND
BLOP!

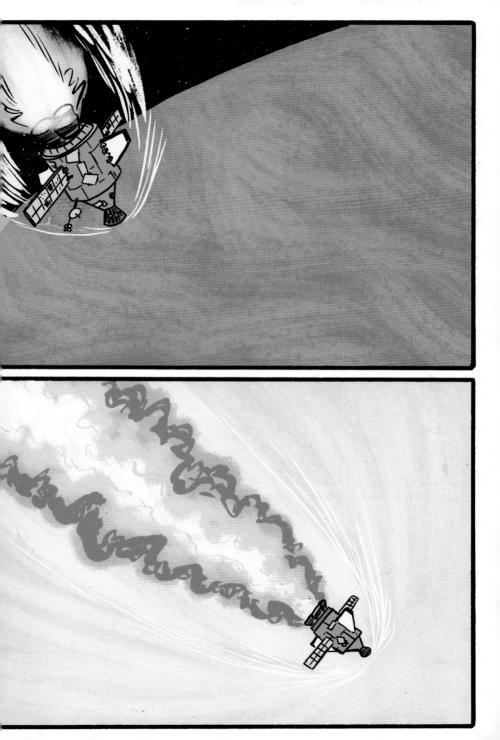

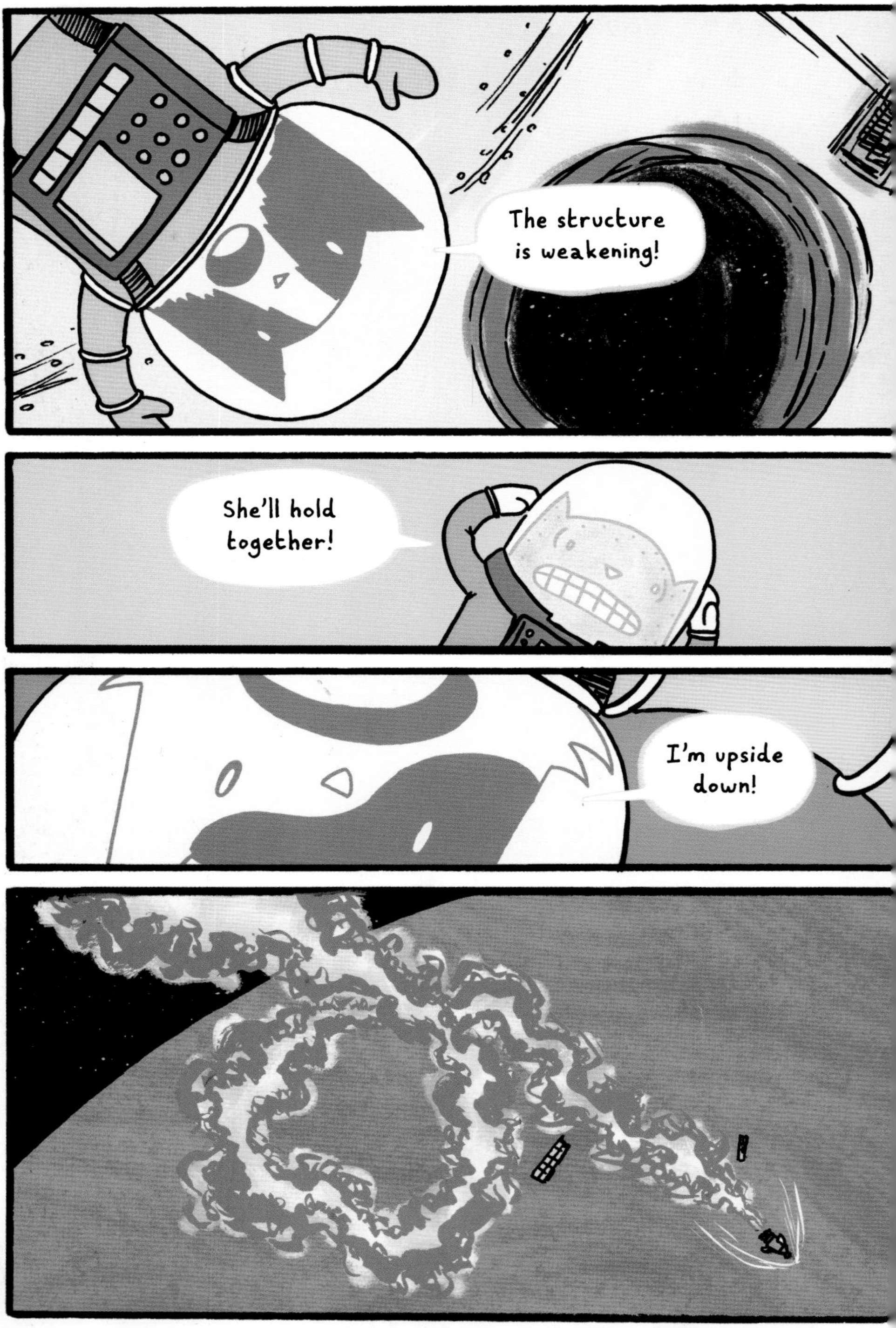
The structure is weakening!
She'll hold together!
I'm upside down!

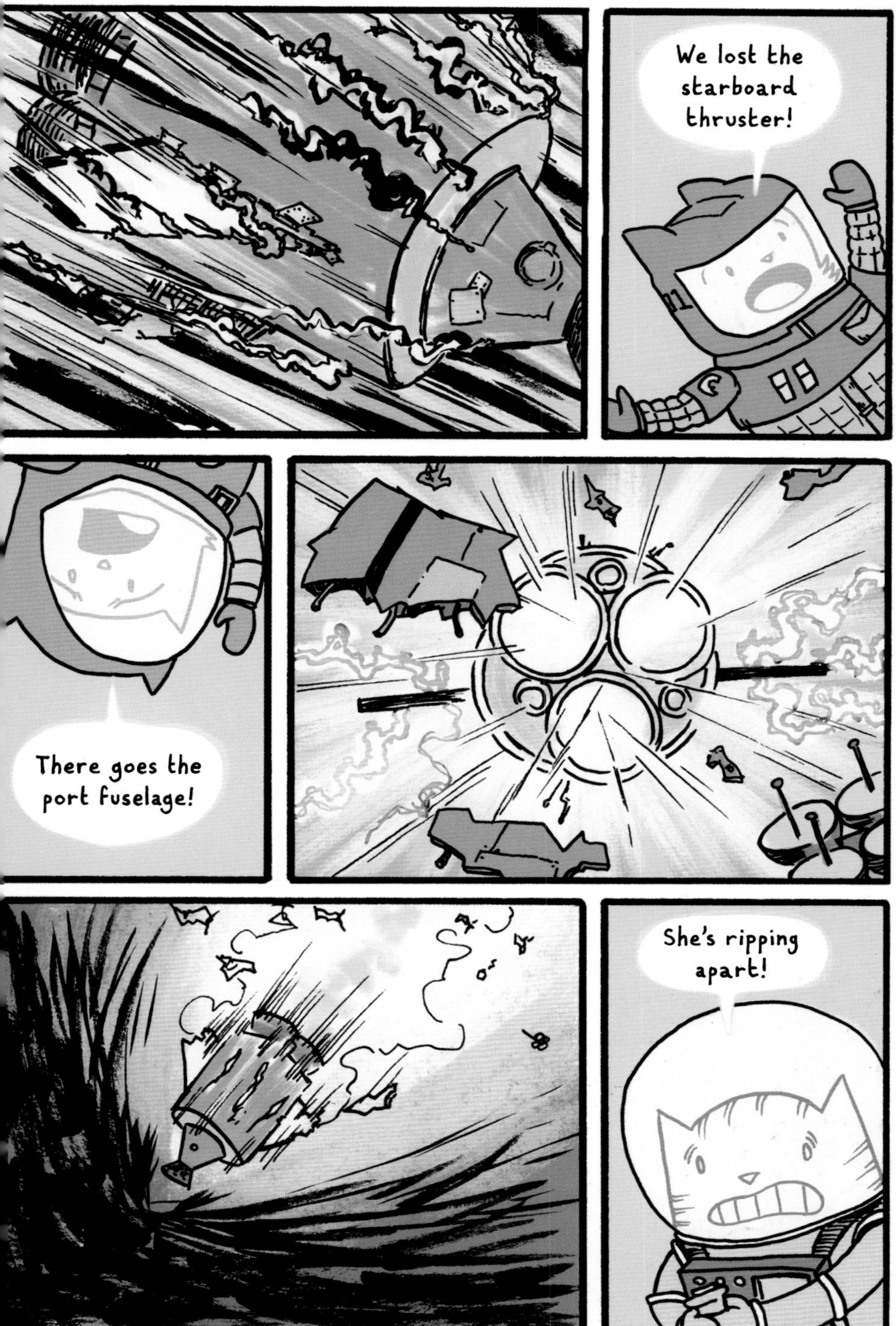
We lost the starboard thruster!
There goes the port fuselage!
She's ripping apart!

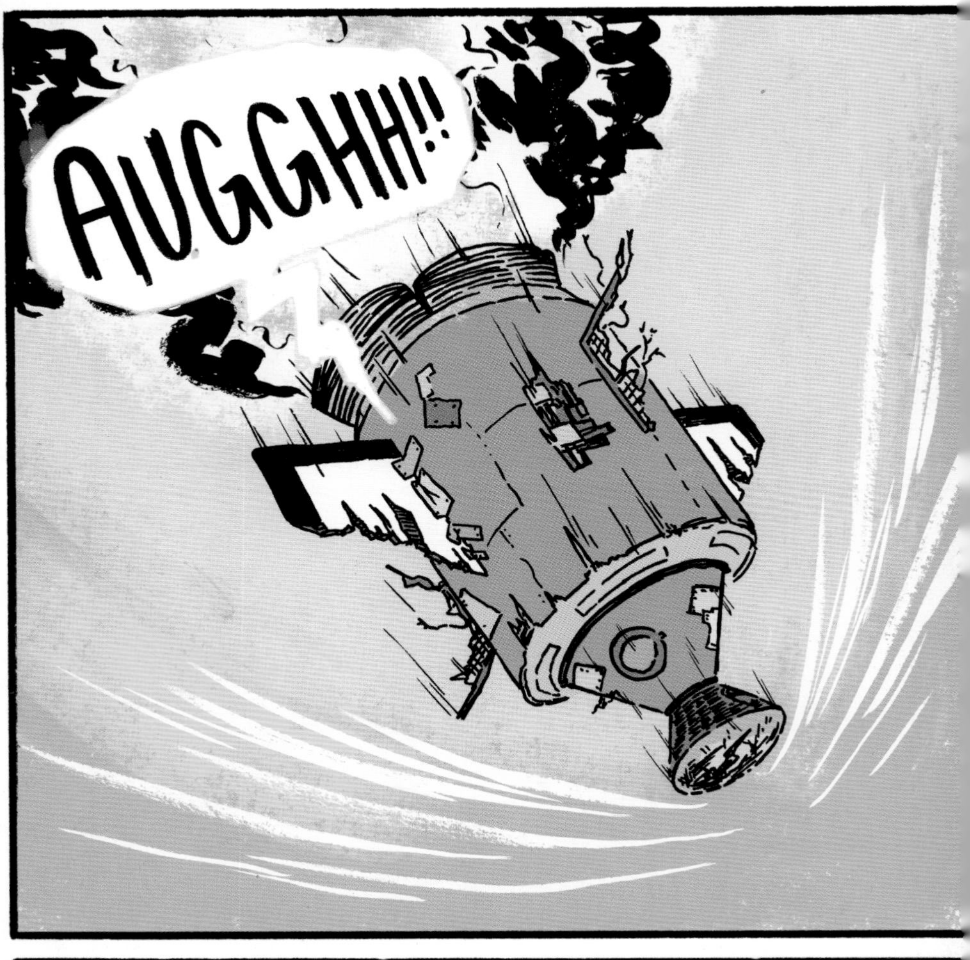
AUGGHH!!

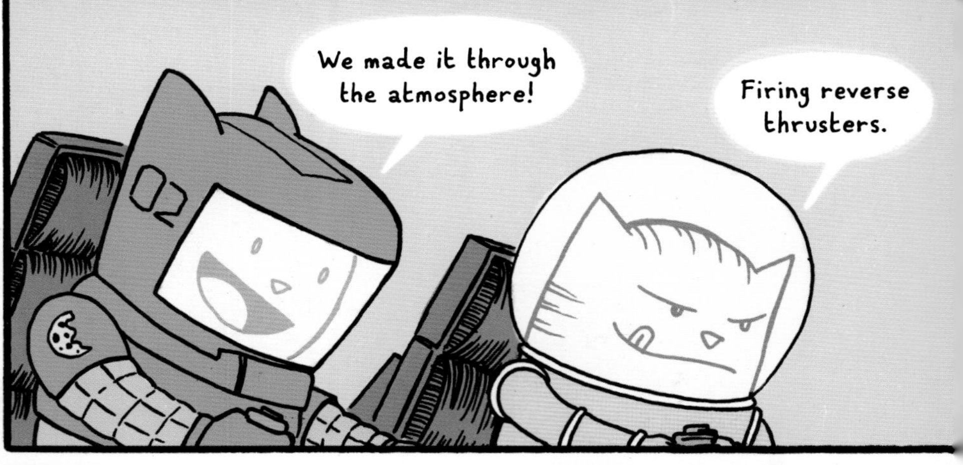
We made it through the atmosphere!
Firing reverse thrusters.
02

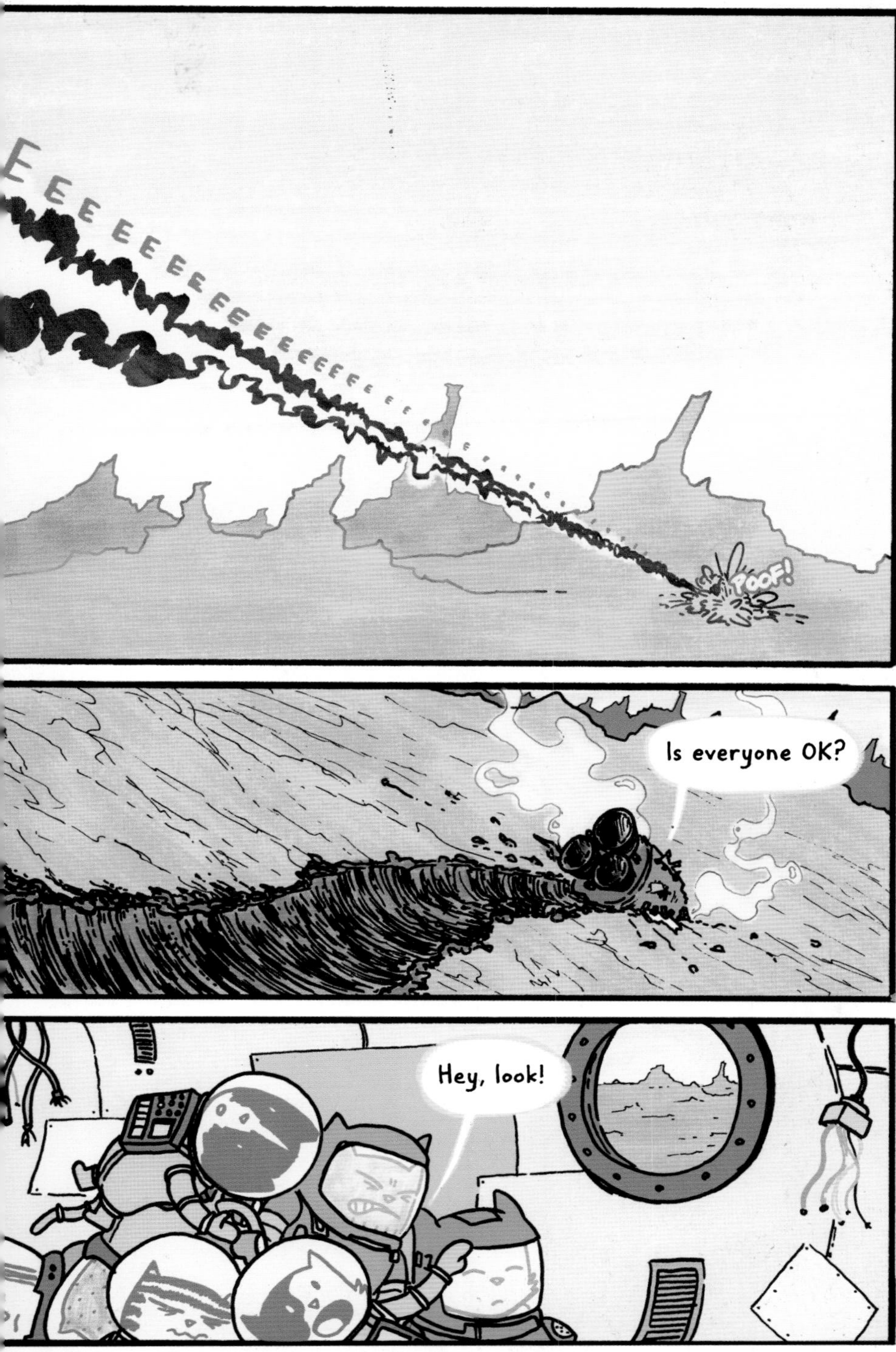
EEEEEEEEEEEEEEEEEEEEEEEE
POOF!
Is everyone OK?
Hey, look!

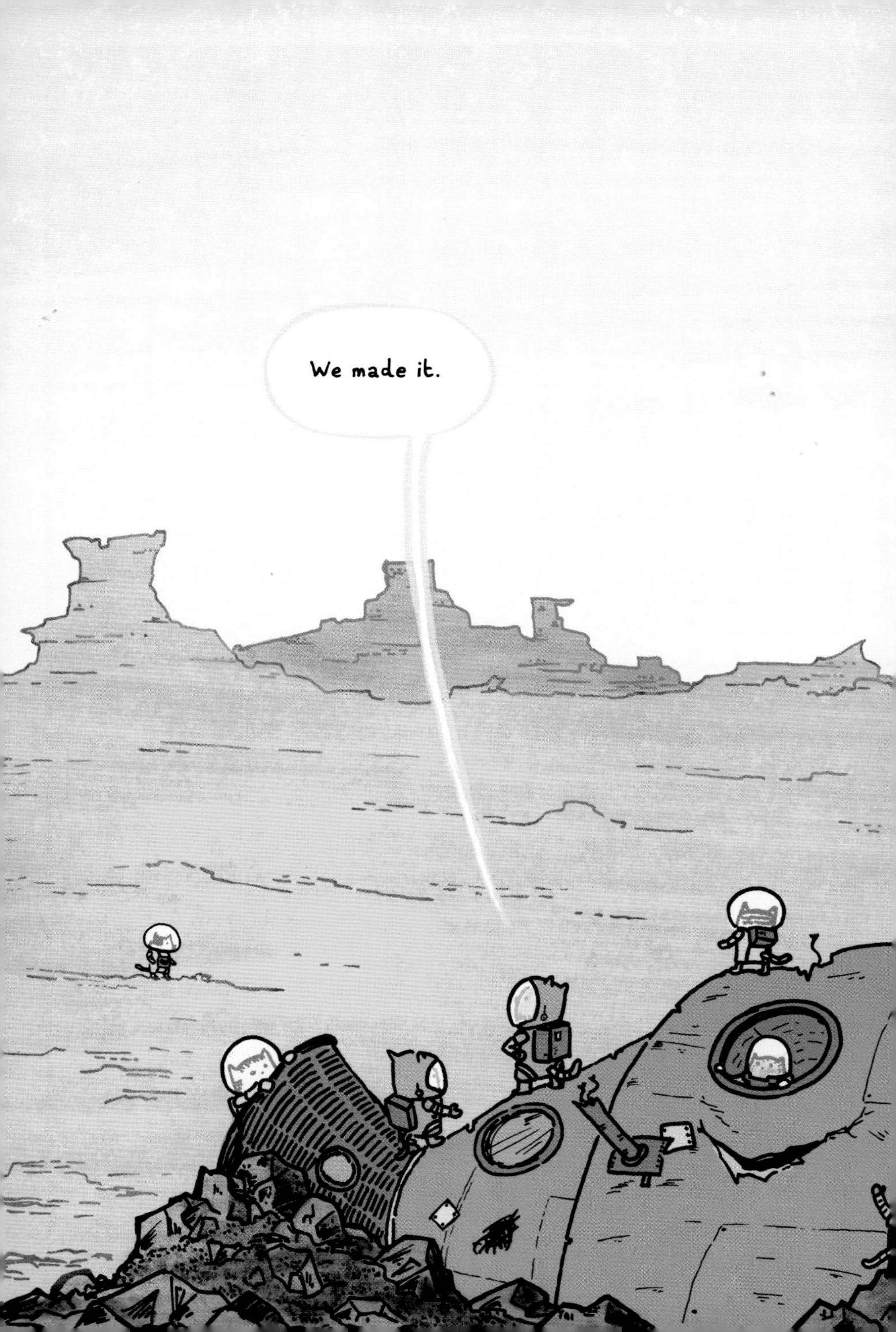
We made it.

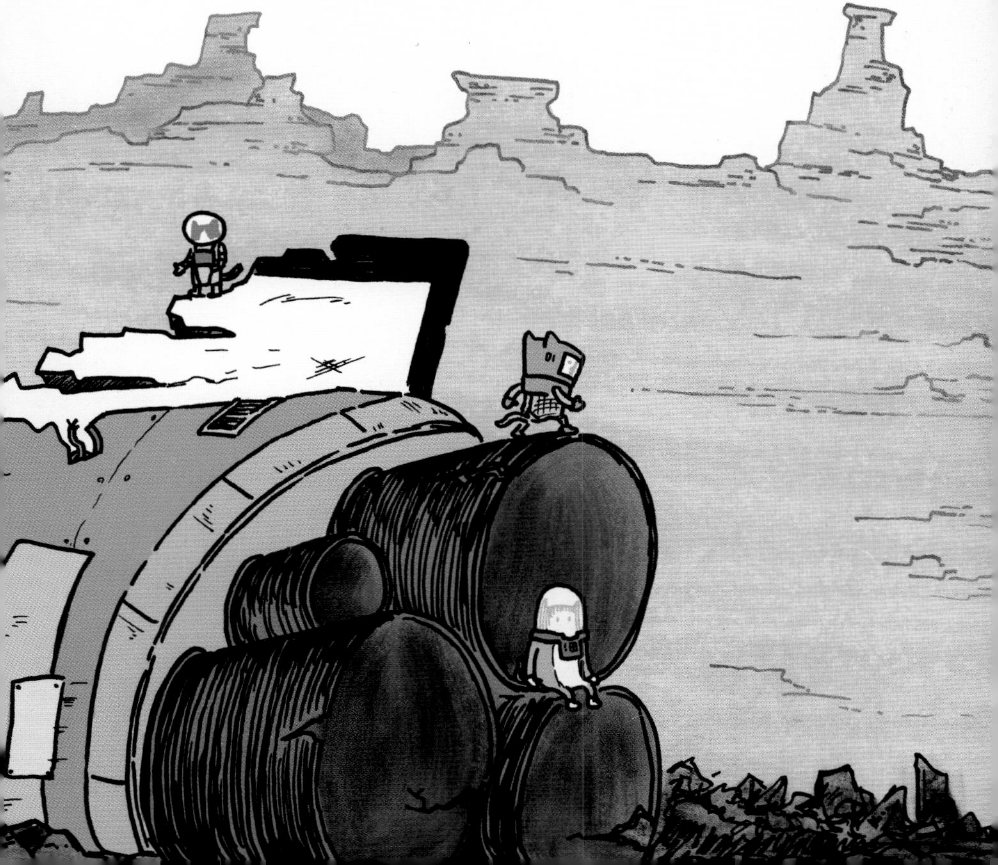

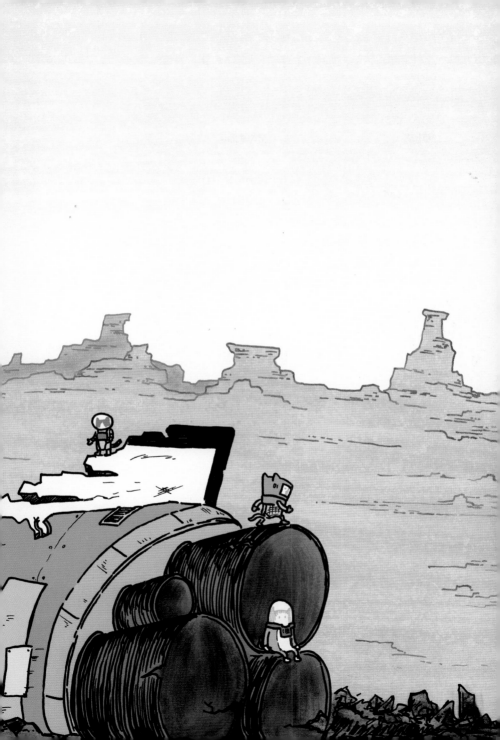

CHAPTER 10

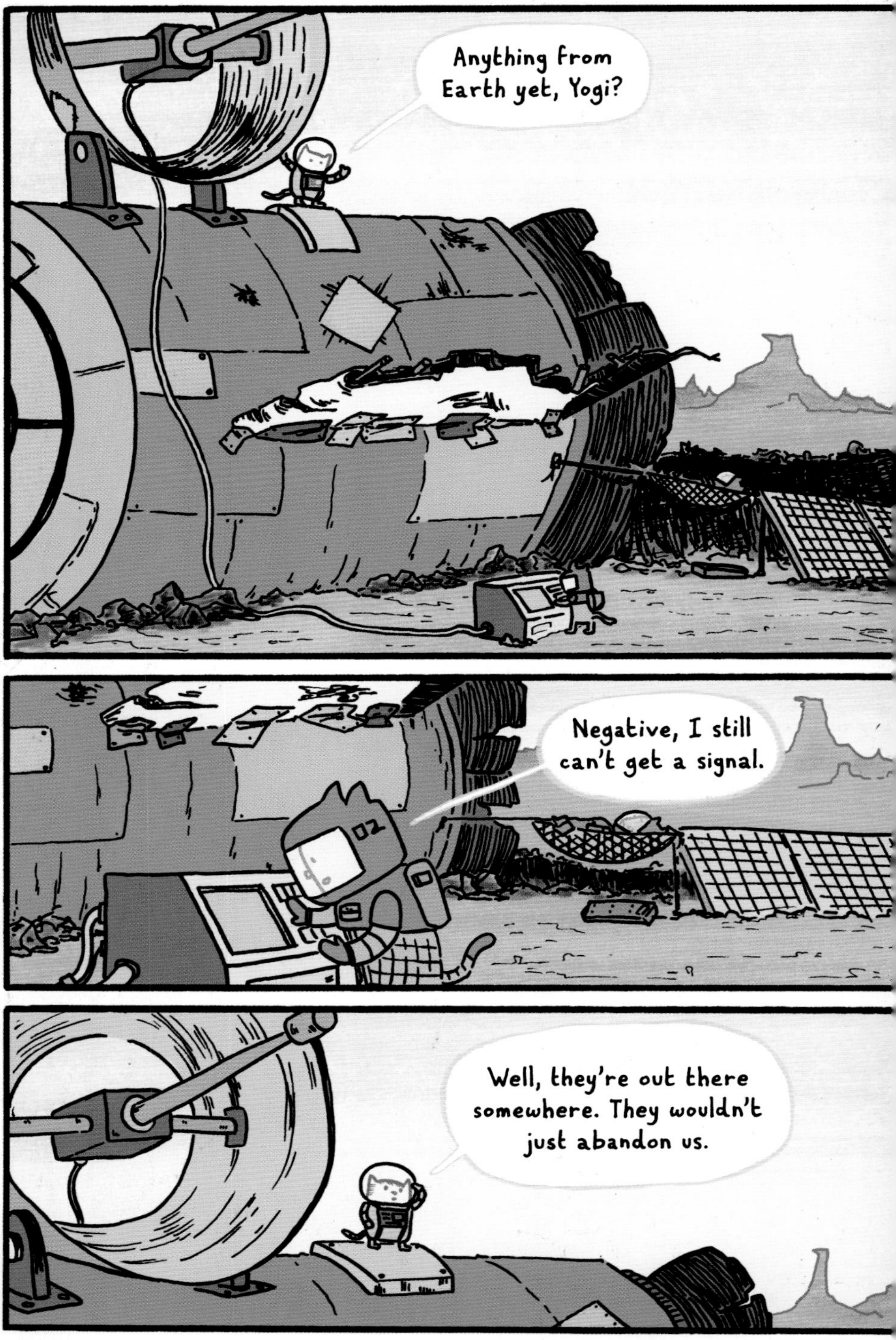
Anything from Earth yet, Yogi?
Negative, I still can't get a signal.
Well, they're out there somewhere. They wouldn't just abandon us.

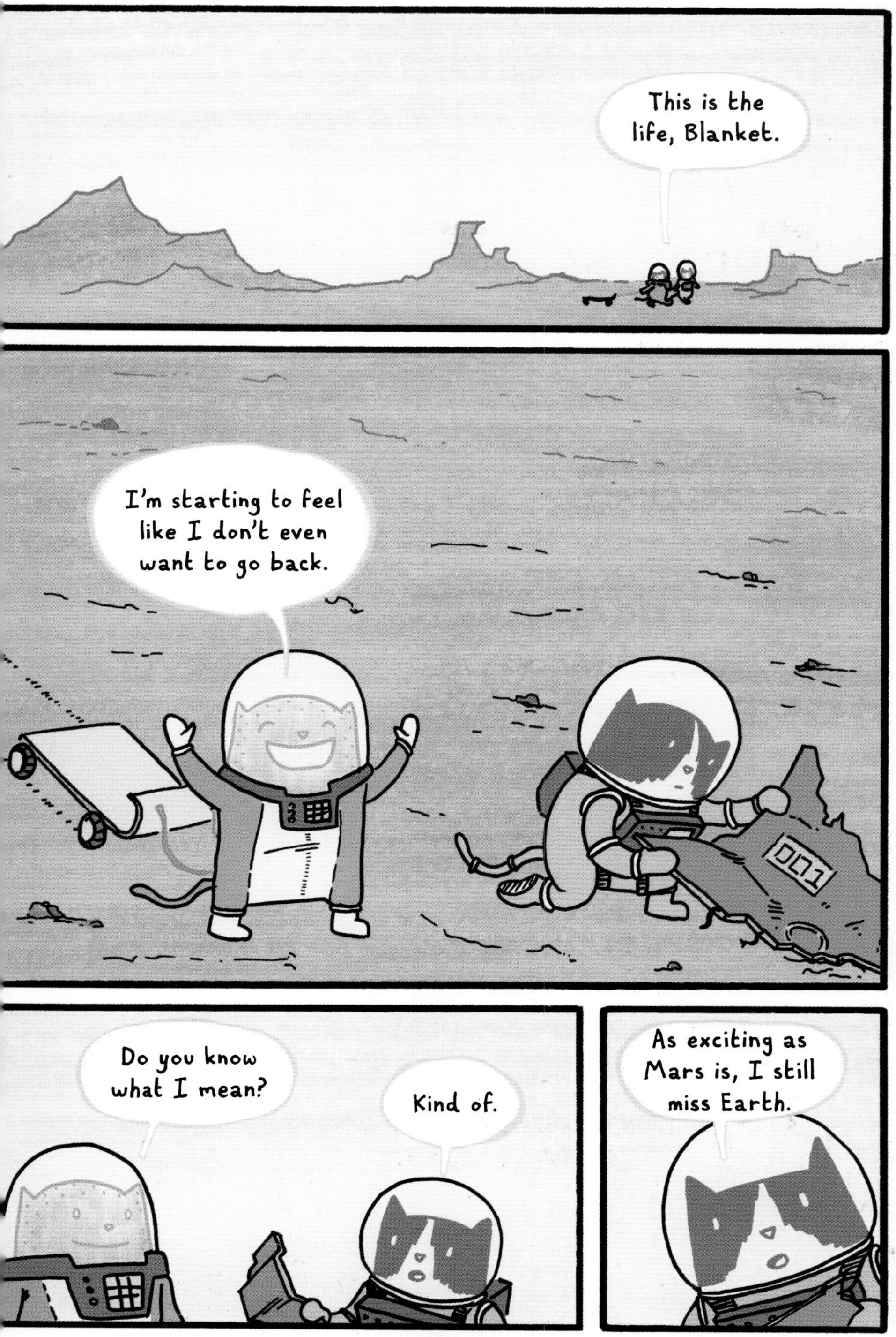
This is the life, Blanket.
I'm starting to feel like I don't even want to go back.
Do you know what I mean?
Kind of.
As exciting as Mars is, I still miss Earth.

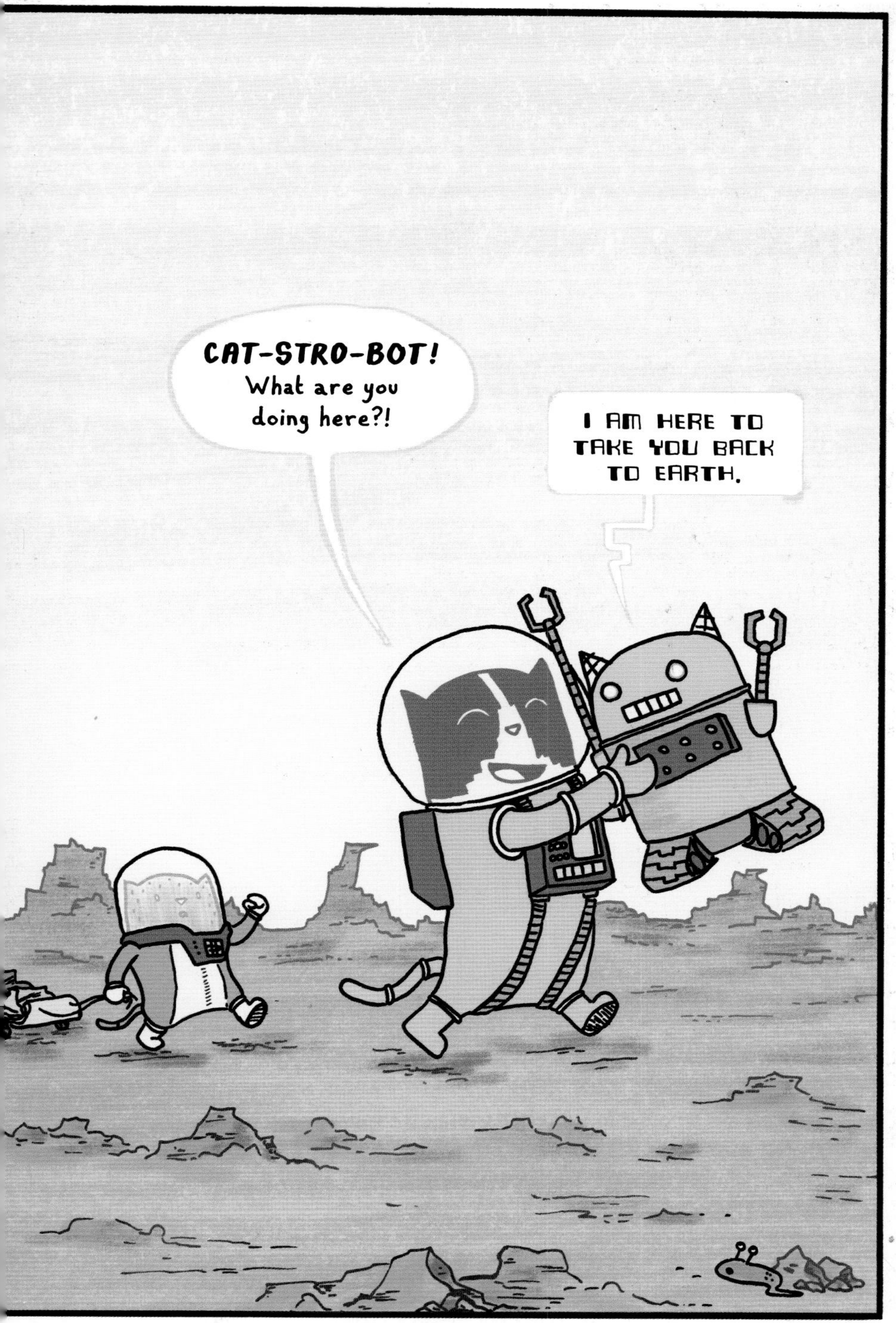
CAT-STRO-BOT! What are you doing here?!
I AM HERE TO TAKE YOU BACK TO EARTH.

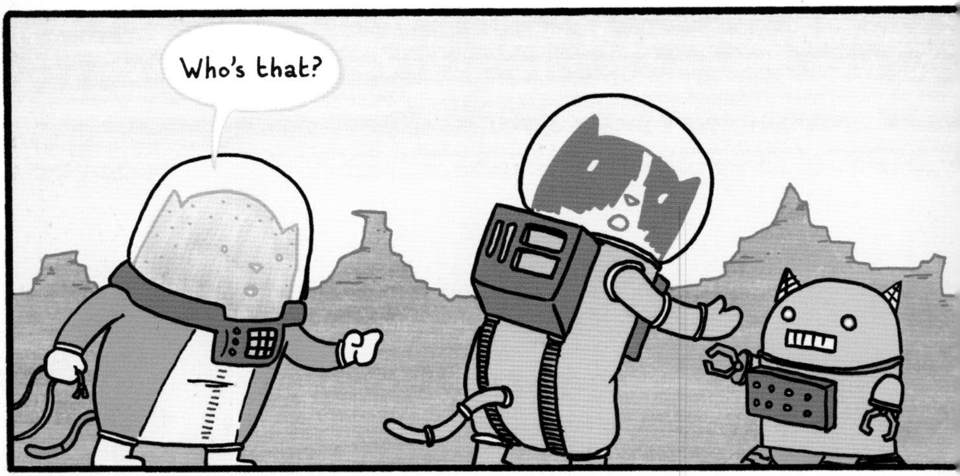
Who's that?

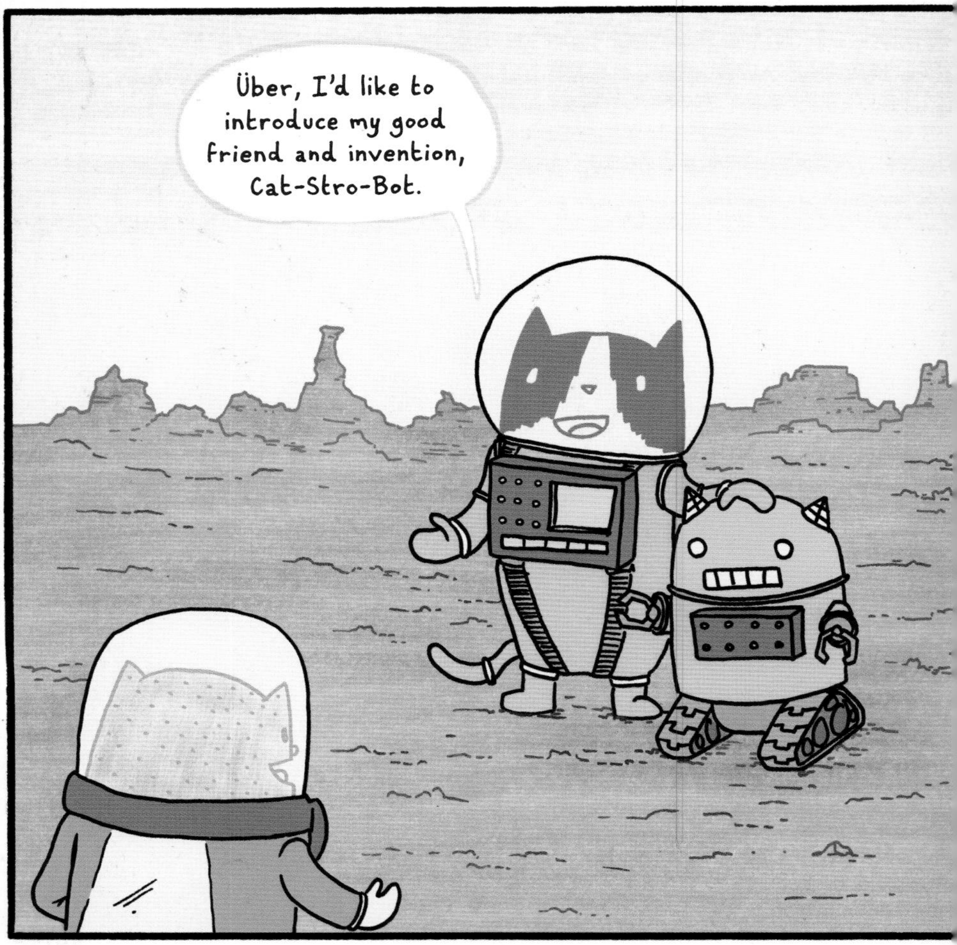
Über, I'd like to introduce my good friend and invention, Cat-Stro-Bot.

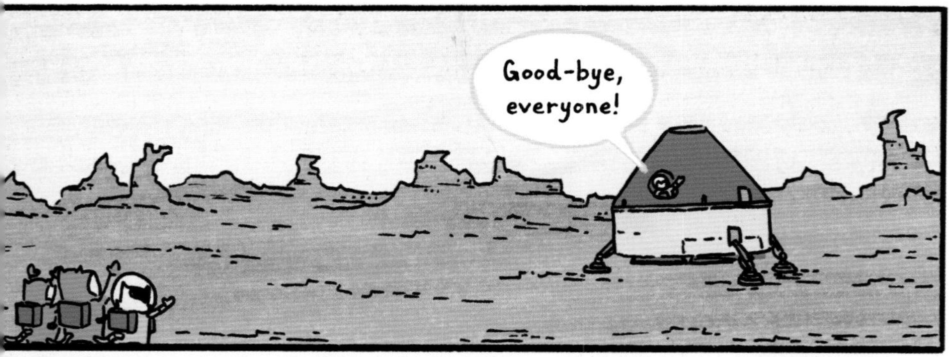
Good-bye, everyone!

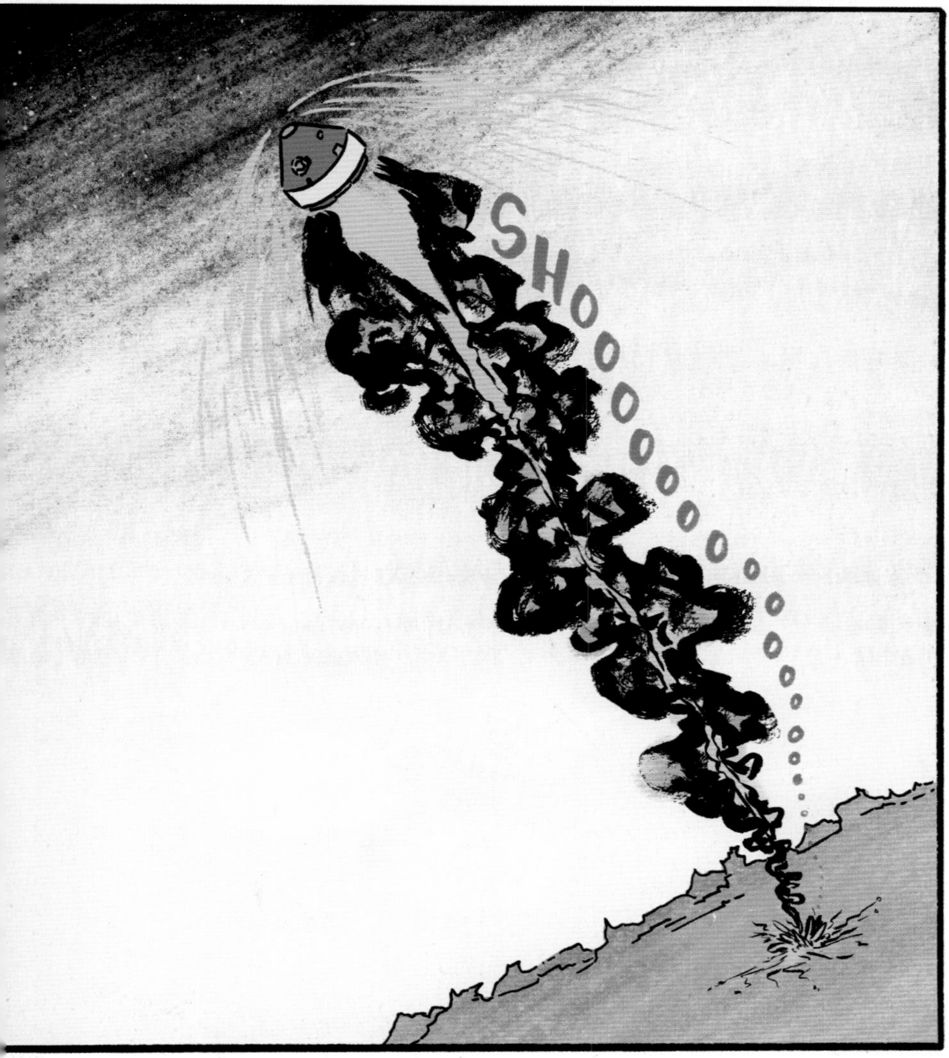
SHOOOOOOOOOOOOOOOOO...

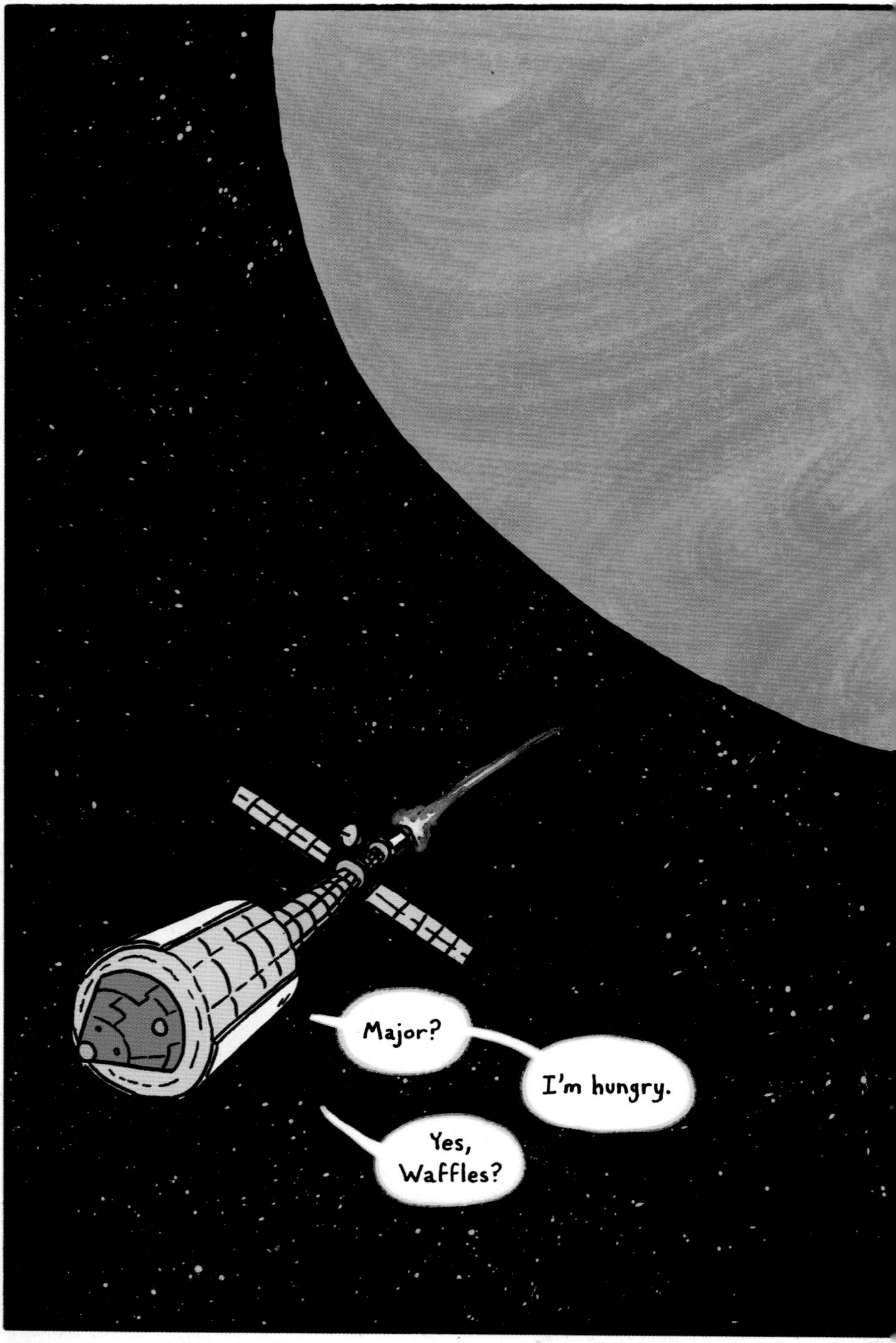
Major?
I'm hungry.
Yes, Waffles?

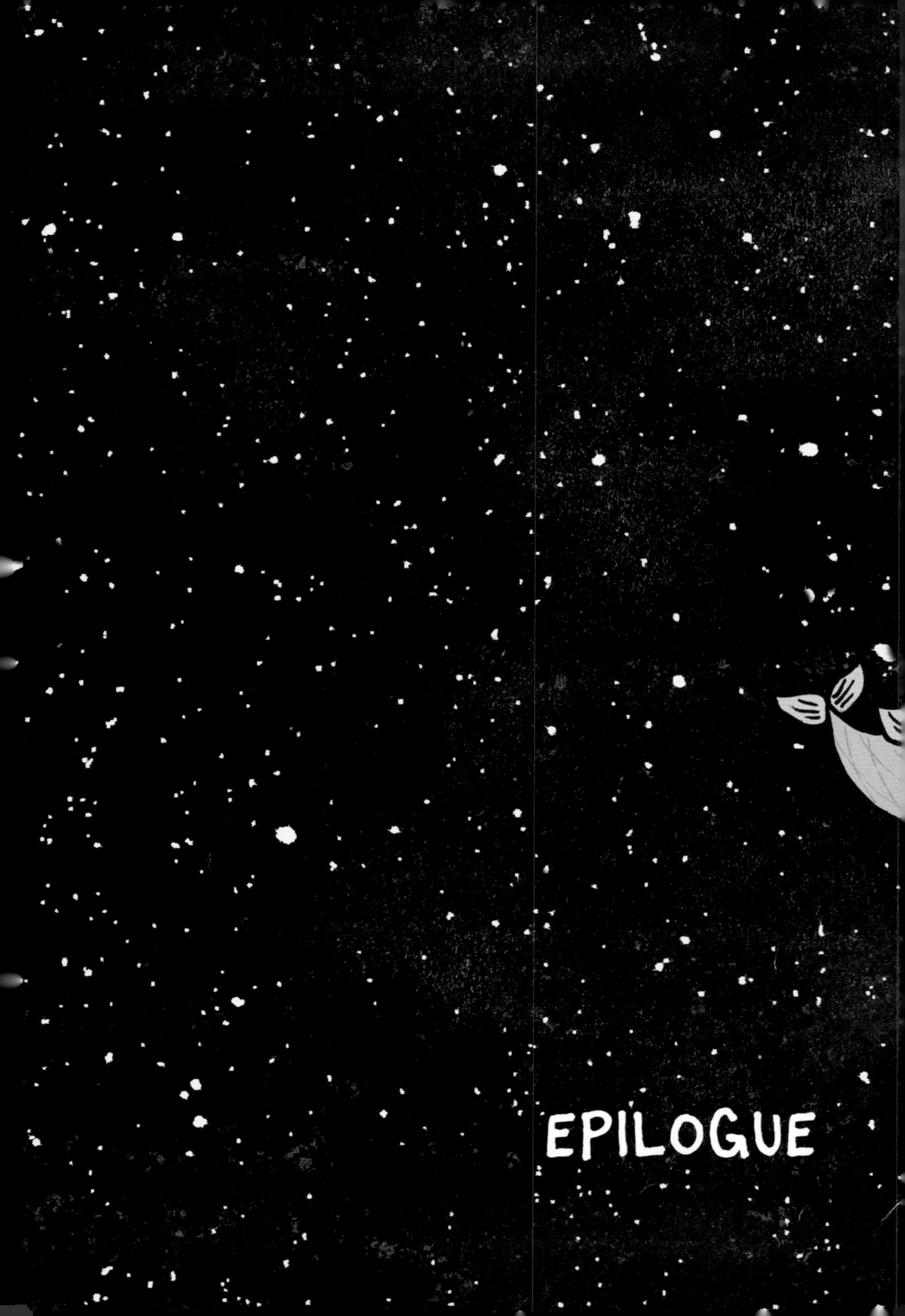
EPILOGUE

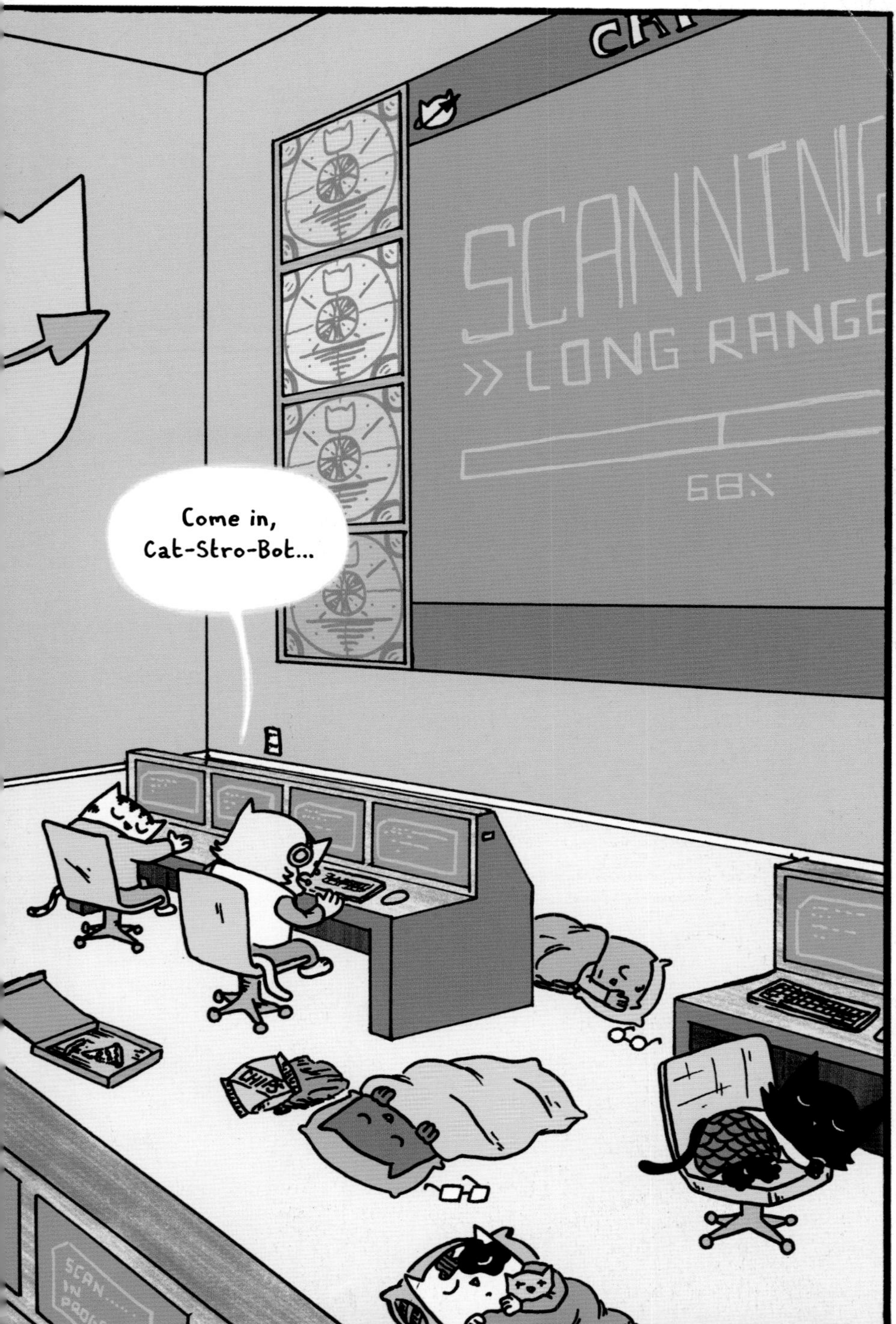

CAT
SCANNING
>> LONG RANGE
68%
Come in, Cat-Stro-Bot...
CHIPS
SCAN IN PROG

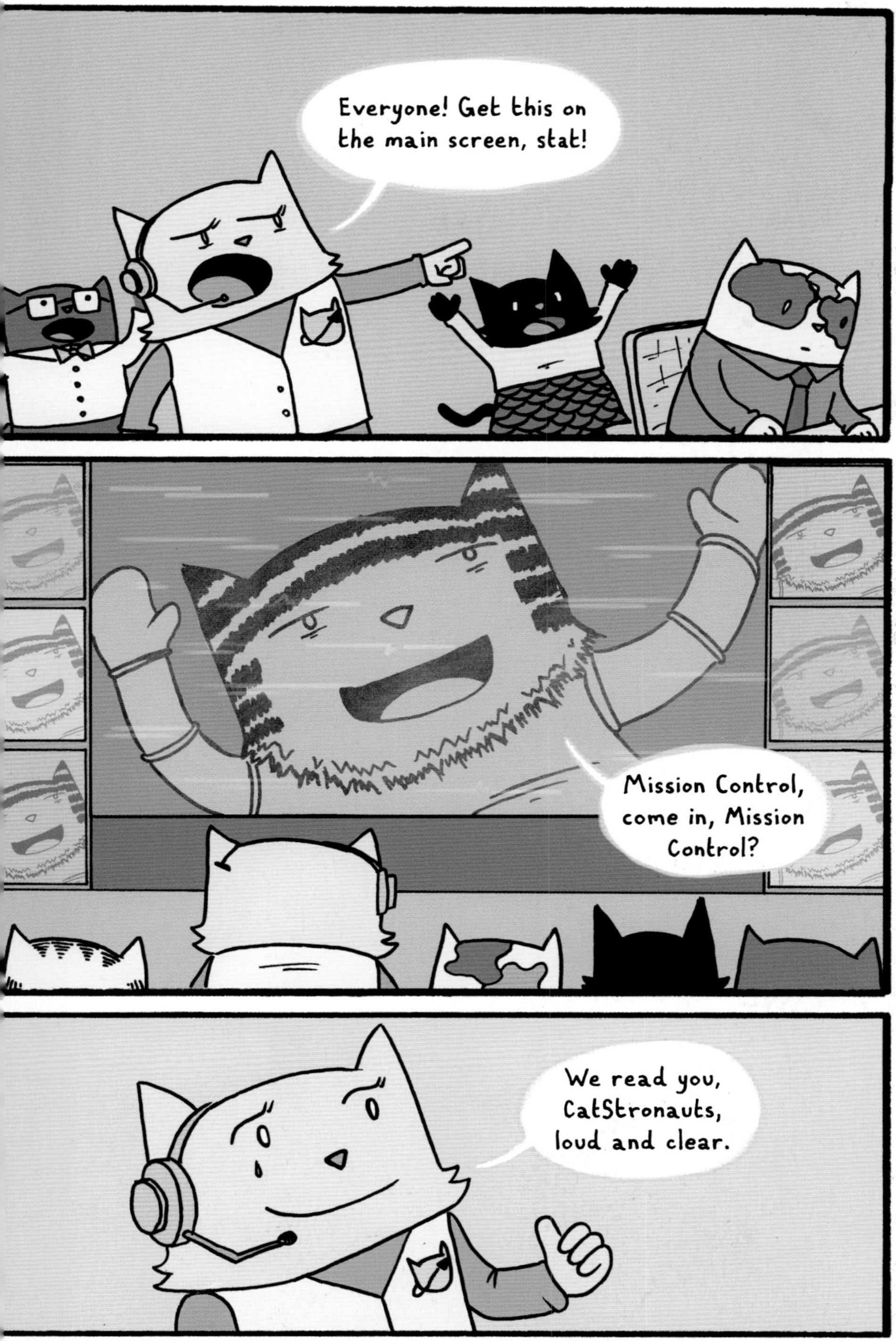
Everyone! Get this on the main screen, stat!
Mission Control, come in, Mission Control?
We read you, CatStronauts, loud and clear.

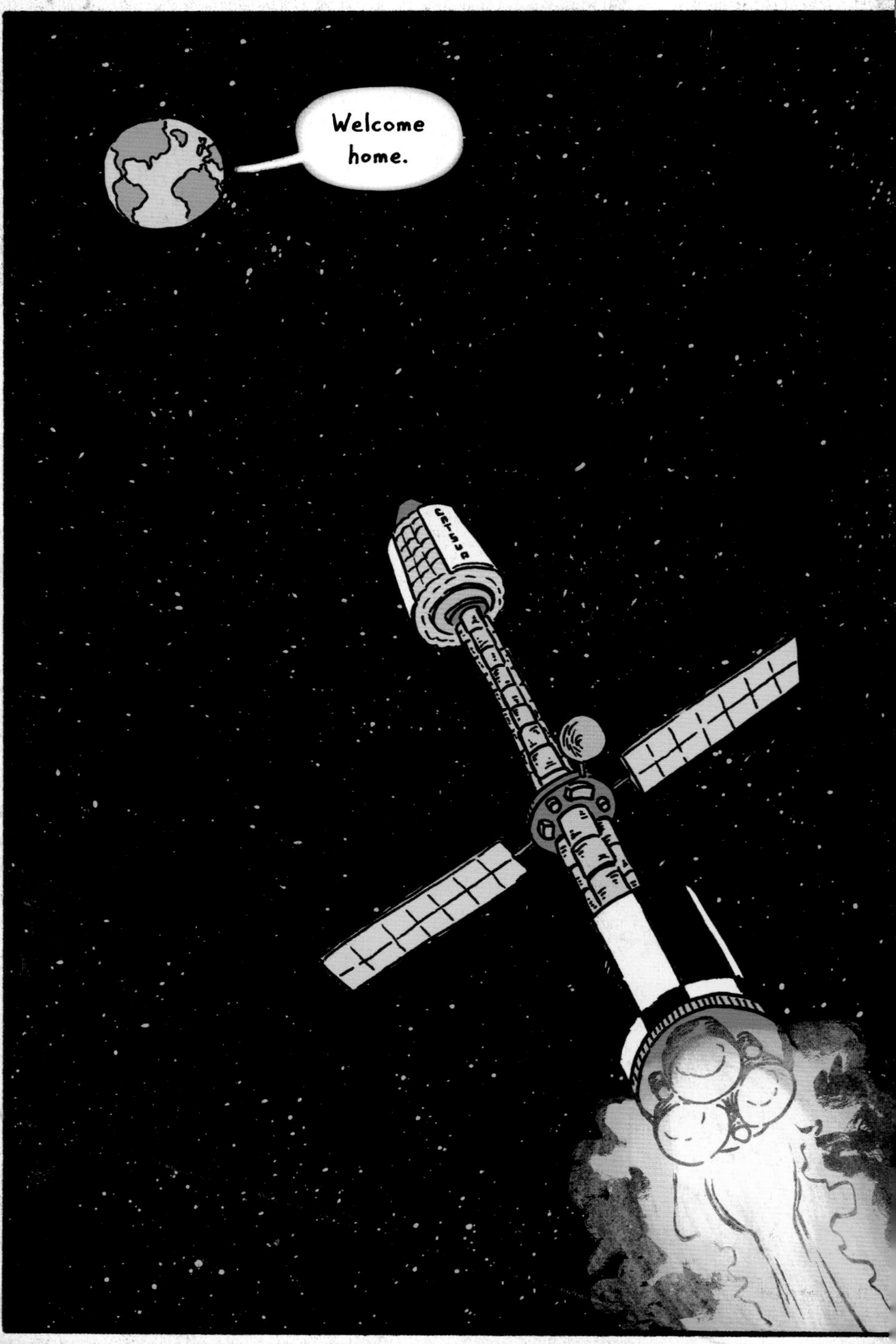
Welcome home.

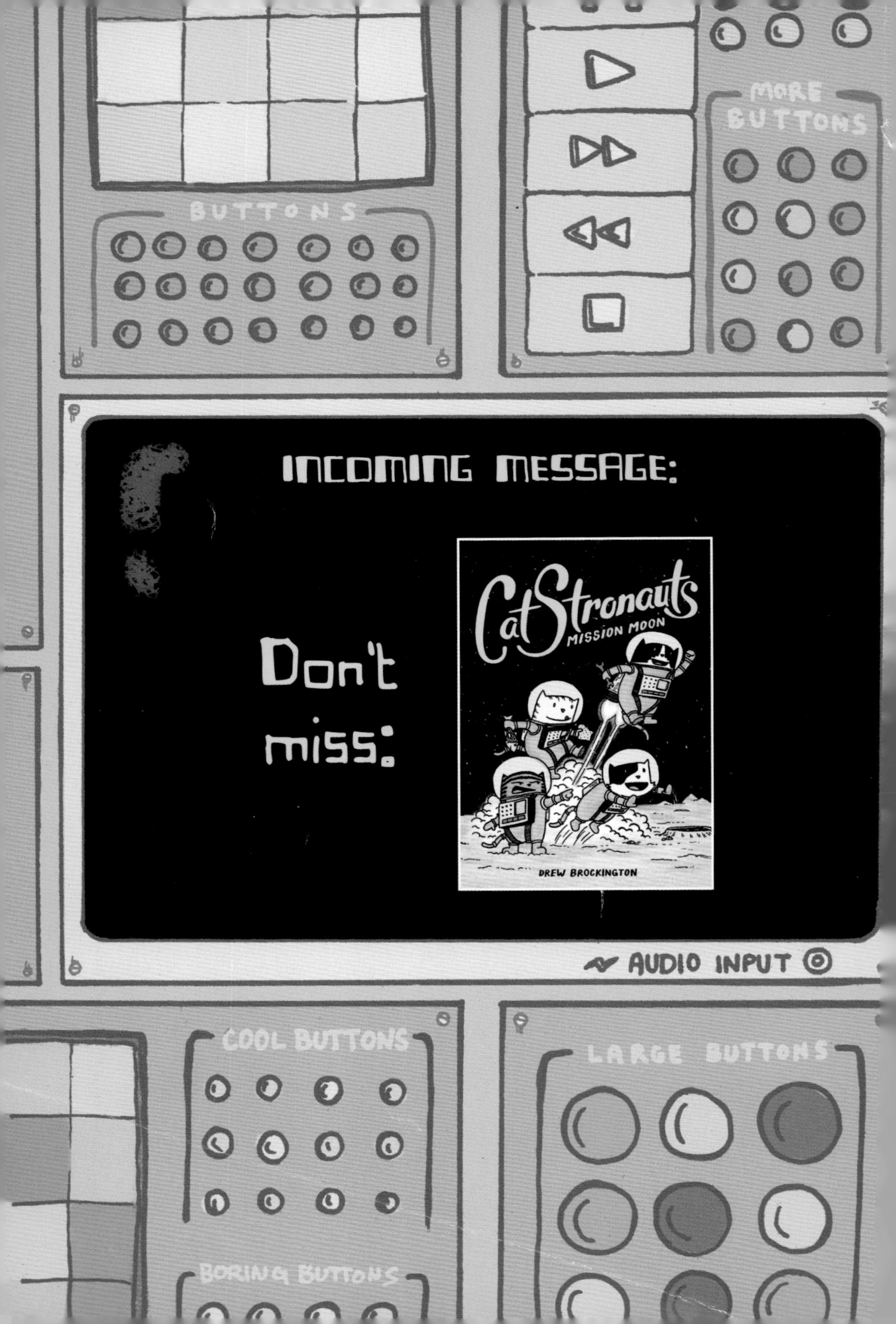
BUTTONS
MORE BUTTONS
INCOMING MESSAGE:
Don't miss:
CatStronauts
MISSION MOON
DREW BROCKINGTON
AUDIO INPUT
COOL BUTTONS
LARGE BUTTONS
BORING BUTTONS

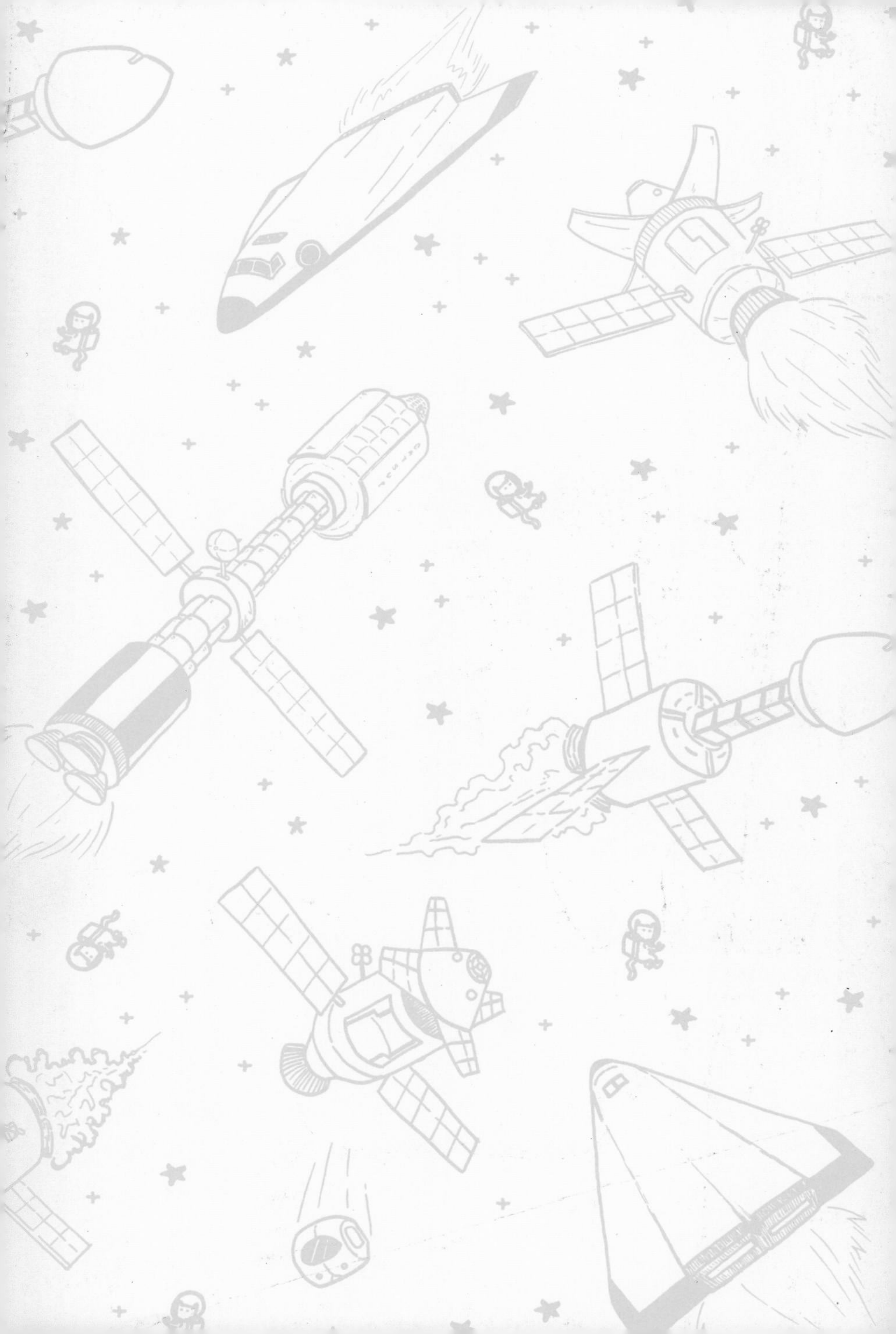

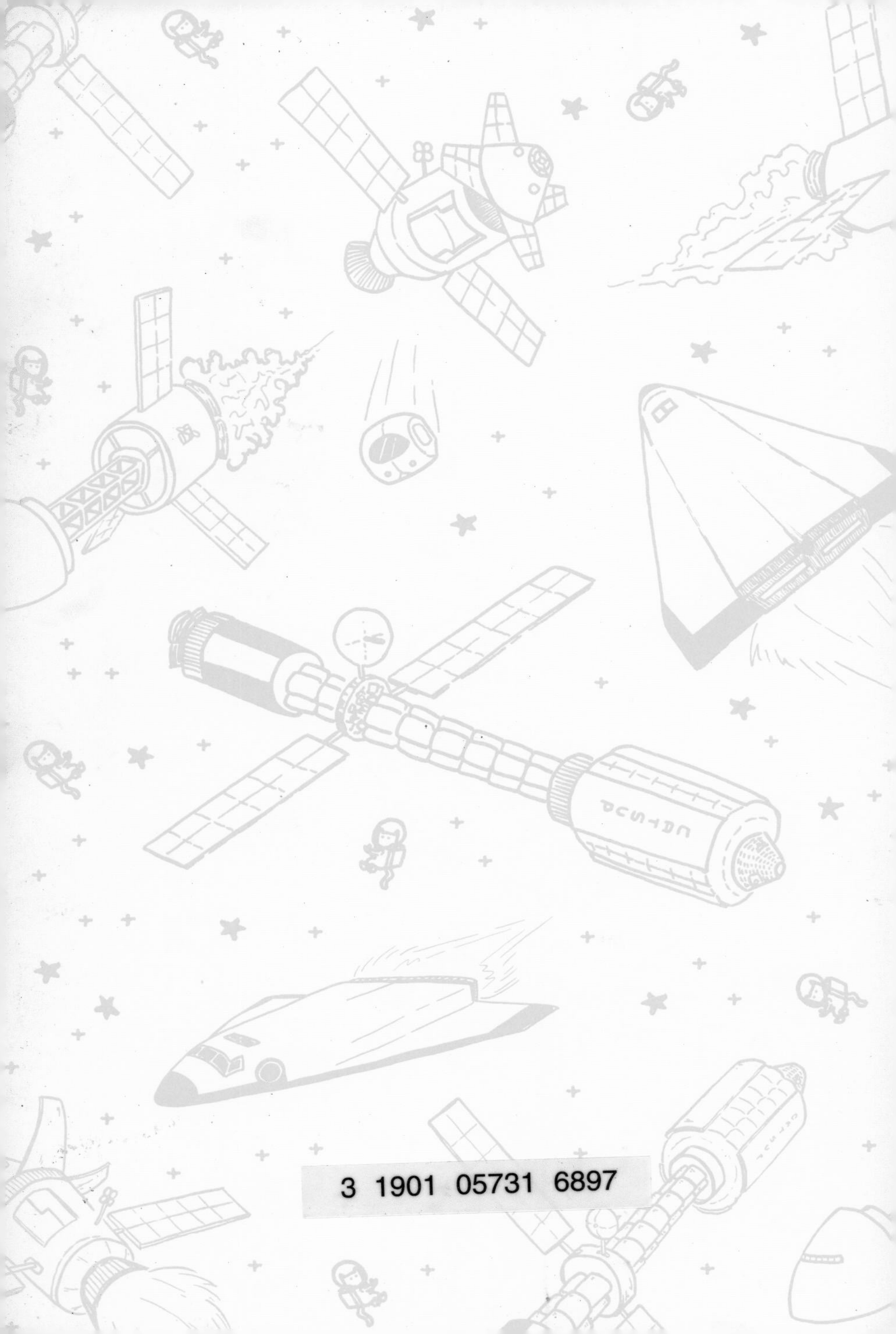